I0606594

The bomb was in place, now all he had to do is wait...

He arrived in Puerto Vallarta two days before the high mass was scheduled in the cathedral where Archbishop John Riley would officiate. He saw the cathedral with the cast iron dome from the beach and walked toward it. It was noon and the regular mass of the day was in progress. He sat in the back, reciting in Spanish the prayers of the Eucharist.

After a late dinner in an excellent German restaurant full of German ex-pats drinking themselves into hilarity, he wandered back toward the cathedral. Earlier in the day, he noticed an alley to the left side of the main entrance and a service door with an old and useless lock. It was locked but a gentle tug to one side opened it. They had made it all too easy over the centuries, as one interest held sway over another, and no one ever gave even the slightest attention to security detail. He would return in time to set in motion the mission for which he had been chosen.

He had left the door ajar the previous night and found it exactly as he had left it. No one had checked it the next day. He walked over the marble on the main altar and found the trap door—one piece of marble with a hole drilled in it. He lifted it and shone his flashlight into the crawl space under the altar. There was nothing but a series of wooden beams, the wood flooring under the marble, and the stone face on the sides. He was done setting the bomb in place in less than fifteen minutes. He left quietly.

John Riley, installed as the archbishop of the Archdiocese of Seattle to bring order and discipline to the Church there, is murdered while saying mass in the cathedral in Puerta Vallarta, Mexico, there as a guest of the powerful and ultra conservative Opus Dei. The United States Government blames the drug cartels. The Mexican Government claims it's a US set up to blame the Mexicans. And the Vatican, inspired by the convictions of a very wealthy and influential member of Opus Dei, Harold Brown, is certain it's the work of a radical, leftist LGBT element within the Catholic Church.

Grady Marcs, former army ranger and entrepreneur-turned-cyber-crime-specialist, is retained by Brown to find out who really killed the archbishop. Grady travels to Mexico where he uncovers more than he bargains for—putting his own life at risk.

ACKNOWLEDGEMENTS

I wish to acknowledge the assistance of a co-worker and friend Josh Willis in helping to define areas of the culture wars that are not only still active but that will erupt even further. We thought we were in the post-culture-war era, but sadly we are not.

DOUBLE CROSS

By

Shawn Rohrbach

A Black Opal Books Publication

DEDICATION

I dedicate this book to Barbara and David Siekkinen,
parents of my husband Andy,
for all of their support and love for the past twelve years.

Prologue

June 2006:

They never really fired a bishop from his job. He was normally convinced to retire, and they installed new blood, someone more to the liking of the current pope and his cardinals.

Harry Boyle went down fighting.

The United States Catholic Conference had negotiated with him on behalf of the Vatican, but to no avail. Cardinal Daniel Day of Los Angeles was summoned to Rome when polite didn't work. He was sent with the mandate to convince Boyle, in order to avoid an ugly public fight. The Italian cardinals underestimated the stubbornness of Bishop Harry Boyle, no matter how politically left his beliefs.

Harry learned of the meeting and was ready when they called, determined not to budge. The evidence that was delivered to the Newark police, implicating his vicar general in a teenage male prostitution ring, was so bogus that Boyle's cousin in the New Jersey State Police laughed when he saw it. Bishop Boyle became furious and more determined than ever. He knew this was all predicated on his position on married priests, ordaining women, and extending to homosexuals the same welcome given to any other Catholic. He was not going to be forced out of anything for believing in the inclusiveness and forgiveness of the Gospels.

Assistant Bishop John Riley called Bishop Boyle and said that meeting Cardinal Day at the Newark Hilton was simply a preliminary fact-finding mission, prior to a direct conference with the holy father, something the pope had expressly wanted to avoid. It was Day's job to convince Harry to leave without forcing the church to take public measures. Day was ready.

So was Boyle. He brought with him a file containing numerous letters of support from noted theologians the world over. He would sacrifice himself for the truth he believed in so passionately. It was time the dinosaur entered the twenty first century. By the time they arrived in Rome, Boyle would have convinced a few Vatican insiders as well. He grinned through gritted teeth as Assistant Bishop John Riley escorted him to Cardinal Day's suite. They rode politely and fraternally up the elevator.

Assistant Bishop Riley was effervescent in his politeness. His graying hair and broad grin took away some of the nervous edge, and Bishop Boyle was happy to be among at least polite company. With a light knock at the living room door, Riley nodded to Boyle. Good Luck, maybe? Harry smiled back as the heavy door swung open.

Harry was taller than Cardinal Day, but something about him deflected attention away. Some called him gaunt, others said he was just too focused to take care of himself properly, but no matter, he always look rumpled and tired. He glanced across the room, expecting to see Cardinal Day seated regally in his crimson cassock, but instead his own mother sat alone, waving at him, with a wide grin on her face.

Boyle stood, wanting to hug his mother and slam his fist in Day's face.

"Son, I'm so glad you are okay. I was so worried at what they said you have been through. Come to Seattle and rest. God forgives, but only if you ask for it and make amends. Son." Her voice was shaken, her face white and her hands shook.

"What are you talking about?"

Cardinal Day entered the room with fast, precise movements. Riley followed and moved across toward Harry. Harry looked Day squarely in the eyes. Quiet, to Day's face, he seethed, "Day, you stinking bastard. What did you tell her?"

"Enough." Cardinal Day did not smile. He was worried about the rage in Boyle's eyes, not a simple case of Irish temper.

"Son, it's okay. I understand. Come back to Seattle with me. Cardinal Day was so kind to purchase a ticket for you." She struggled to stand. Boyle was staring at Cardinal Day.

Riley helped the feeble old woman to her feet.

Harry dropped his folder, spilling the letters, and leaped toward his mother. "You keep your hands off of her."

Part 1
Present Day

Chapter 1

The February sun in Puerto Vallarta danced with the waves of the Pacific Ocean. The streets and walkways were full of American, German, French, and even a few Mexican tourists. The fabled cast iron dome, and the awkward phases of construction of the cathedral, informed these visitors of the power and architectural whims of the long succession of archbishops, who had occupied the Episcopal Chair of Puerto Vallarta, each one putting his own stamp on the shape, function, and style of the cathedral.

Ignacio cared less about a visiting archbishop than he did missing two days of his summer vacation. Their trip to the ocean was delayed because the archbishop was saying mass in La Iglesia de Nuestra Senora de Guadalupe and he and his brother were in rotation to serve. They called twelve other altar boys and if they are home, they scoffed at the idea of serving mass in the middle of a summer day.

The four altar boys listed to serve were told to meet at La Iglesia de Nuestra Senora de Guadalupe, the official name of the cathedral, at eleven in the morning for a two o'clock mass. They moaned that they had served so many masses this was nothing special. And he was just an archbishop. Ignacio had served mass for the pope. They decided to arrive at one.

The master of ceremonies was frantic when he rushed out into the plaza looking for them, finding them playing soccer around frenzied tourists. Ignacio bounced the ball off the head of a fat German who picked it up and kicked it into a crowd of tourists sipping coffee. The boys laughed as they retrieved the ball, leaving the German to explain himself to the offended American tourists and an amused policeman.

Ignacio and Javier ran into the cathedral, down the side aisle, and into the vestibule. They stopped and stared at the tall, white haired archbishop. He was not Mexican—that, they surmised instantly. He greeted them with a broad, load hello. American. A thin, nervous priest was practically running from one end of the vestibule to the other, whining out commands in English. The boys laughed. They didn't understand a word and the commands were not obeyed.

Several old men in nice suits were milling around the vestibule. Two other priests were getting ready to say mass with the archbishop. The archbishop was not at all concerned about the boys or the other priests. He shook the old men's hands vigorously, laughing loudly and whispering to them heavily. Ignacio didn't understand anything that was said.

It was Ignacio's job to light the lower candles and Javier, a year older and six inches taller, lit the candles on the high altar. They genuflected with very little reverence as they came and went from the vestibule. An elderly woman chastised them when they returned. Show more reverence? She was not missing her break, and Ignacio shrugged. He saw the amplifier was already turned on when he opened the small wooden door. Odd. But he was more concerned with getting out of there than he was in reporting on another altar boy for carelessly leaving the amplifier on since the last time the main altar was used.

The archbishop patted each altar boy on the head and spoke in English to the nervous priest. He laughed loud and crude, looking at the boys. The nervous priest laughed, too. Several of the old men smiled politely and stared at the boys. Javier translated in a tight whisper, thankful now for his three years of English. "He says we look like street urchins with our long hair."

Ignacio was not amused.

The clock approached two. The archbishop clapped his hands twice, a signal the boys didn't understand. The nervous priest hissed something at them Javier could not translate. The archbishop angrily waved them to lead the procession to the back of the cathedral. They stood with the processional cross, incense, and books, waiting for hand gestures and eye contact to begin. The boys were not nervous. They had been serving mass for eight years, once even for the pope.

They knew what needed to be done better than most new priests did. Ignacio once had to remind an aging priest to get up and read the Gospel. The wait became boring.

A meager choir followed the lead of a staff organist and the procession began. They walked with precise measured steps and arrived at the altar two minutes later, exactly as they were trained. With mechanical precision, the processional cross was set in its proper place. The archbishop's crozier and miter were reverently carried to the side and set down. Ignacio waited at almost military readiness with the incense burner, handing it to the archbishop exactly where he expected, and followed one-half step behind as the archbishop surrounded the main altar with billows of smoke. Without looking at Ignacio, the archbishop shoved the burner at him, incense filling Ignacio's eyes and nose. The processional hymn had stopped and the archbishop walked heavily to the chair to sit. Javier was on his right, and Ignacio's empty chair was on the left. Ignacio carried the incense burner away to burn out and then turned to walk back up the five steps to take his seat.

Ignacio was pushed back down the altar stairs by the explosion. He instinctively wrapped his arms around his head. He was barely aware something terrible had happened. The pain in his ears was more frightening than damaging.

The smoke was thick and then it diminished, the dust settling, and then there was only the muted screams and yells of people escaping. As Ignacio stood, he saw them panic as they pushed each other and trampled sacred objects. They clawed their way toward the two unlocked doors.

The Knights of Columbus, dressed in their ceremonial uniforms complete with sabers, fumbled over the thick wooden pews and held the sabers drawn high into the air. A senior Knight barked out meaningless commands for order and calm.

Ignacio was aware that the other side of the altar was affected very badly. There were broken chairs, large chunks of marble debris and bodies under this and off to the side. Ignacio had never seen death in his fifteen years and did not recognize it. The other acolytes lay in their black cassocks and white surplices, now soaked with red blood.

Ignacio stumbled over to them, brushed debris away, and saw they were not moving. He saw his brother's blood on his hands, and he could not move. This was death.

Chapter 2

Grady Marcs always cleaned his guns before Grady Jr. got home. He believed in the triple lock system. The first lock was on the steel door to the storage room, the second lock was on the gun safe bolted to the cement floor, and the third lock was on every trigger of every gun he owned. As he reassembled the antique, single shot, twenty-gauge shotgun his grandfather gave to him, he wondered if it wasn't time to get rid of a few of the guns. He had not shot any of them, except for the nine millimeter, in at least two years, and the last time was just for adjustments. He heard a key unlock the storage room door. That would be his wife, Sandy, the only other person with a key to the room. She graced the doorframe with her own slender six-foot frame. Grady was an inch taller but never felt like it.

Grady replaced the trigger lock, set the twenty-gauge in its slot, then shut the cabinet door and locked it.

Sandy was holding a check. "Hashimoto likes what you did. He paid an extra ten thousand. What did you do?"

"Hash? He's great. He likes his art, and what I got back for him was worth five million at least, and it was still in good condition."

"Ten thousand dollars is usually what someone gets paid for killing someone else."

"I would charge more than that." Grady smiled as Sandy shook her head and turned to go. "You know I'm kidding, right? I don't do that."

"So you say. The problem with this extra ten thousand is the IRS. You keep getting more of these, and we're going to look suspicious. Especially if you keep going to Mexico."

"Oh, Mexico," Grady sang.

"And there are a few receipts I can't enter as deductions. You can't deduct scribbled cash receipts paid to informants who never give you their name. Just writing 'paid two grand for running a trace route to Regulator15.' Who is Regulator15? The IRS would very much like to know so they can collect taxes from whoever that is. It's not a high-priced hooker, is it?"

"I was hacking a server and this guy who helps me once in a while found the next server on the network we needed to get into, and that's risky, so I paid him a lot of money for a several minutes of work. We found the emails and letters we needed to track down the paintings. I don't want to know the guy's name, and he doesn't want to know mine. It's safer that way. It's a pseudo name, you know, an Internet moniker."

Sandy shook her head again. "Nope. If I can't send a ten-ninety-nine, you are out two grand that we cannot deduct."

"Okay. I'm out two grand. It got me an extra ten grand."

"I can live with that, but just don't expect scribbled notes about money going to people who have no name to work as receipts." Sandy walked out of the storage room and then back in. "This one was from Harold, right?"

"Hashimoto? Yeah, Harold referred him. The police

took their reports and told the poor guy he would probably never see the paintings again, so Harold referred me."

"And we took on a new client without a deposit?"

"Yep. I got a few thousand up front in cash, but no check. I am sure I told you that. I know I had to go quick, but that was one detail I was sure I told you."

"You're probably right, but I thought you were working directly for Harold, and he knows he can't even call you without writing a deposit check up front, right?"

"You're not making sense. What's really wrong here?"

"I don't like Harold, and you know that."

"The man pays a thousand a day, no questions, even if I don't resolve the matter, and he knows I don't do wet work. I think our personal feelings about the man can guide us as we walk through his minefields. At least he hasn't killed anyone."

"I'm not so sure of that. He was pretty close to that group who shot the abortion doctor."

"Okay, he's tight with some very conservative Catholic types. That doesn't implicate him in murder."

Sandy raised both hands in frustration and walked away. "Junior's almost home. You going to snack with him?"

"Yeah, I'll be right up."

"Don't forget Jimmy and Latoria are coming over tonight. Get a shower. You need to get him to hire you for those FBI things again. He hasn't called you for work in ages."

"Yeah, well. You know they don't pay well, and then they don't pay for a long, long time. At least Harold pays." Grady turned off the light and locked the storage room.

Chapter 3

CNN reported that, in addition to Archbishop John Riley of Seattle visiting Puerto Vallarta for a conference of members of Opus Dei, four adults—two of them attending priests and two lay persons in the congregation, who were not Opus Dei members—and two teenaged acolytes died in the explosion." Harold Brown hesitated. "The lay persons were trampled to death. A German journalist was almost killed as he tried to open a third door."

Cardinal Day breathed deeply and did not respond.

"CNN also reported the dead elderly tourists were American and notice of their deaths appeared next to an article about a brewing scandal, allegedly involving illicit business relationships between the Vatican and known members of rival drug cartels in Mexico. The writer praised the efforts of the police for gaining control quickly and saving even more lives from the panic. The writer noted the body of Archbishop John Riley was returned to Seattle, too emaciated for an open casket. They correctly reported he had been archbishop for only three months."

Harold shuffled through some more notes. "The Mexican government stated openly in a press conference that their efforts to capture the criminals who were responsible would be swift and effective, and they were casual about the fact that they had no idea who could have done this. The Director of the FBI, on early morning television, suggested they had some solid leads and offered any assistance necessary to find the perpetrators. The Internal Minister of the Mexican Government replied in subsequent comments that there were no such leads to his knowledge. He wondered why the FBI was jumping so quickly to conclusions and wondered if this wasn't an effort to appease the Italian people after the American military dumped live ammunition in bottom of the Gulf of Mexico during hurricane Katrina, now potentially able to kill innocent Mexicans."

Cardinal Day sighed. "One of our citizens, an esteemed member of the Roman Catholic Church is brutally murdered and it all gets lost in politics. Who says the inquisition was such a bad thing?" He sounded tired and edgy.

"An editor at Der Zeit wondered about the American demand for more effective police work. They are so good at demanding, at putting the pressure on, and getting results. Are they skilled enough in finding the truth?" Harold stopped again. "Your Eminence, we need to do something."

"What? We cannot get involved in these politics, especially since the Vatican Bank is being investigated for laundering drug cartel money."

"Let me continue and maybe it will become clear who did this. Mexicans interviewed on the streets of Puerto Vallarta were amused at the delay on the part of the Mexican Government, reveling in American indignation at having to wait for everything. Let me read this aloud to you. 'Common Mexicans become heroes when they can tell slightly exaggerated stories about Americans, who become furious at having to wait and start yelling, becoming ever more enraged. The Mexican hero simply responds with a smile and slower service.' The *International Herald Tribune* wondered why American officials were kept waiting for forensic reports and, when received, they were incomplete. A Mexican official claimed it was an oversight that could be easily rectified if only they could wait a few more days. The first forensic reports arrived, complete, within twenty-four hours. Der Zeit claimed it was evident the perpetrator's methods used were unknown to all law enforcement agencies investigating. They were original and very effective. The material blew out directly at the archbishop, the area behind the bomb reinforced. The bomb was essentially pointing at the Episcopal Chair where he would be sitting at the precise moment of detonation. The debris was propelled at him as if it had been shot from a canon. The strategy is location, placement, and timing—all aimed at a precise point and time. When asked, the FBI refused comment on this speculation. Harold coughed lightly.

"What can we do, Harold? We have radio talk show hosts yammering on about it about it in these terms—frightening, a direct assault on the sovereignty of the United States. They saw the perpetrator as a terrorist who might even be capable of threatening the life of the President of the United States during an upcoming visit to Mexico and Central America. I understand the FBI immediately commented, claiming this was not State terrorism, but rather a transgression aimed at the Roman Catholic Church.

"The investigating agencies offered to remain, but suggested it is a matter for the Roman Catholic Church to be more involved in, financially anyway. The investigating agencies were not authorized to work on behalf of the Vatican but, given the new form of technology, would gladly complete the investigation, but at what cost? This question was left without any answer for everyone to ponder. What is going on?"

"I need to be involved, Eminence."

"Not publicly, but quietly, behind the scenes like we have done in the past. Your love of the Mother Church is admired, and we appreciate your willingness and ability to step up to the plate and help."

"There is no one in the church capable of leading an investigation, and you do not have the financial resources. I do." Harold leaned forward in his chair. "Did you know that the L'Oservatory Romano quoted Cardinal Jiminez of Mexico saying '...since so many Americans were killed, and that this was an obvious attack directed at an American prelate, it remains an ecclesiastical matter. It would serve the greater interests of the safety of Americans worldwide if American resources are employed in bringing justice to these heinous criminals.' He pointed to a long standing working relationship between the Vatican and the government in Rome and now would not be the time to interrupt that.

"Diario Oficial reported the police investigators assigned to the bombing were one day answering to their bosses, the next day they met with Cardinal Jiminez and representatives from the Vatican, and perhaps that same day they met with agents from the Federal Bureau of Investigation. Then they were called upon by special representatives from the Seattle Police Department who were investigating connections in Seattle. They asked, 'Is this the way major crime is always investigated in Rome?' The Mexican police asked the Seattle police detectives specific questions, and these detectives were advised by the Central Intelligence Agency to allow the CIA to see the responses before delivering them to the Mexican police. One embittered Seattle Police investigator was overheard talking into this cell phone about how the investigation was like watching the keystone cops. The keystone cops, Eminence."

"Okay. I cannot publicly sanction your work and will deny it if it is revealed."

"As usual, Eminence."

"I want a news conference in Puerto Vallarta, with Jiminez. I'll handle that. You contact the families of the victims and survivors, and I will tell you when and where to gather them."

"I am at your service, Eminence. I think you and I know already who we will find behind all of this, and we had better stop this now." Harold Brown failed to mention that in all of the press reports, there was no mention of Ignacio or his brother Javiar.

ⁱ⁣ↄↄↄ

Victims and impatient survivors of the dead met privately with Harold Brown. He told them he understood their frustration with the confusion over the lack of progress. He promised a press conference with Cardinal Jiminez of Mexico and Cardinal Day of Los Angeles that would ask the world through the press what was stalling the investigation. They would not announce they were hiring a private investigator. They would find someone with solid police and international credentials to carry out an independent and secret investigation on behalf of the Vatican.

At the press conference, an elderly woman asked about the Ignacio boy and both cardinals looked at each other then at their aides. Cardinal Jiminez said he would pray for him and the press conference ended abruptly. Harold dialed the number of Grady Marcs.

Chapter 4

They fall behind, and I wait longer and longer, and I'm getting pissed off. It's like, I ask them how much climbing they've done and you'd think the way they talked they climb Everest every weekend. They have the lingo down. I say it's a difficult ascent, ice patches, we have to keep the crampons on. They wave it off like it's no problem."

Grady stopped talking and gulped the last of his beer. He cleared his throat. "They told me they just did something in South America just like this. I say fine. I get to the last pitch, and I'm not comfortable. It's mostly talk. They're not for real. They went to some climbing school in Boulder, spent three weeks in the Rockies, but they don't have it. I say we go back, and they bitch like hell. No way, they paid me to lead them, and they want the top.

"Yeah, right. So I lead. Worst decision I ever made. I place two protection points and run out to a third, a safe distance away. I tell them to climb and clean the route."

"You want another Guinness?"

"Yeah. Thanks. So, they fiddle around, and then he starts climbing. They get past the first protection okay. It's a number eight chalk. Pulls right out. The next one is a four-inch cam. I stuck it in there pretty good. She tries to pull on it, won't budge. I say leave it. What's forty bucks? Then she unties from the rope. She actually unties from the rope.

"I yell down—like tie, on. She goes for the cam. Jay's climbing, and is not in a position to see what she's doing. Susan walks on the ledge, not tied on, and pulls on the cam. It comes loose and she's gone."

He snapped his fingers. "Like that. Gone. Jay stops and looks back. I know what's going to happen next. I tie the rope and, sure as shit, he's trying to get down to where she was. Can't believe she's just gone. He doesn't go far because I've tied the rope off. I rap down, and he's trying to untie. I hold him and he's freaking out. He shoves me, and then I slap him hard, chill him out. I radio down for rescue for her and him. He's a basket case."

"Grady, the phone," the bartender yelled.

"Is that my wife?"

"Yep. When are you going to get a cell phone? Why does your wife always call here?"

Grady wiped his hands clean on a napkin and picked up the receiver. "That's basically it. She's dead, and he's suing me." Grady shifted forward on to his elbows. "If your phone is off limits, I'll stop drinking here if you want. Hello, dear."

"Dear? It's only three in the afternoon and you're calling me dear? Let me guess, four beers down and the fifth is sitting on the bar."

"How can I assist you, my sweetest?"

"Harold Brown called. I knew if I muttered that devil's name the other day, he would call."

"What does one of my wealthiest clients need today, dear?"

"Something happened in Mexico. He didn't want to say much, and he wants you to look into it."

"Mexico. Hmmmm. When is Grady Junior's mid-winter break?"

"Nope. We're not going to mix work for Harold Brown with family time. Never going to happen. You find out what this is all about, figure out the end game, and we'll talk about Mexico as a family. When are you ever going to carry your cell phone?"

"Yeah, yeah. You're starting to sound like these bartenders. I'll call Harold and talk with you when I get back there." Grady dialed Harold's number before the bartender could take the phone.

There was a deep sigh, a wheeze, and then a soft clearing of the throat. "Harold here. Is this Grady?"

"Yes, Harold. Sandy said you called."

"Am I wrong, Grady, or does your wife simply not like me?"

"Let's not go there, Harold. How can I help you?"

"I need your services."

"Local?"

"No. Not quite. Mexico."

"What do you need?"

"Did you receive payment from my friend Mr. Hashimoto?"

"Yes. He gave me a generous bonus."

"Well, you did some fine work recovering those paintings. I need you to help me with this grizzly murder of the archbishop."

Grady opened a small notebook and borrowed a pen from the waitress. "Who am I working for?"

"You will work for me."

"You working for the Church?"

"I am working independently. I serve the church in any way I can. I can afford your services and will turn over whatever information you find to the Vatican."

Grady wrote the words *Opus Dei* in his notebook with

two question marks. "We should talk about this a bit, Harold. I have a few questions about this organization you belong to."

"Opus Dei? How do you know this?"

"It's my job."

"You need to meet me at the Rainier Club. Tomorrow for drinks at six. We'll have some dinner after."

"Right."

☙❧

Grady chose a high-backed leather chair, facing the city away from the patrons at the bar, aware he was the only non-white person in the room. The others looked, side long, hoping he wouldn't notice them staring. They saw he was not white, also he was six foot five inches tall, weighed about two and a quarter, and his short jet-black hair cut to the skin on the sides and flat on top. He struck out among these pasty white men in suits, their soft hands fondling the crystal and silver. He looked like his father. He smiled and sat, ordering a rum and Coke on his way down.

Harold shuffled across the gray wool carpeting, approaching Grady from behind. He sat without any verbal exchange. He looked sixty-five, short, meticulously dressed, black square-framed glasses, and a bit overweight. The gold crowns flashed in his mouth when he smiled.

"Grady, so good of you to come. It is always good to see you."

"Harold, how nice." Grady's hand was massive compared to Harold's. "We haven't talked since the matter of that boy in Los Angeles. I guess I'm lucky I didn't take the job. I hear the guy you hired took it in the head from the kid. There was something about that case that just didn't suit me. You know I don't do gum shoe very well. I'm happy with cybercrime."

"All resolved. All resolved." Harold waved his right hand, smiling. "No one was ever in any danger, and I have come to appreciate men like you who are meticulous and careful. That other fellow, Jack something, he just messed up."

A waiter appeared with the rum and Coke and a single malt scotch, water back. The delivery was silent, and Harold nodded with a slight smile.

Harold sipped his scotch carefully. "You know this business about the archbishop."

"Yes. Sad, isn't it?"

"You need to find out who did it."

"Let the Mexicans and the FBI solve this."

"It's not going well."

"Let it go badly then."

"Messy politics."

"And you want me to get in the middle of that?"

"We need to find the truth. I have good information that these people have a larger agenda."

"Which is?"

"I don't want to prejudice your mind. I want to see if you draw the same conclusions."

"I assume this agenda is intended to adversely affect the Catholic Church. Anything else? And what part of the case is cyber-crime?"

"I was approached two days ago by a special representative of the Vatican."

"Who is it?"

"You work for me. I will make all contacts with them. Here is your contact in Puerto Vallarta. Captain Olivia Moro."

"What is she?"

"She is a captain in the local police, in charge of the

investigation in Puerto Vallarta. She knows who to deal with."

Grady was silent as he considered how this was unfolding. "She's also friendly to Opus Dei, right? I haven't accepted this work yet, Harold. Your organization helped the Nazis get to Argentina. I may have a problem doing this. I'll need to think about it."

Harold sipped his scotch and stared at Grady. "They say you are a seer, someone who uses the devil's power to read people's minds. I may be at some great risk here."

"Harold, I do not do the devil's bidding, and I personally would rather not know what people think."

Harold smiled politely. "Can we work together?"

"I don't know. Let me get down there and see what's going on. In the meantime, convince me Opus Dei isn't something to stay away from. And why are you employing a cybercrimes specialist in an act of terroristic murder in another country?"

Harold breathed deeply. "There is so much good to our organization, much I cannot tell you. But be assured we want only to advance the word of God through the holy father." Harold looked at his watch. "It's time to go into the dining room to eat. We have much to talk about in there. I will be leaving for Puerto Vallarta tomorrow morning, and I will set things up with Captain Moro then."

"Back to the cybercrime thing, Harold. Why am I going and not some other private eye who does street work?"

"I'm sure you will appreciate my wisdom in sending you when you begin to dig into this thing."

'Maybe, Harold, and maybe you'll not want me to tell you what I find."

"I doubt that. I have seen much and very little frightens me."

Grady followed Harold, gracefully keeping pace with a man slower and much older. "Also, Harold, there is a rumor floating around that you funded a skunk project to first bad mouth an abortion doctor and then you paid to have him shot. Any truth to that?"

Harold did not look back at him to answer. He continued to walk toward the door, but stopped and turned around. "Grady, I have many theories, some more well founded than others, and I do not want to pollute the waters with them, especially if you are going to argue with me. I will tip you off on one of them. There is a group of very radical homosexuals in this city with the financial resources to do what they want. Normally, they spend money on political campaigns, and that has been effective, but recently, especially with the installation of Archbishop Riley, things have taken an ugly tone. I am wondering if we are not looking at something here more dangerous than a political advertisement. You decide if you want the work and call me. I think we need to act quickly on this, so please do not hesitate in your decision process. Thank you and have a good evening. Please say hello to your lovely wife for me. I'll have your advance delivered in the morning."

Chapter 5

Captain Olivia Moro did not want the case. She had worked with the Americans before and found the experience not at all pleasant. She had argued that the murder had taken place not in her jurisdiction, but in that of Captain Salazar. The minister did not listen. "We want it solved."

The fact Moro had the same last name as a murdered Italian Prime Minister always evoked the question, were they related. Yes. Her father was an Italian diplomat to Mexico and a first cousin of the murdered prime minister who decided to move permanently to Mexico to avoid the same fate at the hands of the Red Brigade. He met Olivia's mother, while a diplomat, and married her. The actions of the Red Brigade, and especially the murder of her father's cousin, inspired Olivia to enter the police academy, even though she held a degree in Economics.

Her career as a captain in Puerto Vallarta was more challenging than she had ever expected. With the drug cartels active to the north of her state of Jalisco, and the ever-irritating presence of poor people migrating from Central America to El Norte, Moro was not thinking of retirement any time soon. Besides, she was determined she would find the cartel members who killed her son.

The call from the minister was expected. Olivia Moro had earned the reputation necessary for a minister to call when such a politically sensitive case was to be solved. The call from Harold Brown was not expected at all.

"Olivia, I am aghast at how things are falling apart."

Captain Moro hesitated. "You are involved somehow, Mr. Brown? Tell me now."

"Do you know who did this?"

"Mr. Brown, I do not have time for this. Why are you calling me about the case of a murdered American Archbishop?"

"I am hiring a man who is familiar with your work and your area. Former army ranger with very strong investigative skills. I am sending him to help you with your investigation."

"I have things under control here, Mr. Brown. No need."

"He's familiar with Mexican procedures, movements of various people you track down."

"Who is he?"

"Grady. Grady Marcs or something. I don't know his last name really well."

"Mr. Brown, I am not going to waste any time on this. I cannot. I will check him out with our people, and I'll call you in a couple of days and let you know if he can shadow our investigation."

"I am working secretly for the Vatican on this, Olivia. I am keeping the pope informed."

Captain Moro frowned and rolled her eyes. "If you say so, Mr. Brown."

Inspector Juarez graced the entrance to Captain Moro's office. She looked up and smiled. "Carlos. Just the person."

The inspector set a plate on her desk with two thick slices of rosca de reyes, a cake normally eaten at Christmas time but two or three times a week year round by Captain Moro. She smiled broadly. She explained to him what she needed. He took quick, clean notes and said he would have information on Grady in an hour. Moro sat back in her chair. "Don't hurry. Whenever you get it is fine. I think he's coming down here next week. By the way, I was given these tickets to the carnival, and I just don't want to go. Do you want them?"

Inspector Juarez smiled. "I don't have anyone to go with and that's not my crowd."

"Maybe this guy Mr. Brown is sending will have that right stuff you keep looking for."

Juarez shook his head gently. The only thing worse than being a gay Mexican cop was having a boss who was always trying to find you a date.

In exactly one hour, he sat in front of Captain Moro again. "He's an American. He was in the army rangers, intelligence, mostly in Central and South America. He's been in Mexico quite a bit over the years, speaks fluent local dialects. Last mission was into Afghanistan before the Nine/Eleven incident. Lots of controversy over what he was doing there. Retired his position, seems his wife helped him grow a software company and they sold it, so now he freelances mostly to the FBI and the Department of Defense. Pretty serious cybercrime investigations."

"Interesting. Cybercrimes, huh? Anything specific on what he did in Mexico?"

"That's all we have. He kept a low profile, no matter where he went. No one seems to know why he was ever here, no specific reasons."

Moro sighed out loud. "He'll need to be watched. Keep his hands out of the usual candy jars, that sort of thing. Find out why a former army intelligence cyber-crimes investigator wants to take on a private investigation into the murder of a Catholic archbishop."

"Yes, ma'am."

"And if you like him, that's okay too."

"Sir?"

Olivia laughed and waved him out of her office. She looked at her watch. It was late enough to call Gabrielle in Monterey. He would be eating breakfast. Her first husband had died in a car accident. It was a head on with a delivery truck. She waited almost ten years before she allowed herself the company of a new man.

Gabrielle worked as a business manager for two not-well-known factories. He was abrupt, the meetings were not going well. He said he would see her in two days and hung up.

Olivia raised her right eyebrow and proceeded to eat her rosca de reyes.

ↄ∞ↄ

Grady had left instructions for Grady Junior to wash the vehicles. As he approached the house, returning from his meeting with Harold, he could clearly see Grady Junior sitting on the curb and two younger neighborhood kids doing the washing. A regular Tom Sawyer. "Hey, I told *you* to wash the vehicles. Not them. Whatever you promised them is coming out of your allowance, now get up and finish. You guys are done."

Grady went upstairs to his office and started his search on Captain Moro. The official Jalisco State police web site wisely did not provide any photographs, but extolled her career as one of the first and most successful female captains on the force.

He dialed the number of his former commander, Colonel Mark Burnett, US Army, retired. "Mark, I am trying to get some intel on someone in Mexico. You still have those connections?"

"Grady, I was just thinking of you yesterday. When did you get back from the cabin in Jackson Hole?"

"Well, Grady Jr. had to get back into school so Sandy flew back with him mid-January. I stayed on another week and drove back. I've been home all of February."

"That was such a great week. We really enjoyed it. Thanks."

"And who would have thought that after serving under you I'd still like you."

'Well, you didn't frag me, so I guess you at least respected me. Who you looking for"

"Captain Olivia Moro. State Police, Jalisco Mexico, stationed in Puerto Vallarta."

"How quick do you need it?"

"As quick as—"

"Give me an hour."

ഇരിരി

Grady looked down on the progress of the car washing. Grady Junior was applying the wax and buffing as he went. He opened the window to yell down to his son. "Good job, but it's getting dark. Finish in the morning."

Grady knew how hard it would be to teach his own son the value of hard work in a society placing too much value on leisure and recreation. He would not know how much he had until he was out of college and established in a career. He would also pay his own way through college. They would help on the tuition, but everything else was on him.

Mark called back in less than an hour. "Interesting woman, Captain Moro. Related to the murdered Italian Prime Minister, Aldo Moro. Has a record of being fairly brutal, and I can understand. She believes the cartels are responsible for the murder of her son. That's a good motivator, I'd say. No connections other than informants. She's clean. What's the case?"

"Murdered archbishop from Seattle. This is more an explosives case, maybe brutal terrorism, but not sure what the cyber-crime angle would be. You know I'm not interested in regular cases like this. All that forensics and blood."

"Yeah, that was interesting when I read about that. Hey, do me a favor and keep me posted when you can."

"Roger Wilco."

"Grady, do you know how stupid that sounds?"

Grady dialed Harold's number and got him on the second ring. "Harold, Grady here. I checked her out. One of the things that would have prevented me from doing this would be any connection between her and the cartels, and she seems to be pretty clean."

"Good. I didn't tell you I mentored her when she was in college. She comes from a very fine family. I knew her father very well, worked a bit with him on some church related projects."

Grady hesitated. "Harold, why is it with you—you never give me vital information up front."

"I give you the information you need when you need it."

"Fine, Harold, make the introduction. I am going to make arrangements to get down there day after tomorrow."

"I was thinking it would be better if you—"

"I have a family, Harold. I leave the day after tomorrow. You can have the tickets and cash dropped off here any time."

Part 2
Several Months Earlier

Chapter 6

reg Lucas blew snot from his nose as he rode his bicycle past several tourists standing in line to buy lattes. Jackson Hole was now nothing more than a perpetual traffic jam of expensive sport utility vehicles and fat yuppies escaping what he figured was the urban decay they had caused with their unbridled greed. New money, mostly, who would gladly pay four dollars for a poorly made latte.

He needed to get safely across the highway through thick, stalled traffic. He slipped in front of a large Suburban and pedaled between the opposing lanes of traffic. A man in a Range Rover leaned out his window. Greg could plainly see he was getting ready to spit at him. Greg pretended not to notice until just before the man blew then clenched his left fist and slammed it square into the man's face. He knew he had done some damage, but didn't stop to look. He slipped through the other lane of traffic and was off toward his cabin.

By the time the man's wife dialed nine-one-one on her cell phone and screamed for the police, Greg approached the last steep hill before his cabin. The ride had been good, except for that brief encounter. The endorphin rush made him smile. Officer Jerry Garcia of the Jackson Hole

Police Department waited for him at the cabin. The sight of the police car dulled the pleasurable edge.

"Lucas, what the hell did you do this time? They sent me up here to talk with you about a gentleman in to—"

"Gosh, Jerry, I'm impressed. Last month when those kids down the street were breaking into my cabin, you guys took two hours to get here. Then some fat-sucking yuppie calls you about something, and it's hop to. They must pay the taxes around here or something." Greg wheeled his bicycle into the roughhewn basement of the cabin. "Come on in if you want."

Officer Garcia followed. "What did you do to that guy, Greg?"

"I was riding through stalled traffic, the kind of traffic you guys can't seem to figure out how to clear up, trying to get to the other side of the road. I was cutting down in between the lanes. You know that's the safest place to ride. My head is down, I'm watching tail lights and wheels, not faces. I look up and see fat boy leaning out the window of his monster mobile trying to see what the holdup is. He's not looking at me. They never do. Bicycles are invisible. Well, too late. I brush him aside with my elbow and keep on going. Did something happen to him after that?"

"Seems he got pretty beat up. Says you took two or three swipes at his face. Blood all over everything. He's on his way to the hospital, stitches maybe. They're pissed as hell." Jerry smiled. "They described that butt ugly jersey you wear, so I knew who to talk to."

Greg pulled off the neon pink and lime green cycling jersey. "Hey, I know it's ugly. But, I get noticed more and run over less."

"Greg, what are we going to do? This is not the first time. The chief is getting pretty upset with you. I may have to bring you—" Jerry started slowly.

"What the hell would have happened to fat boy if he was leaning out his window to check on traffic, and a logging truck swooped by and slammed him with the extended mirror? No more mister fat boy, right? What the fuck is the guy doing leaning out of his truck, anyway? I know. He was going to spit on me. I made a pre-emptive strike. It's that simple."

Jerry held up his hands. "Okay, I'll talk to the chief. But you know he hates to piss off the tourists. And hitting someone is a crime. Don't leave town today until I sort this thing out, okay? In the meantime, just chill out and leave the tourists alone."

Greg mustered a sloppy, back-handed salute. "You still coming over to play poker tonight?"

"If I don't have to arrest you and throw your ass in jail, sure." Jerry waved as he got into his patrol car.

Nothing ever came of the tourist who was, quite illegally, hanging out of his truck as he was trying to drive it. There were certain laws in the State of Wyoming that just couldn't be ignored. And when Officer Garcia ran his California plates, he discovered a warrant for a no-show on a DWI hearing. The chief advised the man to make sure the doctors in town took good care of him and…well, to take care of that arrest warrant when he got back home. The man was happy to get out of the station.

Detective Jerry Garcia insisted on bringing the cards. He said he never trusted a known felon. Greg would remind Jerry he had never been convicted of anything and his reputation far exceeded any reality. Jerry arrived early when Greg said he had some interesting evidence, guaranteed to be better than the trust fund bilking case— Internet mail fraud. Not the cheesy Nigerian bank scams, which still worked by the way, but more sinister, targeting recently widowed women with phony love interests.

"Don't the old ladies see past that BS?"

"You'd think so, but it seems to work. I think he's raked in a cool two mil so far on this scam."

"Do I know the perp?"

"Yeah."

"Who."

Greg was about to respond, but was interrupted when Jim Burns burst through the front door of the cabin. Greg handed Jerry a flash drive, smiled, and winked. Jerry raised his eyebrows and looked puzzled.

Jim liked Greg's poker games. His life as a New York attorney had always been proper and moneyed. His specialty was mergers and acquisitions. He felt that these weekly games salted his life a bit. He always said it was time to unbutton his shirt a bit, chomp a cigar, and live like a man. He retired at forty-eight and moved to Jackson Hole to feel closer to the Earth. He claimed, in a moment of weakness, he had finally begun the vision quest for his life and had heard the clarion call of the wolves—the siren song of the wilderness. Greg asked Jim if he wouldn't like to go out on a weeklong ski tour with him to really experience the wilderness. Jim promised that one day he would, but always insisted there were loose ends to business deals that needed his urgent attention.

Genelle was the first person Greg had met in Jackson Hole. She was thirty-nine, a Lesbian committed to the same woman for fifteen years. She arrived in Jackson Hole twenty years earlier with a pair of skis, a duffel bag of clothes, and, in her words, a shit load of healing to go through. Genelle was selling real estate when Greg arrived. She sold him the cabin and introduced him to extreme skiing.

It was during those first weeks in the winter of 2004 when Greg really learned how to ski. He also began to learn how to respect women. Genelle's biting charm, slow drawl, and no-bullshit attitude delighted Greg. Too bad for him, she was a Lesbian.

Greg dealt the cards for a round of five-card draw. Jim sipped his Maker's Mark.

"Those dear folks from California get on back home okay?" Greg asked sweetly.

"Seems the old boy was in a bit of trouble back home. Something about a no-show on a DWI. We thought he shouldn't waste his time around here with such an important matter like that waiting for him in California. We told him we don't care much for drunk drivers around here. We like our kids and don't want them run over or anything. He was real polite after that." After a pause, Jerry asked, "What makes you so violent, Greg?"

Greg looked at his cards and poked his lower lip out. "Is this a psycho-babble alert?"

"No, friend, I just want to know what puts you over the edge. Maybe help keep you out of jail. It's very nice you are able to help us out with your computer expertise, but you need to button up the anger."

They all looked silently at their cards.

"What did you do before you were a cop?" Jim asked.

Genelle looked at Jim and then at Jerry. "Are we here to play poker or analyze Lucas?" she asked sharply, getting a thankful smile from Greg.

"Just asking. I'll bet two bucks on this hand."

The others threw their two dollars on the table to stay in the round. Jim took two cards, Genelle one, and Jerry three. Greg did not take any cards.

Greg flipped his cards through his fingers. "It's a long story."

Jim affected a bad southern accent. "I hear tell you was special forces."

"I quit the forces. I have, well, something of an edge, and I hate assholes, especially assholes in charge. I was teaching in a private school in Los Angeles, and I beat the shit out of some rich kid in the school. He was a shit-for-brains little brat who thought he could do anything he wanted. I caught him putting firecrackers in a dog's ears. He killed the dog, and I was going to kill the kid, except a couple of other priests pulled me off. The kid's dad proceeded to sue the school, the Jesuit order, the local diocese, and added about five million dollars to their family fortune. I was told to leave." The table was silent as each person pondered their hand.

Genelle folded and the other three bet their way through. Jerry won the hand, and Jim took the cards to shuffle and deal.

Jerry winked. "Bad boy."

Jim was always the first to quit. When the whiskey bottle was empty, he would stretch and say it was time to hit the sack. He cashed in his chips and said good night.

After another hand, Greg motioned at the computer disk in front of Jerry. "Pretty good stuff on there."

"Yeah?" Jerry asked, picking up his cards.

"Local guy."

"How local?"

Greg did not look up. "Well, we may need to find a fourth player for our game."

"Jim? The hell you say." Jerry stared at the disk "Can I look now?"

"Sure." Greg reached over and booted the computer. "He uses the screen name Ralph Crand, Esquire. He finds funeral records on line, does the math by zip code to determine if there's any money in the family, and makes contact by finding them on social networks. He plays like an old friend or business associate of the husband and apologizes about not making the funeral. Exchanges a few emails and then offers to stop by and visit on a business trip. He fakes some lie about forgiving a debt from way back and usually gets the woman to offer something, so he fakes some paper work usually a direct loan or an unpaid consulting fee depending on what he finds out in the obituary and where the stiff worked," Greg said as he slipped the drive into the computer. He brought up the email messages he had saved.

"What makes you think this is Jim?" Jerry asked as he read a few of the messages. His eyes widened.

"I set him up. I routed my messages through Genelle's computer so it had a woman's name and a local computer address. I create the profile of a woman who would fit the profile and baited him. I use a simulation software to make it look like the emails are coming from someone else, that being the woman. I don't think that's illegal, yet, so don't worry. I got him to want to come and see me. Look at these messages here." Greg found the section where he had invited Ralph Crand Esquire to Denver. "He's the one who suggested the steak dinner at Ruth's Chris, keeping it quiet so as not to upset the family about having an outstanding debt, hush, hush, and all is forgiven."

"How old did you say you were?"

"Sixty eight. He likes that number. Twenty years older than himself, but then he likes mature women, right?"

"Did he show up?"

Greg nodded. "Showed up right when he said he was going to. You tell him the rest, Genelle."

Genelle slowly shuffled the cards and dealt another hand. "I invited my kid brother George over. He lives down in Cody. George is in cement contracting, bigger than anyone I know. Ole' Jim shows up at the door, knock, knock, and Big George asks him what the hell he wants. Jim stammers a bit, checks his little book, and, sure as shit, it's the right address. He apologizes, gives some bullshit excuse, and leaves. He parked a block away for about three hours watching the house. Waiting to see if a little woman came home or something? You be the judge."

Greg placed a bet on the table. "You in this hand?"

"So, Jim," Jerry said quietly. "You just never know. And he's ugly as a monkey, no I take that back, monkey's run when they see him."

"I know you probably can't use this as evidence because it's a set up. But now you know where to look. Nail that little shit-sucking lawyer before I kill him."

Jerry smiled and nodded, looking at his cards. "I can keep the disk?"

"You bet. Won't little Jimmy be surprised. Thinks he owns the goddam valley with his five-thousand-square-foot house and his bank full of money," Greg said smoothly.

Genelle smiled.

Jerry set his cards down and looked up at the clock.

"His email postings were all done between ten p.m. and midnight. It's ten-fifteen. He's over there right now doing it, isn't he?"

Greg smiled. "That's why you're top cop around here, Jerry."

Jerry picked up Greg's phone without asking and dialed a number. He walked into the kitchen and spoke in a quiet tone for a few minutes. "The chief is coming out here," he informed them. "How can we tell if Jim is on his computer now?"

"Wouldn't it be great if there was a computer program like this one?" Greg clicked on an icon. "Something that would allow us to get into a person's computer and see what he is doing right then." He smiled. "I wrote a program for that. Now that I know his address, I can make direct contact with his computer, and I can even tell you what he's doing as long as his computer is on and he is using his modem."

"Can you do that now?"

"Right now? In the middle of the game?"

"Well, uh, yeah. T—this is like i—important—" Jerry stammered. "I told Chief Greig that—"

"I'm kidding, Jerry. Yes. I'll be into his system in less than five minutes. You tell your chief to come here if he wants proof."

The telephone rang and Jerry answered. He explained to his chief what Greg was doing.

"Is this illegal? I mean, we don't have a warrant to tap his phone line. Are we tapping his phone line?"

Greg rolled his eyes. "What is illegal? Besides it's cable, not telephone, and he's using unencrypted wireless." He showed Jerry what was then appearing on his screen. Jim was logged on to one of the commercial Internet access providers and engaged in a private, on-line chat with someone, a woman. Ralph Crand, Esquire, invited her to Jackson Hole.

"He's doing it right now," Jerry yelled excitedly. He leaned close into the screen.

The chief of police arrived. "Lucas, you working for us full time now?"

"You hiring?"

"No. What's this all about?"

Jerry showed him the computer screen. They followed the on-line conversation.

The chief made a short call on his cell phone and slapped it shut. "Okay, Jerry, let's get him. We have a warrant. No Wyoming justice, got it? I want him alive. Keep Gardner outside and don't let anyone get close to him in the holding cell."

Officer Garcia nodded.

Greg sighed. "So, I guess this ends the game. Damn it, Jerry. Now what do I do?"

☙❧

Jim was still logged on and in the middle of the very same conversation when the police arrived. The search of the house yielded boxes of files of both former victims and potential marks, video recordings of houses and the women who had been or would be victims, photographs, and a diary.

Jerry did not look at the evidence—he just stuffed it into plastic bags.

Chapter 7

Bishop John Riley thanked the Papal Nuncio with weak enthusiasm. After hanging up the phone, he spat the word "Seattle." The old liberal Schwarz died, probably from Sclerosis of the liver he drank so much. And the archdiocese of Seattle was a mess. A bastion of gay priests, married priests, abortion doctors, gay activists all lined up to go to mass and shake the fat old man's hand and slip him money to fight for their agendas. He was finally dead, but why did they have to send Riley to clean this crap hole up?

His absolute fidelity to the mission of the Mother Church, as defined by the pope and his attending cardinals, won him many influential friends all the way up to the corridors of the Vatican. The holy father himself warmly greeted him upon his return from the suffering heat of Central America. He thanked him for so many saved souls for the Mother Church, so much work to stem the hedonistic and secular influences among the faithful.

Being picked to replace the liberal Archbishop of Seattle was a clear indication he had not influenced enough of the right people.

John Riley walked away from the phone and looked out over the steaming city of Los Angeles from his air-conditioned office. He opened the cherry wood cabinet that held his supply of single malt scotch, fingered for a Waterford Crystal glass, and poured out a generous portion. The first drink was long and heavy. He swallowed hard, allowing the alcohol to bite at his nose and throat. He wiped the excess from his lip with the back of his left hand, took another sip, refilled the glass, and sat hard in his high back leather chair.

Riley dialed the number of Bishop James Sanders. "Seattle," Riley grumbled. "They've appointed me to Seattle."

"Seattle?" James coughed a slight laugh. "I had heard a rumor that you were headed for the northeast. Remember what they did when Santini was named assistant bishop under Schwartz. Chewed him up and spit him out. My God, Seattle. At least the coffee is good up there," he added with a sharp laugh.

"It's not funny, James."

"Seriously, congratulations, John. No one deserves this as much as you do. I mean, any other assignment right now would be as a bishop, you know that. How would you like to be the bishop of Helena, Montana? Got an alcohol problem? If you don't, you will."

"Yeah, right. Very comforting thought. Thanks a lot."

"We'll see you at the conferences, won't we, John. Or maybe you plan on going native."

"What do you mean by that?" Riley demanded.

"Ease up there, friend. I'm trying to help you laugh through this. You're going to need a sense of humor up there."

"I'm sorry, James. This is my last assignment. I have worked my ass off for something really good. Seattle does not get me noticed when Day retires," Riley said quietly. "They'll look at San Francisco or some other archdiocese. This is the end of the road, James."

"It's God's work, John. You've been lucky, and now, at fifty eight, you get tapped to lead. Look at this for what it is, John."

"I know you're right, James. I know it in my heart, but—" Riley covered his eyes with his free hand. "We're still on for the house at Laguna Beach, aren't we?"

"Yeah, yeah. The Macmillans will be in Spain for the month and they said we could stay there. The domestics even speak English. Is Bishop Johnson still coming with us?"

"Are you kidding? It's late October now, and we don't go until the week after Christmas, and he's in Nebraska. He's already called me three times this week just to make sure he had a room."

After hanging up, Riley sat quietly for a moment. The sun was low, shedding soft gold across the vast city of Los Angeles. Lights began to twinkle. He noticed the air conditioning had stopped. He guessed that the temperature outside was cool enough for a quick run.

He fingered for the atlas on his bookshelf and opened the book to the map of Washington. He was surprised to see Seattle was not right on the coast. It appeared to be farther in situated along a large inlet. He was surprised to see that Portland was so far south. He had always thought that Portland was closer.

"'Average rainfall, thirty five inches,'" he read out loud. He winced. "Average January temperature, forty three degrees." He did not smile. The telephone rang on his desk.

"John, how lucky," Cardinal Day said loudly.

"What do you mean, lucky, Eminence?"

"Well, Seattle is a booming city. I know many people who *want* to move there." Cardinal Day emphasized the word want. "You know who is up there, don't you?"

"Yeah. Our friend, Harry Boyle, former assistant bishop of Newark, New Jersey. Retired. Living in the lap of luxury under the liberal theological protection of Archbishop Howard Schwartz. Now, tell me again why I'm lucky."

"Because the holy father specifically told me he wanted you for the job up there." Cardinal Day responded firmly.

Riley stiffened. "The holy father?"

"Yes. He's just plain sick and tired of what's going on up there and…well, the truth be known, he was looking for someone he could depend on. Someone with some backbone, who would set things right and, just like you did so wonderfully in Central America, keep the holy father informed. The papal nuncio wanted that fool Barringer up there, but I argued like a crazed Banshee. Barringer is a softy, a fop. He talks loud, but he gives in. And he's drinking again. We need someone who can shut Harry Boyle down for good and fix what Schwartz screwed up," Cardinal Day said loudly.

Riley was quiet. He had misjudged Cardinal Day. He had taken him for an ineffective old man, given more to visiting grade schools than running the church. He now saw the cardinal in a whole new light.

"You have a mandate here, John. Bring her back into the church, for the holy father. He's old and tired and doesn't want to fight those liberals up there anymore. He wants the place run the way it should be run. And he wants someone to keep an eye on Boyle and the following he's got. The holy father doesn't want a new church springing up in Seattle because no one was man enough to keep things organized."

Bishop Riley, soon to be Archbishop Riley in the Holy Mother Church, set the phone down gently. He poured another drink and called his friend William Sanchez, member of the Knights of Malta and always good for a celebratory dinner. "William, good news, I am going to Seattle, as their new archbishop."

William Sanchez said something about praising the Lord and thanking God for a clear-sighted pope. They agreed to meet at the quiet little spot, just off Rode Drive, Riley liked so much, 208 Rodeo. William offered to have his driver pick Riley up, but Riley thanked him and said he wanted to drive after dinner and reflect on his new opportunity.

When he arrived at 208, William—dressed in a dark suit and tie with an ornate medallion around his neck—was handing his keys to the Bentley to the attendant. He waited for Riley—dressed in clerical black with a large gold cross hanging around his neck—as he handed his keys to his Audi over. Some people walking past gawked and stared. Willian and Riley walked inside. William was immediately recognized and ushered past other waiting customers to a quiet table.

The Knights of Malta claimed to be a charitable organization running hospitals around the world, and openly discussed their history as a military organization and, at one time, an independent country on the island of Malta. Today their headquarters were in Rome and were recognized by the United Nations, again, as an independent country, much like the Vatican. While there were disputes about what their real work was and it was subject to many conspiracy theories, it was undisputed that the members were mostly extremely wealthy and influential members of their community and to be on casual dining and conversational terms with a bishop, or even the pope, was expected of them at their station. And they picked these hierarchical connections based on their level of conservatism and adherence to traditional church teachings.

Routinely, their discussions centered on the Church

and her mission, rarely venturing into secular issues. William, over the years, did not talk about money but, instead, listened as Riley expressed a need. Quietly, the next day would proceed to put the money where it was needed without any discussion. This night they could not avoid talking about how bad the archdiocese of Seattle had become.

William had one drink and a modest glass of wine from the bottle with his dinner. Riley had two more scotches, finished the bottle of wine, and sniffed a brandy as they picked at the desert. William offered to call his driver and get Riley home. Riley refused and said he wanted to drive up the coast and look out at the ocean.

Riley drove his car from Rode Drive out to the coast highway, driving through two red lights. As he slowed for the intersection to turn north on the highway, a LAPD cruiser flashed its lights, but Riley did not immediately stop. He turned right, not paying attention to the flashing lights behind him, and then heard the siren. He pulled over so far to the right, his Audi scraped against the post of a traffic sign. He rested his head on the steering wheel as the officer motioned for him to roll down his window.

"Sir, are you aware that you drove through two red lights back there? Have you been drinking?"

"No, officer, I have not been drinking. I received some bad news today and it is very upsetting."

"I see. Can I have your license and registration please?"

"I don't have my license with me. I went out to dinner with a friend who usually pays and I rarely carry a wallet."

"What is your occupation, sir?"

"I am a Catholic bishop."

"I see. Would you please step out of the car? I am going to ask you to consent to a breathalyzer to determine your blood alcohol level. If you do not consent, I will need to take you in so we can determine if you are not drunk and okay to drive."

"I am a bishop. I will soon be an archbishop, and I do not take breathalyzers. I am going to get back in my car and drive home."

The action of his hands being forcefully brought behind him and cuffs clicking on and then pinching his wrists distracted him from hearing his Miranda rights. He was barely aware of the fact he was sitting in the back of a patrol car, hands tightly cuffed behind him as another patrol car and a tow truck arrived to remove the bishop's car. When they arrived at the station and waited for the processing to begin, Riley admitted to the officer, he had been to the 208 Rodeo. He had a classic filet mignon with a twenty-year-old bottle of Cabernet, he liked so much, the brandy he always liked was a hundred dollars a glass, and that he most certainly did drink too much. Anyone would if they just found out they would have to work the rest of their career in Seattle. The officer shook his head.

Chapter 8

Father Joe Gatz, Archbishop Riley's personal assistant, informed the chancery secretary Mary Conners that he would review the archbishop's appointment calendar and would approve or deny all future appointment requests. Mary wondered out loud if the archbishop wanted things done this way. Father Gatz stared at her and sternly said yes. Archbishop Riley entered the office, thanked Mary for his coffee, and walked into his private office. Father Gatz followed, smiling at Mary Conners.

The door closed solidly. Mary Conners stood staring at it.

"How did Father Carroll take it?" Archbishop Riley asked quietly.

"Oh, they all take it hard. You know how they are. Take money away from AIDS victims, and they all get emotional on me." A tight smile appeared on his face. "I think he's rather attached to his pals."

"What's his office number?" Archbishop Riley asked quickly.

Father Gatz flipped through his small book and handed it across the desk. The archbishop dialed and waited as it rang.

"Father Carroll, Archbishop Riley here." Riley had a smooth, pleasant voice when he wanted it.

There was a silent pause on the other end, and Father Carroll cleared his throat. "Yes. Archbishop."

"Father Carroll, I would like to invite you to have dinner with me tomorrow evening, my residence. Say, about seven? I want to talk to you about some ideas I have for your new assignment. I'm excited. I've heard a lot about your work, and I think that you have the right potential to organize some very effective programs."

"Seven. Tomorrow night. Very good Archbishop. Thank you for calling." Father Carroll was polite.

Archbishop Riley leaned back in his chair. "I want that office dismantled today. As of five p.m., it no longer exists. Lay off the entire staff. Tell the lawyers you're doing this on my direct orders. I don't anyone to think they can call out and alert the press or anyone else, so make sure the phones have been disconnected. Give Carroll a few days off. If you can reassign the staff, fine. If not, let them go. Give them two week's pay. We don't contribute to unemployment insurance, do we?"

Father Gatz shrugged. "I'll find out."

"If we do, fine. They can all go on unemployment. Get Harry Boyle's number for me."

Father Gatz flipped the pages in his address book and pointed at the number.

The phone rang and Riley cleared his throat. "Bishop Boyle," he said sweetly, politely. "This is Archbishop John Riley. I wanted to see of you have some time to spend with me over lunch, say tomorrow. Twelve thirty? My office. Yes. Fine, fine. I look forward to meeting you." Riley set the receiver carefully in its place. "If I was sent here to put the reins on him, I'm going to break his balls."

⸙⸙⸙

Harry noticed the archbishop had aged since the last time they had met in Newark. Even though he was four inches taller and considerably thinner than Archbishop Riley, the handshake was firm and lasted several moments. Father Gatz was sent on an important errand, and the two bishops were left alone, the cold lunch set out on the small conference table. "You care for a scotch?"

Harry nodded.

"Club Soda?"

"No. Straight up."

"Ah, yes. That's how we Irish do it, right?" The smile was broad, genuine. The archbishop touched Harry's glass with his. "Oh, yes, before I forget, during the transition, I was shown, let me say it politely, a few minor financial irregularities. The books for the AIDS awareness project, for example, are not quite, oh, up to date. Clerical errors, I'm sure. But so much so, I had to close the office. It was becoming something of a cash hemorrhage. Were you in on that stuff much?"

"No. I had nothing to do with the finances."

"Pretty loose affair, really. Father Carroll is joining me for dinner tonight. I have to find out who was writing checks, giving out assistance, who received it. That sort of thing."

Harry set his drink carefully on the desk. "I'm sure Father Carroll will be very helpful to you in solving this problem."

"Oh, that's not the main reason he's coming over. I need to reassign him into something more spiritually productive. The parishes out on the Olympic Peninsula are in need of fresh young blood."

"It's such a terrible shame that the best and brightest priests are always sent to such remote and isolated areas. Too bad priests can't get married. They end up such lonely people, and the risk of alcoholism is so great."

Archbishop Riley carefully pondered what he called the poisoned logic of the left. "Alcoholism is a treatable disease. Many experts believe it exists already in the victim and can be triggered in isolated loneliness or in the middle of a vibrant and entertaining culture as well." The words were heavy and cold. "Your opinion on the marriage of priests is well known in Seattle, am I right?"

"When asked, I exercise my constitutional rights and express my opinions."

"Do you understand, Bishop, that your elevation to the office of bishop, no matter where it took place, is a permanent state? No matter what your circumstances, people will believe you are speaking as a voice of the Mother Church."

Archbishop Riley sat back in his leather chair and finished his drink. Bishop Boyle sensed the inquisition had begun. How nice for it to happen over good scotch and a catered lunch. Many others who believed in a faith other than that expressed by the Holy Roman Catholic Church were treated with much less grace and dignity. If it was going to get bumpy, he wanted another drink. And how bumpy could it get?

They forced him out of Newark and left him without a bishop's chair. They had already done the hatchet job on him. What could they do now?

"I have never defied what the Catholic Church teaches or requires of its priests. I have always said it is an issue that demands reconsideration."

"Reconsideration?" Archbishop Riley leaned forward on his desk. "Reconsideration? That's defying what the holy father himself has only recently said, that the issue is not to be discussed and the matter is closed to debate. Reconsideration?"

Archbishop Riley needed a commitment from Boyle, not more hostility. He leaned back in his chair. "Father

Carroll looks to you for guidance. He thinks the world of you. I am told many other priests in the archdiocese have become close to you as well. You have been a great spiritual inspiration to many of them, got them to say their daily breviary more regularly. That's the thing that kills a priest faster than liquor, when he stops saying his prayers." He looked at Harry for a moment. "You want another drink?"

Harry hesitated and finally nodded. "A small one."

"Small, hell. We have to understand each other, and right now we're about as uptight as we can get."

It worked. Boyle raised his eyebrows and smiled when Riley said that. It always worked. His Irish father taught him that. Make a personal connection and you will win over your worst enemy. The pouring was loud and a bit clumsy.

"That is indeed a large drink," Harry did not touch the glass. He smiled.

"We need to understand each other, Harry. I am the local ordinary, not Archbishop Schwartz. He allowed you to function in many capacities, many that I would not allow and will not allow. You were removed from the Diocese of Newark, and you live here to care for your mother. We welcome you as a member of the Church of Seattle." Archbishop Riley sipped his scotch loudly, siphoning off much of it. "But I will be clear. I will not tolerate public opinions about theology and church policy that are contrary to the official positions of the Roman Catholic Church. I am asking you as a fellow bishop to stop."

The room fell silent.

Riley was also taught that, when a room goes quiet during negotiations, the next person to speak loses. As much as he wanted to ramble on and drive home his point, he remained disciplined and sipped his scotch.

Harry spoke next, intuitively aware he was the loser.

"I care for these people, Archbishop. I just want to see them love the church."

Archbishop Riley wanted to laugh. Instead, he spoke calmly. "I am certain you do. I admire anyone who has given his entire life to the service of God's people. But I have work to do, and you are in the way."

"I want to remain in Seattle to care for my mother."

"I admire that, too." Riley took another long drink of his scotch and knew it was time to tighten the rope. "It will be helpful to have you around to clear up any questions about the little financial problem we have. There were some things I saw, some entries that were paid out to you. We'll want to know what that's all about. Do you want to eat now?"

Harry sat back in his chair. "I'm not hungry." He had always wanted to be cunning, to be good at duping and tricking people. All he was ever good at was basic holiness and that never got anyone to bend over and pick up a stray dime. It would be hard to explain the money.

Archbishop Riley ate his sandwich and salad in silence as Harry nursed the large scotch. He thought that, for such a slim man, Riley ate like a horse. There was a light knock on the door.

"Yes" Riley bellowed.

Mary Conners opened the door. "Archbishop, there is a man by the name Harold Brown who has been trying to reach you all morning. Do you want me to take another message or put him through?

"Ask him to hold, Mary." Archbishop Riley looked at Harry and smiled. "Opus Dei. Harold Brown is Opus Dei. You ever have much to do with them?"

Harry set his drink down. "As a matter of fact, I was recruited before I went into the seminary. I always served mass and one day a kind, elderly gentleman approached me after mass and told me he belonged to a service organization that was founded on the principles of a monastic life, but it was for people who were not particularly interested in the priesthood or entering a convent. I visited their residence where the recruits lived and thought it resembled a prison more than a residence for charity volunteers. I think my time in the seminary, as strict as that was, was a better choice."

"Could be. But they have the money and can make things happen that otherwise would never happen."

"Oh, I've heard the stories. I'll be off so you can take the call. Thank you for the lunch." Harry let himself out.

℘℘℘

Archbishop Riley arrived at the home of Harold Brown, retired president and CEO of First Fidelity Securities. The list of corporate boards on which he sat was too long to recite. His proudest accomplishments were those achieved as a member of Opus Dei in service of the holy father the pope.

The house was modest for the neighborhood, three doors down from Microsoft co-founder Bill Gates. It was a well-manicured, classic twenties-era Craftsman with a large covered area extending from the front door to allow guests to be dropped off out of the rain. The drivers were sent to a parking area at the entrance to the property. The archbishop was greeted personally by Harold Brown and escorted into the house already filled with guests. "So, good of you to come, Archbishop."

"Harold, I am the one to thank you. What a lovely home."

"My grandfather had it built." He motioned for the archbishop to walk into the main room from the foyer. "I believe you know William Sanchez."

"Of course I do. William, how nice to see you again."

The archbishop leaned toward William and whispered in his ear, "Thank you for the attorney. Everything was dropped. Such a dumb mistake."

William smiled, nodded, and shook his hand.

After his guests had enjoyed refreshment and cocktails, Harold stood in the middle of the living room. "My guests, may I have your kind attention. It is a special privilege for me to welcome the newly installed Archbishop of Seattle, John Riley to my home. I am greatly honored, Archbishop, and thank you for joining us. I further want to announce we have invited Archbishop Riley to be the keynote speaker at a special meeting of Opus Dei members in Puerto Vallarta, Mexico. This invitation, I must say honestly has been presented by Opus Dei at the specific suggestion of the holy father in recognition of Archbishop John Riley's loyalty and fidelity to the Mother Church and the holy father."

There was long and polite applause.

Harold hastily arranged an impromptu receiving line so his other guests could have the opportunity to shake the archbishop's hand and introduce themselves. One of the more elderly guests shuffled slowly toward him and handed him a business card without shaking his hand. 'Cardinal Day asked me to spend some time with you, William, and Harold this evening, at your convenience of course."

"Of course."

Just as the receiving line began to thin, Harold escorted the archbishop to a finely appointed library on the other side of the house. William and the elderly man stood when he entered the room and sat after he did.

"Archbishop, I am George McGurdy, and I am Cardinal Day's liaison with the Vatican Bank. He and many of his associates—and I am hoping to finally include you— have accounts, and I help manage those. You and I have never met because those affairs have little to do with the daily life of the visible public church. The holy father and others, especially Cardinal Day, think you will be extremely helpful in the future mission of the Vatican bank in Mexico. You are fluent in Central American Spanish, you understand the politics, and you are a high-profile member of the church. You can help us influence certain events we feel are important as we move forward serving the people of Mexico."

"What exactly does Cardinal Day—"

"The holy father requested your participation, and we will discuss specifics at another time. I simply wanted to introduce myself this evening, and Harold was gracious enough to invite you. I will be in contact with you, Archbishop."

Chapter 9

Jerry Garcia called Greg. "Hey, Lucas, thanks. Little Jimmy is singing so sweetly. Got his ass nailed to the wall. This is number three asshole you've helped us catch. You're okay. You…uhm…just have to do something about your anger, pal. Let the tourists go."

"Right. Well, make sure you lock his cell door really tight, okay?" Greg hung up the phone.

Denise was sipping a Maker's Mark as she sat next to Genelle lying on the couch.

"Well, they got him." Greg sat back in his chair and picked up his whiskey glass. "I wish I had gotten him first."

They were all quiet for a moment

"What drives you, Greg?" Denise asked. "There's something about you, a duality. I both love and hate you at the same time, and I don't know why."

Greg hesitated. "I'm a strange man, that's for sure. I was in the special forces at the tail end of Vietnam. I was ordered out just before the fall of Saigon. They sent me to Central America, ostensibly to do some drug interdiction. But, mostly, I helped screw up attempts of government take overs by communist sympathizers. I propped up right-wing dictators. Killed several communists—kids like me, mostly. I was educated very well in El Salvador. What the media told you is not what happened there. We trained the hit men and picked the targets. We gave them the guns. We gave them money.

"I saw a very corrupt element there, especially in the Catholic Church. They sided with the money, with the power. They didn't give a rat's ass about the people. I watched a zealous priest by the name of John Riley finger the more radical elements, and zap, they'd be gone. He was one heartless little bastard.

"That's why I'm pissed off. I saw perverse power used to hurt the innocent. Jim Burns was doing basically, the same thing to his victims. I saw it on a daily basis. If it wasn't for money, it was for influence or just raw power.

"I had a childhood that taught me absolute justice and that also wrecked holy hell on me. It was perverse how badly people would treat me. I ran away from it, my father, his friends. The Church. On the face of it, these people were so good. My father treated my two brothers with a gentleness and concern you would expect from a good father. But me. Whew."

"You don't have to do this—"

"That's all right. It helps me remember, and then I can focus better. I didn't know a person could be like that, both really good and really bad. Maybe I got it from him, this thing you see in me."

"What happened after the forces?"

"I ended up pandering to wealthy brats and a social order that perpetuated the domination of the poor and the weak. And I was killing so many people. Then one day I'm sitting in a bar in Guatemala. No one knows we were there then. El Touriste, that's what we called ourselves. Baggy pants, floral print shirts, Rolex watches, lots of gin. I'm sitting there listening to a nun describe how she was kidnapped and tortured for several weeks. Military types, commandos. Our friends. They killed some other nuns who appeared to be sympathetic to the communists, and they kept torturing this poor woman. I realized I had trained the guys she was talking about. She described the unit pretty well, and I knew it was the guys I had trained. That's when I flipped." Greg spoke slowly, without emotion. "Yeah, I get a little extreme sometimes. I know that."

Genelle appeared to be asleep in Denise's arms but woke and sat up.

"The dead has risen." Greg offered a drink but Genelle declined.

"You sound like my brother." Genelle wiped her hair from her face. "He's just like you, except he doesn't have your health."

Greg motioned with his hand. "I'm missing something."

"He's got AIDS. He had the fight in him for a while, but now he's sick. Sicker than a dog. He was going to set things right. We had him lined up to help change the way the church does business, but he's too weak."

"What are you talking about? There are medicines for that now. I've heard of people living twenty years or more with a diagnosis and no end in sight for their productive lives. Tell me I'm wrong. It's not a great thing to have, but it's no longer an absolute death sentence."

"You are right for the most part and the state does a great job of paying for the medications. But some people need different kinds of medication that the state does not pay for, and we have to find private or charitable resources, and we are running out of options." Genelle sat up on the couch. "We were funded in Seattle by the old archbishop there, Schwartz, but the new guy, Riley, shut down the operations and my brother is out in the cold, and now we're scrambling."

"I see. I guess you can add that to my list of what's pissing me off."

Denise sipped slowly from her whiskey. "What do you focus your anger on?" she asked quietly.

Usually questions like this set Greg's jaw tight. Denise didn't bother him that way, though, so the question deserved an answer.

"I focus on bad people. Like Jim. I knew he was stinko when I met him, that's why I kept inviting him over. I wanted to know what his stink was. I caught wind one night when he was drunk and everyone else went home. He talked about his elderly friends. Not women friends or even girlfriends. His elderly friends. He used the word 'elderly' a lot. 'I like the elderly, they are so mature and have such great wisdom,' something like that. I went into automatic pilot and kept up surveillance until I caught him. I focus on bad people."

"Are these people always bad?" Denise asked

Greg thought carefully. "By my standards at the moment, yes." He set his drink down on the coffee table. "What the hell are you two talking about?"

"We have a project we're working on. Actually we're financing it. We are hoping to do a little payback. What we fund is not turning the other cheek. We intend to hit back. We'd like you to meet someone. You know Mike Gerard, right?"

"Yeah, I do. We go way back."

"He's involved. We asked him to call you because I think you will appreciate his perspective. Is that Okay?"

"Sure, anyone can call me."

❧❧❧

Jim Burns was in jail and Jerry was on duty, so there was no regular poker game. Greg telephoned Mike

Gerard, former special forces commando turned leftist Maryknoll priest, spending his days in a spiritual bliss that Greg always envied.

"That's it. It's confirmed. I think about you and you call. Lucas, how the hell are you?"

"I started thinking about you. Hey, this is good psycho-babble. Your friends up here told me you would call, and I was bored, so I called. How's the world of religious subversion?"

"You know how I told you the people in Peru wouldn't let me work with them if I wasn't married? They gave me someone that I really fell in love with. She's living here in Berkeley while I finish my doctorate, then I take her back."

"Nice arrangement. Superiors approve?"

"Superiors don't ask, and I don't tell. There is something that I want to talk with you about. Friend of mine wants something done…uhm…maybe a little covert like."

"How covert?"

"I don't know. He was a bishop. Not a nice situation. In some trouble up in Seattle. Can I give him your number?"

"Why don't you do it?"

"My doctoral thesis is on the various spiritual avenues to peace. I can't really go around cutting throats anymore, can I?"

"Do what you want to do. How's your mother? She always sends me a Christmas card. I finally got one off to her last year."

"She's really well. She met Maria and she likes her. They get together once or twice a week."

"Yeah, give this guy my number. What's his name?"

"Last name Boyle. Harry."

"FBI?"

"What? I said he was a bishop."

"Irish name. Is he foreign-born Irish?"

"Got me there, buddy. I haven't heard that for a while. No. Jersey."

"And he doesn't have connections for this sort of thing?"

"Greg, I don't know *what* the man has. I turned him down, and he sounded desperate. I'll give him your number. Hey, I haven't told you. I'm off to the Patagonia for some rest, and then we're going to be in Peru for six months. Can't get hold of me. No phones, nothing. I'll get in touch when we get back."

Chapter 10

The driving was boring and, in a daydream, Greg saw Father Gary Gordon approach the classroom door, stop, and scowl. He stared momentarily at Greg and then at the other students. "Welcome to your first class with me. It's true what you hear. This is a very difficult class, and I am not here to be liked." He fixed his gaze on Greg again. "What's your name?"

"Lucas. Greg Lucas."

"You're a pretty young man, aren't you?" Father Gordon said after a pause.

Greg looked down at his desk and then side to side at the other students. Most were looking straight ahead. Some were laughing quietly.

"Greg, you're probably gay and, at best, just very stupid. Your kind usually doesn't make it through my class."

The words fell hard on Greg as he looked at Father Gordon through squinted eyes.

"What does your father do Greg?"

"He owns a plumbing company."

"Ah, yes a tradesman. We all know about tradesmen, don't we?" Father Gordon glanced around the room, beaming, then again at Greg. "All that rigorous work, big meat and potato dinners. Not much time for a good book,

huh? Let's see if the tradesman's pretty son can read."
Father Gordon wrote *SHIT ROLLS DOWN HILL* on the
board. "Read this to me, Lucas."

Greg did not yet know how to defy a priest. "Shit rolls
downhill."

"Excellent job. You've graduated. Now go out and
buy yourself a new pair of overalls and get on with your
career."

☙☙☙

It was getting harder to control these dreams. He lay
awake with his arm wrapped over his eyes. He had been
sweating. He eyed the mostly empty bottle of scotch on
the nightstand. He probably drank too much, but it was
better than the sleeping pills. Damn things gave him
worse nightmares than the real ones. He glanced at his
watch. He was going to be late. After breaking three traffic laws, his Scout rolled smoothly into the driveway of
the St. Walburga Monastery near a remote town in northern Colorado. The bell in front of the chapel was ringing
and the nuns scurried inside through the front and side
doors.

He sat in the back of the chapel as the mass began.
They sang a hymn as a tall, white-haired priest entered
alone from the back of the chapel. He kissed the altar as
he approached and the hymn ended. He continued with
the mass in an informal manner, chatting with the nuns as
he progressed. His sermon did not address the Gospel
reading much at all and spoke more of a need for a revived, progressive spirituality. He ended the half-hour-
long mass and left by way of the vestibule. One of the
nuns motioned for Greg to follow her, and he did in silence, to a small, wonderfully smelling dining room.
There was hot cereal, eggs done over easy, some bacon,

toast, coffee, and juice. He ate slowly, listening to the nun and one other guest talk about the farming chores that needed to get done. Greg guessed they were trying to appeal to his manliness. She emphasized the difficulty of digging the ditch. He was embarrassed when the nun started talking about how she was going by herself. So much for needing a man around the place. The nun told him to follow her outside, and they walked across the compound toward a group of small Quonset huts. She knocked on the first door and opened it. "This is Bishop Harry Boyle." The nun motioned Greg in.

"It's Harry to you." Harry was the tall man with longish, wild white hair who said the mass. His large, sharp nose and graying temples gave him a sophisticated look. The nun, wrapped in traditional clothing, smiled sweetly, bowed slightly, and silently left the room. "I've been waiting for your call. I hear you were a jar head, am I not correct?"

"No, special forces."

"Right. Just another kind of efficient killing machine."

"Yeah, right," Greg said quietly. "What's this about?"

"You've been here before?"

Greg looked around the modern Benedictine monastery shaking his head. "You?"

"Necessary R and R. Life can get you down and my cousin is a nun here. They don't ask about my situation, even though they know everything." Harry opened the door to step outside and breathed the pine scent. "They let me fish in their stream. Bring any gear?"

Greg nodded.

The food in a Benedictine monastery was always good. Steaks, fresh fruit and vegetables. Creative side dishes. Greg had traveled through Europe with Mike Gerard just after his ordination, and they stayed as guests in several monasteries and religious houses. It was the best he had ever eaten in his life. He could smell the kitchen.

"First, it's happy hour."

They walked to a small Quonset hut that had formerly been one of the main structures of the monastery during construction of the new facility.

Harry raised the glasses and bottle of scotch. Greg touched his glass. "Nice of you to think of bringing something good."

Harry drank back. "If we run out, there's more inside."

Greg sat in the aging but comfortable chair. "Where you at these days, with religion I mean?"

"Good question." Harry glanced at him then back to the fire. "I have a personal relationship with—" He paused and waved his right hand. "—God, if you want to me call it that. Where I lost it all was when I went on a sabbatical. I was ordered out into the field to study the Dead Sea Scrolls. I started asking questions about what I saw, about what the archaeologists and biblical scholars were finding in the scrolls. They pushed me away, clamped down, and became secretive. The Vatican started an investigation on me, roughed me up with a visit from a cardinal, and told me that it was dangerous to ask too many questions about something I knew very little about. It was downhill from there."

"You said something when I met you. About an efficient killing machine."

Harry sipped from his glass. "Commentary on the United States government. Not you."

Greg nodded. "Your little story about the scrolls. I've had a passing interest in that."

"If you have integrity, you have at least a passing interest."

"I want to hear more."

"You will." Harry stood and stirred the fire. "You and

I are here together for a reason. Mike described you and told me about your history. Suggested you might be in the freelance business. I need something."

"What?"

"We have a few days. Let's pace ourselves."

⌘

Greg found himself on the second day a hundred feet downstream from Harry. They acknowledged each other, their fly rods quietly whipping. They did not speak other than to comment on a catch or to acknowledge how cold the river was.

Greg lost a fly. He went back to shore to tie another. Harry came and sat next to him on the log. Greg tied the fly on the hook. He looked at Harry and smiled. "Something I picked up in the special forces. My master sergeant could tie fifty eight different kinds of flies."

"I sense you can be an intense man, Greg. You afraid of something?" Harry asked.

Greg smiled again. "That's a bit off the wall." He went back to tying the fly. "I just get that way when I'm starting to get pissed off."

"Pissed off about what?"

"I know you mean well, but leave it." Greg continued to prepare his line.

"No, if you don't mind, I don't think I will. I think you and I are pissed off about the same thing. I also think we're afraid of the same thing," Harry said quickly.

Greg looked sharply at him.

"I just don't have your professional ability to focus my anger and fear into high octane energy. I knew some people who were in the rangers, the special forces, and the navy SEALs. Pretty much the same training. They all went out on secret missions, behind enemy lines, things like rescues, cutting communications lines, that sort of thing. Some are even trained to kill. Just simply trained to kill." Harry paused. "What was your specialty?"

Greg looked at Harry, this time not smiling. "What's this?"

Harry looked Greg in the eyes. "I've been around your type. I was a chaplain in my early years as a priest. You'd see a guy at mass every Sunday and then you wouldn't see him for three months. Then you'd see him again. They'd never talk publicly about where they had gone. I started to find out, though, in the confessional."

Greg nodded. He paused for a long time, watching and listening to the river. He swallowed hard. "My fear, Harry, I don't know what I'm afraid of. I'm afraid of them."

"Who is 'them'?"

"I saw what happens when the Church gets cozy with the power and money. Some bishops try to convince themselves they are really giving something good to the people, others don't even pretend. I met too many of them in Central America driving Mercedes and looking the other way as we selectively killed.

"There was a tight little circle of friends who liked the money and the power more than anything. That's what it's all about, isn't it? Money and power. Religion has become a justification for keeping money and power in the hands of the few who know how to play along."

"And you fear that," Harry teased. "I fear that people actually think you know Jesus loves you if your wallet is full. Do you fear what men do with words that may or may not be true? They use these words to acquire power and hurt innocent people."

"Don't let it get you down."

"I don't intend to." Harry paused a few moments and took a deep breath. "I told you there's a reason you and I are here together. Denise told me about you, says you don't talk much about yourself."

Greg shook his head. "My life is my private affair."

"Denise knows how deeply I have been disturbed by all of it, and she wanted me to meet you. She told me what little she knows about your past. I have some ideas and I need to share them with someone who can help me. I want to get them. I've been part of the Jesus Seminar. Smart people with good hearts, but they lack the balls to do anything. I've been advocating open dialogue on a number of issues, and they sent John Riley to shut me down."

"Harry, you'll never get those guys off your back. Power and money are a lot more fun than the truth."

"Funny you should say that. This new archbishop in Seattle. John Riley. You knew him before?"

"Oh yeah. Has a hard time concealing the shark fin under his red cassock."

"Mike told me you knew him. He's got the Opus Dei guys going through my personal affairs for public embarrassment. Checking out my finances, connections, sympathies. They are on me in a big stinking way."

"What are they going to find?"

"Not all of it good. I'm a man, just like you. I live my life. My real issue is to stop these bastards from harassing good priests who are doing the real work of Jesus Christ."

"All right. But what connection is there between me being here with you and John Riley?"

"What's left for you? Thirty more years of being pissed off writing your little computer games? No desire to act on the obvious wrongs you saw in Central America?"

Greg turned slowly to look at Harry. "How extreme?"

"Well, they had Archbishop Romero killed. It was a message from the powerful alliance, the right wing dictators, the other conservative bishops, and the United States to cease and desist Communist infiltration of the peasantry. It worked. The Communists shut up pretty tight after that. Sure there was some mild complaining in the United States, but it had an effect, right?"

Greg nodded slowly. "It had impact."

"Impact, indeed. Then when the nuns were murdered, those seven nuns—"

"I knew them. If there is a hell, I know a few church people who will go directly there for that one," Greg said loudly.

"An eye for an eye. We start with Archbishop John Riley," Harry said quietly, looking away.

Greg took a long slow look at Harry. "Who are you, like really? What's this all about?"

"Mike didn't tell you?"

"No. Do you really know what you're asking me to do?" Greg picked up his fly rod and walked toward the river.

Harry paused and crossed his legs. "I don't agree with the Church on many issues. Marriage of priests, ordination of women, advocating for the recognition of lesbian and gay marriages. Just to name a few. They took away my diocese in Newark, New Jersey."

"Sounds like I'm getting involved in something personal."

"Perhaps. They used my mother. I am angry about that. But deeper in me is a dichotomy. A spiritual war I fight inside of myself every day. On the one hand, I still love the best things in the Church, and on the other hand, I no longer have any tolerance for the worst elements. I get so angry. I have never been like this. I see those people who kill abortion doctors. I don't want them to do it because I see nothing wrong with abortion. But I can understand why they feel like killing. If you believe pas-

sionately, and you try and try and try to make some progress, and they keep leaning on you harder and harder.
Do you know what I'm talking about?"

Greg eyed Harry carefully.

Harry looked desperate. A man being pulled apart by
love and hate. "They lied to me so many times."

Greg patted him on the knee. "I don't do bar mitzvahs
or personal vendettas. Do you know what I do?"

"Hell, yes. I know what you secret military types are
capable of."

"No, you don't know what I do. What you heard in a
confessional somewhere is just the tip. I'm not interested.
It isn't worth it."

"At least give it some thought, will you? If you think I
am wrong, tell me. Tell me why. Make a rational argument and I'll listen. But be fair, as well. Be fair to all of
those who have been hurt, destroyed, murdered in these
modern days of so-called civilized existence, in the name
of spreading a Gospel I doubt they really believe in. I
know a few people who really believe in the message of
the Gospels, and they never get into power. It's like the
government. The real patriots never get near the control
levers. Those are reserved for the greedy power-lusting
few who consider themselves the elite. Will you at least
give it some thought?"

Greg was silent for several minutes. "How are you going to pay for this?"

"Our mutual friends, Genelle and Denise. They gave
me money. A lot of it. They said retire or retaliate, and I
think I'll do a bit of both."

Chapter 11

The call from George McGurdy to meet in Los Angeles at the Hilton near LAX was an odd request. Upon arrival, Father Gatz made an inquiry of the desk clerk who gave him directions to a conference room one floor up. Father Gatz led the search for the room and found it. He pushed the door open and found a large conference table with twenty-five or thirty chairs around it and George McGurdy sitting alone at the far end. George rose stiffly as Archbishop Riley entered the room. The archbishop motioned him to sit back down. Father Gatz walked behind the archbishop, carrying a black folio, as they approached the end of the conference room table where George again sat.

George straightened his glasses. "Who are you, may I ask?"

"I am Father Joseph Gatz, the archbishop's personal assistant."

"You can't stay here. I need to talk with the archbishop privately."

Father Gatz looked down at George silently, waiting for the archbishop to intercede on his behalf. The archbishop looked at him and gave a slight wave of his right hand. Father Gatz nodded silently and left the room.

"I apologize if that appeared rude, Archbishop. I am under strict orders from the holy father to speak with you alone and to insist you do not share our conversation with anyone who is not on this list." He slid a sheet of paper with five names typed on it, at the top was that of George McGurdy.

The second, third and fourth were Hispanic names Riley did not know. The fifth was that of Louis Garcia, a Honduran national attached at different times to various Central American armies. Louis had been useful in the past, and Archbishop Riley studied George carefully. Cardinal Day was not on the list.

"This comes directly from the holy father," George continued. "Are we clear on that? I am certain if you felt you could not fulfill the holy father's humble request, he would look cheerfully on that and respect your wishes."

"I am most certain that if the holy father makes such a humble request, it is for the absolute good of the Mother Church."

"Archbishop, we have a problem. The Institute of Works of Religion, what the uninformed press casually calls the Vatican Bank, does not like cash transactions. People would begin to suspect something untoward, and we are associated with the Holy Roman Catholic Church and cannot tolerate being seen in such a crass light. We are welcoming new clients who may be interested in the various investment instruments we offer and find organizations in Central America, and most importantly in Mexico, who have liquid assets that they need to invest quickly, but unfortunately these assets are in various forms of cash. These consist of the US dollar, the Canadian dollar, the pound and so forth. And they are not insignificant amounts."

Archbishop Riley wanted to ask a question to which he already knew the answer. Who are these organizations, and where did all this cash come from? He squirmed in his chair.

"I understand you have worked with Mr. Garcia in the past, in our efforts to neutralize the Communist effort against the Church in Central America."

"I know Louis Garcia, yes."

"Excellent. The other people on your list are associated with financial institutions with branches throughout Central and South America. All of them good Catholics, members of various charitable service organizations like the Knights of Columbus, Knights of Malta—"

"On our side. I get the picture."

"Excellent. Mr. Garcia has done business with the three other men from time to time, small amounts of money transferred, or processed through when exchange rates were favorable. They all understand fully well how money moves internationally. I could explain all of the technicalities, but you really don't need to know that."

"What do I need to know?"

"You already know what you need to know. You are a highly placed prelate with direct connections to the holy father. That's all you ever need to know."

"What is it the holy father wants me to do?"

"Yes, it's time for that. You see, the initial deposit the depositing organizations wish to make is equivalent to six billion US dollars, and like I said before it is spread out over several different currencies. We need these three gentlemen to help us find discreet channels for these currencies so we can register a singular deposit."

"And they will do this because they are good Catholics."

"And because a highly placed prelate who understands their culture and passionate love for the Mother Church has offered them blessings for their quiet service. The holy father would like to meet each of them personally and privately in Rome once we have a good system in place." Now George McGurdy was silent and looked at Archbishop Riley with a tight smile.

"If you say the holy father is himself making this so-humble request of me, I believe you, but I have never seen this side of him and I have met him prior to his coronation on several occasions."

"There are a few of us who advise the holy father, and he insists on using his name and authority in an effort to help the Mother Church remain completely transparent in all of her dealings. Yes, the mechanics of our efforts here are the fruit of these consultations and the holy father has blessed our advice."

"What role will Louis Garcia have in these efforts, as you call them?"

"Mr. Garcia knows the safe path for depositing money in the Vatican Bank, and he knows the principals in the various organizations wishing to establish business relationships with us."

"He knows who has the cash and where it is."

"Yes, you do not need to worry about any of that. We would like you to meet with these three gentlemen and warmly introduce the idea of serving the holy father and the Church in this capacity. If they are amenable, you would then introduce them to Mr. Garcia who will do everything else that we need to have done. Of course, after their gracious and tireless service, it would be wonderful if you could join us all in Rome and they would then have the opportunity to meet privately with the holy father."

"How do I make contact with these men?"

"They have received special invitations to attend your meeting in Puerto Vallarta as honored guests who will be recognized for their service to humanity and the Church. You will be staying at the St. Regis Punta Mita resort, and so will they. This is the host for your meeting. They have agreed to arrive a day or so early in order to prepare for their honorary awards. They know they are meeting with you as a formality and an honor. You will be hosting a private lunch for them in your suite. No one else should be at this luncheon."

Archbishop Riley nodded. "This is all so well planned."

"Archbishop, the holy father has wanted something like this since before his divine election. You were his choice then. We simply needed men of character who love the Mother Church, who are in a position to assist us, and we have found them." He slid a large sealed envelope over to the Archbishop. "Something to read. It will explain the technicalities of your arrangements with the gentlemen in Puerto Vallarta. You should think of a name for a charitable initiative in the archdiocese of Seattle worthy of receiving funds."

Archbishop Riley said nothing to Father Gatz as they boarded the flight back to Seattle. He sat in first class and Father Gatz sat in coach. Discreetly, the archbishop opened the envelope and began to read. Cash from a group of business men in Mexico would be aggregated with proper receipts by Louise Garcia. Each of the men the archbishop was about to meet would receive the cash as individual deposits from legitimate companies, who would then be compensated in cash for any and all taxes they might incur. Archbishop Riley would open two accounts at the Institute of Works of Religion in the Vatican in his name for the benefit of a charitable organization in Seattle and for his own financial benefit. A website address and a password were provided for both accounts. The three men he would be meeting in Puerto Vallarta would donate large sums of money to this account, the money originating from Louis Garcia. Small amounts of the donated funds could be drawn down to finance some charitable activities, and a fundraising effort would be undertaken in the normal method. People tended to give more to an organization that had already been primed by unnamed wealthy benefactors. The bulk of the funds in the account would then be used for loans and other banking activities designed to increase the value of the account. This would all appear to be normal banking activity to give a more solid financial foundation for the charities in Seattle. For his efforts, the archbishop would receive a management stipend to his own personal account in the Institute of Works of Religion. The three bankers would also receive modest management stipends for their efforts. There was no mention of where the cash ultimately originated, nor where it would end up. That much he would never know. The archbishop opened his thin laptop and checked for in-flight Internet. He typed in the address for the Vatican bank. There wasn't much to it. The passwords completed the process and issued two identity keys to be used for both deposits and withdrawals. He created some new spreadsheets, entered the log in information, and started to record the initial financial transactions. He moved two hundred thousand dollars from the charitable account to his own.

 свсә

Father Gatz collected their bags and hailed the taxi. The archbishop looked pensively out the window as they drove into a Seattle rain squall. "Father Gatz, is there a charity we do not have in Seattle that, if funding were available, would increase our spiritual presence in the archdiocese? Is there something more to our liking that is currently underfunded?"

"Yes, the Seattle Family Council. They advise young

women to bring their pregnancies to term and assist in finding adoptive families. Schwartz never funded that and it depends completely on outside funding."

"Excellent. Draw up a proposal to determine their budgetary needs and have that to me day after tomorrow."

Father Gatz would also stay at the Punta Mita resort but would be sharing a standard room with a member of the Opus Dei staff and would not have access to the archbishop's suite. The archbishop would already be in Puerto Vallarta ahead of him. Gatz should leave a message at the front desk upon his arrival and not disturb the archbishop directly. He said nothing but his face reflected his anger. Mary Conners turned away so she could smile after breaking the news to him.

℮℮℮

A week later, Archbishop Riley waited in the security line at SeaTac airport on his way to Puerto Vallarta. He always traveled in a black clerical suit, but did not wear his gold cross after one occasion when the TSA refused him security clearance for wearing an obvious weapon. The ensuing argument and search, no matter his station in the Church, was not worth future embarrassment. He enjoyed the complimentary mimosa in first class and chatted politely with an elderly woman sitting next to him.

She had grandchildren living in Puerto Vallarta, on her dime of course, and this was going to be a surprise visit. "I want to see if they are keeping the kitchen clean, you know?"

John Riley rarely relaxed. Once he landed smoothly in Puerto Vallarta, he stopped the driver the hotel sent for him before he set the bags in the car and took the cross out. Once at the resort, they simply escorted him to his suite and completed his registration there. His two suitcases and the set of golf clubs were set carefully in the bedroom, and a hotel employee was directed to unpack the suitcases and properly set the archbishop's clothing in the dresser drawers and on appropriate hangers. Archbishop Riley walked outside to catch view of the ocean from his private terrace.

In flawless English, the employee informed the archbishop that his room was ready and wondered if he wanted something from the kitchen or the bar. Riley ordered a bottle of scotch and some peanuts. For the next day, in the privacy of his suite, he would not be the Archbishop of Seattle, but once again John Riley. He dressed in his flowered shirt, white shorts, and sandals and sat in the sunshine until a waiter knocked and came in to set up the bar.

"I should have other things also, maybe some good gin, Russian vodka, you know, set up a complete bar, with mixers."

"Yes, sir. I will get those immediately."

There were two options for the lunch. Inside was a table large enough for six people and outside, under the shade structure, one table for four people. He decided on a more informal lunch outside. He would dress in black clerical with the gold cross. It was terrific what the cross did in projecting his position. He sipped his scotch and ate peanuts as he set his laptop up on the desk. The waiter returned with a cart and stocked the bar with quick efficiency.

"Do you know if preparations have been made for a lunch in my suite tomorrow?"

"Yes, Archbishop, all arrangements have been made. I will be serving you."

"Excellent. You will also tend to the bar?"

"Of course, Excellency."

"I'd like to have the lunch outside tomorrow. The view is so impressive. What is your name, please?"

"Frederico Jimanez."

"Well, thank you, Frederico. How do I reach you directly?"

"You tell the front desk you need something, and they will send me for the duration of your visit."

"Excellent. Thank you. I see it's four local time, and I am getting pretty hungry. Could you get me a steak, a filet, medium well; a modest baked potato; and some green salad for my dinner, say by five-thirty?"

"As you wish." Frederico bowed politely and left.

 round

At eleven the next day, Archbishop Riley was dressed in a freshly pressed suit and wearing his gold cross. The eighteen holes of golf went well, and he was able to get through the first nine before having to reveal what he did for a living. His mixed group of American businessmen did not make much of a fuss at knowing this.

Frederico knocked and entered the suite to prepare the outside table for the lunch. He was dressed in a well-fitted tuxedo and wore white gloves. He covered the table with white linen and set out silver and crystal for four. He explained he would return precisely at noon, when the guests were expected arrive, to host the bar. The lunch would be wheeled in for service by twelve forty-five.

round

Frederico escorted three men into the suite and took up the silent position behind the bar. The men introduced themselves to the archbishop, one even bowing to kiss his ring. Archbishop Riley recognized the old-school manners and allowed him to do so. They all wore the gold, ornate cross, identifying them as members of the Knights of Malta. He motioned for them to get what they wanted from the bar and join him on the terrace.

Once seated in the comfortable lounge chairs around a glass table, Archbishop Riley thanked them all for joining him. He wanted to share something with them that they needed to assure him would not leave the room. They looked at him seriously.

"The holy father has humbly requested I approach you three men, specifically you three, to request service to the Church in his name."

The youngest and most earnest of the three nodded his head. "If the holy father wants something from me, I will gladly and freely give it."

The other two nodded. They were now, all three, sitting more on the edge of their seats and listening intently.

"For several years, the holy father has been working with his advisers in the Vatican Bank to facilitate the transfer of funds from several cash accounts to the Vatican Bank. I do not know the specifics, but he found it necessary to contact men such as you, who work in the various banks in the region and whose fidelity to the pope and the Church were unquestioned."

The eldest spoke first. "I am honored to even be considered for this humble work. To think the holy father himself knows of my desire to serve him." The other two were equally humble.

"Tomorrow, the Opus Dei meeting begins with our mass at ten in the morning downtown in the cathedral. I understand there are some meetings through the rest of the day, but, at five, I am inviting you to come to my suite for drinks and meet a man who the Holy Father asked to help you with the logistics. After that, at seven, I understand there is a banquet in your honor." All three nodded, smiling. "I very much look forward to that," Rily continued. "You men have obviously served the Church with distinction and honor." He stood and motioned toward the table. 'I'm hungry. Let's eat lunch."

As they sat and unfolded their napkins, Archbishop Riley set his drink down and looked at each of them. "Once we have in place the plan the holy father has asked us to set up, he would like each of you to fly to Rome for a personal and private audience with him." He smiled and watched as the three faithful servants sat back with gaping mouths. "Now, ask Frederico for anything you'd like, from the bar while we eat."

Part 3
Present Day Again

Chapter 12

Grady stood across the plaza from La Iglesia de Nuestra Senora de Guadalupe. Pigeons gathered around elderly feeders then, with a feathered rush, sprang into the air, only to land again precisely at the feet of their benefactors.

A guard should have been at the door, but Grady was half way down the main aisle before he saw anyone. The size of the cathedral allowed the scraping and lifting of marble debris to carry on, seemingly, without sound. Grady stopped and looked out into the graceful arches. He cocked his head to the side, listening. He ambled slowly toward the main altar. The damage was obvious even from two hundred feet away. Two elderly women rattling rosary beads against the ancient pews made him look sharply.

My own prayers, more like meaningless idle chatter between old people married too long, the same arguments and obvious comments recited a thousand times, stagnant words to fill an empty void.

Two polite uniformed officers approached and asked him to leave. He nodded. He had seen the remnant components of the trigger lying on a white sheet as forensics specialists picked through chunks of rocks, marble, ash, and human flesh. Grady explained his interest in the bombing. He flipped his notebook to Captain Moro's phone number. They drew a tidy, readable map and told him to go there. He left, understanding he was once again encountering the Church, an institution that always defeated him. He walked slowly toward a café for coffee.

Captain Olivia Moro was the same height as Grady. Her grip was certain and she moved with casual confidence. The graying hair belied the lean, smooth face. Grady could not place her age, but guessed late fifties. He had often called some women handsome, and this described her perfectly.

"I don't speak Spanish."

"I don't speak Greek. Lucky for you I speak English," Captain Moro returned. She motioned for Grady to sit.

"You know who I work for?"

"I have spoken to him." She wasn't going to tell this guy yet how well she knew Harold Brown.

Captain Moro's office was long and narrow with a twenty-foot high ceiling. An ornate four-legged desk sat at an angle, facing the tall narrow windows. The view was a variety of building facades, trees, and the incessant street traffic of Puerto Vallarta. It was northern light, even and consistent year round. A photograph of the Mexican President looked down on Captain Moro's work.

"Harold Brown wants me to find something, a larger conspiracy."

"He spoke with me about this. I know only that we have an explosion and five murders in La Iglesia de Nuestra Senora de Guadalupe. I must solve this. I know nothing about larger conspiracies. You have some experience in terrorism. Harold tells me this."

"Army Intelligence."

"You call that…uhm…wait, I have it. An oxymoron."

Grady laughed comfortably. "My job was to know who wanted to attack the United States or its interests around the world."

"You were good. I understand you have some special skills? You can see through walls?"

"There are different ways of getting information. I happen to possess certain skills that are helpful in getting to the truth. Call it acute intuition."

"Yes. I wonder about such things."

"It's not something supernatural or anything like the old belief in ESP. I was never formally trained in computer science but understand it better than most people who have degrees in it. I am blessed with a heightened sense of intuition, logic, able to put pieces together by what I observe. This helps in my cyber-crime investigations. That's all."

There was a light tap at the office door. A young man dressed in black slacks, white shirt, and black bow tie carried a tray of coffee cups, sugar, and cream. He approached Captain Moro's desk. He set a small leather folder on the desk and served the coffee. Without a word, Captain Moro reached for the sugar and stirred in two lumps. The young man bowed, took the pesos from the desk, muttered "Gracias," and left quickly.

"The coffee is local, from San Sebastian up in the mountains. You should visit there, especially on the feast day of San Sebastian. A wild experience. You know the story?"

"Yes, he was tortured by the Romans and he didn't die from their arrows, so they stoned him in the morning."

"Ah, you know your catechism. What they do up there is start the feast day celebration at five the day before with a parade depicting this, and they shoot off a few bottle rockets as kind of a warning of what's going to happen. You see, it's a real vigil and the bottle rockets go off all night to keep you awake. If San Sebastian stayed awake with arrows in him, you could stay awake one night a year to remember his suffering. You should drive up there sometime."

"Perhaps. I will look into that if my wife and son join me down here."

"Ah, how old is your son?"

"Just fourteen."

"Same age as my son. Well, same age he was."

Grady hesitated. "Was?"

"His life was taken in retaliation, I believe, but I have never been able to find him or any evidence. I live with the hope he is still alive."

"I am terribly sorry. Truly, I am."

Captain Moro nodded and sipped slowly from the cup and sat back in the black leather chair. "You left army intelligence. Why? It seems like such a good career."

"I needed my space."

"I've heard this expression. I don't understand it."

"I'm retired."

"I hardly believe that. You are a spy for hire I am told."

"I look into things."

"What happens if you find something interesting? Something your boss does not need but someone else might find useful?"

"I know who will need the information and they get it. They might have something for me."

"I see. As you know this is not the attitude of your FBI and CIA."

"They are not mine. They are answerable to the American public."

"Really. I would like to believe you. As you know, the various agencies are not sharing information. You are the first American I have spoken with since this incident."

"And if we can't work together?"

"Maybe you should take up golf or something in your retirement."

Grady finished his coffee. "What are your thoughts, Captain Moro?"

"It is not the cartels. They killed my son, of this I am certain. They do not kill like this. It is not anyone from Lebanon, Iran, or Libya."

"I agree. This is different."

Captain Moro nodded her approval. "Yes, quite."

Grady placed the English as a mix of formal American education and New York streets. The Bronx?

"I understand the triggering device is new."

"Yes, we have not yet given it to your FBI. We want to look at it for a while."

Grady was silent.

"Have you seen this trigger before?"

"Yes. I saw it in parts as the forensic guys were sifting through for remnants." Grady tapped the desk with his right forefinger. "I saw it before, in South America. I think I also know the man who invented it. It's an assassination tool for the drug-interdiction folks in Central America. Their operations are secret and deep in the jungle. It's hard to bomb from the air, and you simply cannot shoot drug lords at close range and expect to run into the jungle. The trigger was built to detonate from three hundred feet, allowing the assassin to see his subject and then have a head start into the jungle when the job was done."

Captain Moro rubbed her fingers through her hair. She glanced carefully at Grady and then out the windows. The reaction was usually like this the first time Grady gave this kind of accurate information.

"Then you know who has done this?"

"No, I just know what he looks like. This man works outside of the purview of the CIA, NSA, and army intelligence. I need to be at the site of the explosion. If I'm lucky, I'll get a better picture of this man in my mind."

Captain Moro was silent.

"I am not sure this is a Jalisco case, though, Captain. For me, this looks like a US based operation." Grady waited for the reaction.

"For your archbishop, perhaps. I will, of course, work to solve that murder. But I have another more important reason to find who has done this. You go visit this boy. Then you tell me what interest I have in this matter." Captain Moro slid a small white card across the table. "The name of the boy is Ignacio. He is in that hospital. Be careful with him. You know the bomb killed his brother. He is still very upset about this."

Captain Moro leaned calmly back in her chair and dialed a number. She spoke rapidly then hung up the phone. A male officer entered the office. He placed three files on her desk and sat in the empty chair. He was thirtyish, tall, dark haired, and sharp in a tailored suit. Grady was distracted.

Moro cleared her throat "You and I, we have history. The archbishop, we will find he has a history. Much of it not clean, yes? No man of the world is without sin. If you were killed, I would do my job to find who killed you. But Ignacio's brother and the other acolyte?" Moro shook her head. "That is why I am in the police force." She stood and motioned toward the male officer. "This is Inspector Carlos Juarez. He will assist you while you are in Puerto Vallarta. His English is excellent and he will serve as a translator for you."

৩৩৩

Ignacio was reluctant to talk. His mother sensed this and openly asked why Grady needed to speak with her boy.

"He might remember something that will be helpful."

Inspector Juarez rattled the Mexican translation quickly. The mother nodded. Grady noticed a bicycle-racing magazine by Ignacio's bed.

"Who will win Le Tour this year?"

After the translation, Ignacio sat up. His opinion was clear and well founded. Not one of the favored racers, but a younger man. A Mexican would finally win. Ignacio pointed his finger to emphasize his belief. Grady recited the stages of the Tour de France this man won the previous year, and the fact that he almost won the Tour of Spain. Ignacio was impressed.

Grady noticed a photograph of Ignacio's brother. He asked if he was a good brother. Ignacio was silent. After a few moments, he said only that he was dead.

After a few questions, it was clear the boy had no conscious recollection of other people around the altar. Grady knew if he spent enough time with the boy, he would see what the boy saw before the explosion. Grady thanked him and politely left the room.

Grady and Inspector Juarez stopped in the lobby. "Moro is right. This is not about the Archbishop of Seattle. This is about Ignacio and his brother. This is about innocent blood."

They walked out the front door of the station. "When did the captain's son go missing?"

"She told you about him?"

"I shared that I have a son the same age."

"Well, it was all very suspicious. It was a year ago. No one knows where."

Captain Moro saw a different expression on Grady's face as they met late in the afternoon.

"I want to work with the boy. I want to know especially about before the mass, before all of the guests arrived. What did he see? I just need to ask question about what I am seeing when I am next to him. No hypnotism."

Moro hesitated. Her index finger over her lips, she leaned back in her chair. "To do this…uhm…seeing thing, with someone so young, I think would be dangerous, especially when he feels the blood of his own brother. I do not want to do this right away. Perhaps we will take care of that and tell you what we hear."

"Captain, let me make it clear to you. I do not profess to have psychic abilities. I have a very sensitive intuition, and I can—"

"I get it, Mr. Marcs."

Grady stared at Moro. The conversation did not start again when the same waiter knocked lightly and efficiently served coffee, leaving with a hearty wave and a wide smile. The only sound to follow was the clanking of spoons stirring sugar into the thick black coffee. Moro sipped loudly.

"You, of course, have not ruled out that we may be dealing with someone in Puerto Vallarta who has affected the orders of others, and those others are comfortably somewhere else."

Grady nodded.

Moro continued with a heavy sigh. "We can give you details of evidence that may help you, especially the bomb, the triggering device. I will give you what you need. You tell me what you find. Or *see,* whatever." She stood and looked out at the continuous motion in the street. "I understand the police in your country use your services."

"Yes. Not frequently, but the quality of the information is often quite unbelievable."

"Much in life is unbelievable." The sound of hundreds of cars were rattled the windows. Moro paced in front of them. "Look how long it took to find the men who exploded that plane over Scotland. Only after more than ten years did they bringing those terrorists to justice and they let the man go back to Lybia. Imagine."

"Do you think they found those men only through conventional methods?"

Captain Moro looked at Grady and shook her head. "I did not say that at all. But unconventional methods, well, maybe it is better I do not know how. I am capable of finding who did this in Puerto Vallarta, in Egypt, in China, no matter where he goes, using conventional means. I will find the man who put this bomb in La Iglesia de Nuestra Senora de Guadalupe. I have found many murderous men, most especially the man who killed my husband. I spent nine years looking for him, and I found him. I will find this man, too. You go and look for the people who hired him with your methods. You give me what you find and I will give you what you need. Leave the boy out of it."

"Okay. That's fine. Any ideas?"

Captain Moro opened a desk drawer and took out a slim laptop. "This belonged to the archbishop. His assistant wanted to secure it and take it immediately back to Seattle, but we took possession of it. You understand these things, I don't. I can turn it over to our forensics people, or I can give it to you. Which would you like?"

"I would like paper work, which maintains the official chain of custody, so anything I think might be evidence can still be used."

"And here it is, first in Spanish and then translated if you cannot read it."

Grady read it carefully. It was a standard authorization for him to take custody of the laptop with specific instructions on how to handle suspected evidence. He signed both copies and handed it back to the captain. "Anything in particular you think I will find?"

The captain shrugged. "I'm not sure what archbishops

are interested in. Maybe some electronic holy cards perhaps?"

It was just the address of a walk up rooming house. It was a small family-owned hotel in the summer time and safe living quarters to budding actors and escaping beach bums after the tourists had gone home. There was always very good coffee in the morning, served by a congenial mama who nagged the guests, mostly girls in their twenties, for their linens once a week and scolded them when they came home too late. If a guy was real sweet to her and the girls, occasionally there was room at the table Sunday afternoon. She took care of her girls.

Grady stood across the street looking at the ornate entrance.

The day they met, she was as sweet and fresh as the month she was named after. Shy, that's how most people described her. Foxy was Grady's word. Fast, smart, quiet, and often cunning. He thought he saw her, hesitating on the steps, looking at him. Not her, obviously. Just another pretty girl stopping to see who was watching, who was following her.

Grady walked into the coffee shop bar across the street. Absent mindedly, he ordered standing up and then sat down at a clean table. The waiter huffed, out of a tip for sure. Grady looked up and recognized his mistake, then apologized and offered a tip. The waiter refused. *I work for a living. Next time you want a seat, I'll serve you properly, you gross American.*

Grady winced.

When he met her, he didn't know April was using heroin. She used the model's trick, shooting between the toes. Yes, he would have left her then. His job required it.

But how does a pretty girl get into that complex, self-destruction in the first place? And why give her, free of charge, all of the heroin her addiction requires? Market-

ing? Pretty, half-clothed women sell cars, washing ma-chines, carpeting, travel, cigarettes, anything. Why not heroin?

See the pretty girl sticking the needle in between her toes. See the same pretty girl party, falling into the hands of waiting piranha, ravishing her. Now, see the pretty girl walk the catwalk, working—alive, vibrant, and rich. You too can live like this.

Grady didn't know until Captain Michael Healy— Army Intelligence, Mexican Task Force, where they were both assigned—showed him the photographs. Healy passed them up higher and got a promotion. Grady destroyed the photographs someone anonymously gave him of Healy. No, he would not be like that.

He didn't hate Healy. He belonged to a culture of hypocrisy and power, and Healy paid for his career with his self-respect.

Grady looked up when the woman from the steps across the street sat next to him. He nodded and smiled. The waiter approached, smiled at her, and shot a look at Grady.

The woman ordered a coffee. "Gracias," she said when it arrived.

"Si," was the automatic response. So polite this exchange.

Grady leaned back. "I saw you across the street."

"I saw you, too." The accent was Californian. "I recognized you from somewhere."

"Did you know April Meyers?"

"Only briefly, before she went home. Okay, now I know. I'm sorry. I should have remembered. She spoke of your wife frequently."

"Yes, Sandy knew her better than I did. They went to college together and we were always close."

"That's okay. I was just sitting here thinking about

her. Did they ever catch what's his name, Dennis? I hear he went on the run. I'll bet it's hard to find a guy like that."

Grady shook his head. "I don't think they have."

Her name was Stephanie and she was going to a very important audition with a Mexican movie producer shooting something down the coast a bit from Puerto Vallarta. She could sign with the studio if she did well. Her Spanish was native and the fact that she trained in Hollywood gave her an edge over most of the locals. The coffee was a good luck thing. She had two jobs after drinking her coffee here. She had to go. Grady wished her luck.

Dennis Hofburg. German drug dealer, sometimes-incompetent fashion photographer. All around lecherous scumbag who left April in an alley screwed up on smack, and she was raped twice. She couldn't talk right after that. Oh, Stephanie, it was easy to find him and what I did then was easier than that.

As Stephanie walked out, she passed by Inspector Juarez, standing just outside the door. The inspector looked back at the model and smiled as she approached Grady. She motioned the waiter and muttered something almost unintelligible. The waiter nodded graciously.

"Who was she?" Juarez asked. "I've been standing outside waiting for you. I didn't want to interrupt anything."

"She lives in that hotel. A model and actor. Trying to do it honestly. She knew my wife."

"Was your wife a model too?"

"Your English—"

"BA Criminology, Michigan State. Four years. I picked up a bit of the language."

"Indeed."

The waiter set the cappuccino in front of him and Juarez muttered something. "Tell me about her."

"Who."

"I don't care about the model."

Grady hesitated. He motioned at the waiter and pointed at his cappuccino. He nodded. *Maybe you'll get it right this time.* Grady shook his head.

"I met her here in Puerto Vallarta after I was married. She and my wife went to college. It got complicated for a while. Nothing bad. I was stationed in San Diego, special army intelligence unit. I came down here for intelligence work, went to a party and right off, we liked each other a lot. We were great friends. I realized something later. Like, how much can you love an addict? You end up loving the addiction. Life ebbs and flows around the addiction. Whoever thinks they can help an addict in a relationship is delusional. You can't. You just need to get out. Do the other person a favor and get out. You think you're doing something good, but you're not. You have to remember they love the poison more than they love you. You've got to stop buying the junk for them and just get out of the way." The cappuccino tasted good. "She hated that I knew what she was thinking. She tried to trick me, but I would catch her every time. With her, it was like being wired directly to her brain. Every thought, every motivation. I could see it like it was on television. That drove her nuts."

"I don't mean to drag all of this out of you—"

"No, that's okay. This is the first time I've been back to Puerto Vallarta since they found her, and I've been thinking of her a lot today. Had some free time and when I told you where to meet me, I picked this place."

"Memories like this are tough."

Grady shrugged. "She found someone else to pay for the silver needle express. I got out. I was still getting her thoughts, and I had to learn how to shut it off. I had to get away."

"Where is she now?"

"Some bad things happened, and she's wasn't right after a while, mentally. I still wake up at night and I see it. An overdose. I've always thought it was intentional, but strangely I could never be sure."

"I'm sorry. Nobody deserves that."

"No they don't, on either side. I think of her to keep my perspective. Life is hard and mostly it hurts…well, for most people it does. I have to remember that when I work. There are criminals and there is criminal behavior. Do you agree?"

"I'm not sure what you mean."

"Sometimes criminals aren't bad people. They're just trying to make better things happen, right?"

"I don't think I can answer that the way I think you want me to."

"That's okay, I need to call Harold Brown. And then my wife."

Part 4
One Week Before the Bombing

Chapter 13

arry called Greg nine times after the fishing trip. Greg did not pick up until the ninth call.

"I got the package you sent, Boyle. Did you read that article I sent you?"

Harry was quiet for a moment. "About special operations. Yes. He's got to be stopped."

Greg said nothing. Harry talked nervously about the weather, fishing at the monastery, and nothing of significance to fill the dead space. Greg interrupted him after five minutes of it.

"You're probably right. He needs to be shut down. Problem is, he's like a weed. Pull him out and throw him away, and another one just like him pops up tomorrow. It's still no, Boyle."

"Well, can I get Mike to call you tonight? Would you please talk to him?"

"I can accurately guess he is expecting me to say yes. I thought he was in South America."

"Delayed. I could get him to come out to visit you if you want."

Greg hated desperation of any kind. It created unstable relationships both in love and in business. "No. just have him call."

Mike had cancelled the trip to Pategonia and was home when he called. He knew Greg was going to be angry.

"Does Boyle really want me to do this?"

Mike sighed. "Well, I know better than to ask what it is Boyle asked you to do. But, I called to tell you why it needs to be done."

Greg smiled. "Has Boyle ever used an expression like 'terminate with extreme prejudice'?" Mike laughed. "This is not a game, Mike, and I don't think Boyle understands this. You know the drill, once the procedures are set in place, they are handed off cleanly enough so that the operation cannot be aborted. If I do what Harry wants, someone will die, period. Is he aware of that?"

"I'm not sure what he's aware of, Greg." It was Mike's familiar, no bull-shit tone that Greg liked so much and made him prick up his ears. "When I'm done, you decide what you want to do with the information," Mike continued.

He told him about the archbishop's first actions after his installation, closing down the offices that provided services to persons with AIDS. Greg shrugged. Reprehensible, but not deserving death. The files that were kept in the offices contained very private and sensitive medical information concerning the clients. A state run organization, well known for its discretion, requested the files for safe keeping to protect the clients. The Church refused and handed the files over to the office of Catholic Charities where the files were left in cardboard boxes in an easily accessed storage room. Nothing was done about the files, in spite of the fact the clients themselves personally met with the archbishop requesting something be done to secure the files. The archbishop turned the matter over to his assistant, who proceeded to give access to the files to a very conservative organization, which then created a website and published the names of the former clients. Of course, there was a lawsuit. A judge shut the website down, but the damage was done. Families found out about their sons for the first time. Insurance companies cross checked their files and canceled policies. People were fired from their jobs. The local press made something of it, but it blew over and the archbishop skated through. A secretary in the Catholic Charities office was fired.

"What organization made the files public?"

"The rumor was it was an organization called Opus Dei, but the archbishop denied any knowledge of how the files were made public and said only Opus Dei was involved in raising funds for various Catholic Charities."

"Anyone you know get hurt in this?"

"My younger brother."

Greg sat silent for several moments.

"Greg? You there?"

"Is your brother sick?"

"Yes. I delayed my trip. He's got pneumonia."

Greg watched the last sun light flicker behind the mountains.

"You mad at me for pitching for Boyle?" Same no-bullshit tone.

Greg doubted it would have bothered Mike much if he was mad. "No, Mike. I'm sorry about your brother. It's just that this is not my issue, you see? If the archbishop was hiding child molesters, then maybe I'd be more interested. But like I told the gals, this is just a non-issue now. Everyone lives so long. And I am not hearing legal recourse here. Take it in front of a judge, even a prosecutor, and see what they are willing to do. I need more to act at this level, you know?"

Mike breathed hard into the phone. "There's more, and it goes all the way to the top, it has to do with money, lots of it. But that's not my issue. I don't care about money laundering, I care about people."

"I need to talk to someone, and I'll call you back." Greg called Genelle and asked if he could stop by and talk.

☙❧

"You mentioned something about a movement. A strike-back mentality." Greg was talking before he removed his jacket and sat down.

"It's growing. It started with the gay and lesbian community in Seattle, and it has spread. We attract conscientious people who will no longer allow the Church to control, hurt, manipulate, or use us."

"And both Mike and Boyle believe in this."

"Yes. Mike has been useful in providing intelligence, facts…uhm…proof shall we say, that there are powerful members of the Church who willfully behave this way. They are aware of the harm they are doing and consider it minor collateral damage in their effort to transform the world to their liking."

"Okay, I've seen this, but this is a larger effort than just one local bishop. Yes, they want to see the world operating according to their values and only their values. This is nothing new."

"You told me about the nuns and the Jesuit priests who were murdered. We have been aware of this, and we have really done nothing about it. We sat back and shook our liberal heads and they kept doing it, without any accountability, and they walk around with their sweet, hypocritical piety. We decided to hit back. I don't know why, really, Mike and Bishop Boyle are in this. I think Mike is focusing on his brother and Boyle is hurting from a recent scolding. That's fine with us. We don't care what the straw is that breaks the back. We have all been hurt—"

"I get it. Thanks."

***

Harry sat on the edge of his bed, his forehead in his right hand, the phone in his left. "He must be someone special. How did you convince him to do this?"

"He owes me. He took a round in his left butt in Guatemala. Ripped it all to hell. He kept saying leave him, but we both knew the drug lords would pull him apart piece by piece to get information out of him."

"Why did he get out of the service?"

Greg leaned back in his chair and sighed. "Armies and businesses run at peak efficiency when you have a work force of fairly competent and adequately skilled people. This fellow was never just fairly competent or simply adequate at anything. He was so smart, and so good at what he did, he scared the shit out of everyone who ever commanded him."

"What's his name?"

"No, no, no. Not for your ears. Got to be that way, padre. Hand off is clean. I won't even know who this guy gets to do certain aspects of the job."

"Can I ask why he owes you?"

Greg picked up Doug Dorn's file and flipped through some of the pages, ignoring the question. "How convenient they found drugs in his satchel when he went in for a Pentagon briefing. Five grams of cocaine sitting right in front of the drug czar himself. Too close to his work, burned out, the drugs too readily available, that kind of crap. Huge gaps of time he wouldn't account for. They had some photos of him on a recon, and they said it was his personal supplier." Greg shrugged. "They allowed him to resign."

Greg flipped the file shut and leaned forward on the

table. "He wouldn't account for the time because he was slipping in and out of bed with his boyfriend, regular army. Accounting for the time would mean informing on the guy. The guy is still in, a career man, thanks to my friend."

"So, let me guess, he's angry about something."

"Worse than you and me." Greg laughed. "Got him to cut back on the drink for a while and he found a new guy to hang out with. The guy comes from beaucoup bucks, so they live well. He invents things and likes the chance to experiment with them."

"He doesn't need the money so he's doing this because he's angry?"

Harry didn't doubt—it just sounded like that to Greg. "When I call, he responds. Is that okay with you?" Greg's tone was icy, defensive.

"Hey, I wasn't asking like that, Greg. It just seems odd a guy would go off and risk his life at the drop of a hat."

"He does."

⧼⧽⧼⧽

Greg told Harry to fly out the following Saturday.

Doug Dorn stood at the front door of the motel room and knocked lightly. He turned around to look at the Tetons. A midsummer snow capped them, setting them sharply against the deep blue sky. When he heard footsteps, he held the worn leather back pack in his left hand. There was no verbal exchange between him and Greg.

Doug walked around the living room and then quietly sat at the table. He looked at Harry and smiled briefly, saying nothing. His eyes shifted left to right, taking in the room, the two men sitting across from him. Their eyes caught.

"Good trip?"

"Yeah."

Greg busied himself with the scotch.

"You certainly know how to find the shittiest possible motel rooms. You should write a book. *The Absolute Worst Motels in the West*."

"I like places that don't require credit cards and don't ask questions."

"That's where the whores hang out."

Greg smiled. "And?"

"Yeah, I guess we're just a couple of money grubbing whores."

"Doug, you finally get it."

The glasses were set loudly on the table. The scotch was poured with reverence and the bottle set carefully down. No ice. Greg tipped a small bit of water into his and silently offered it to Doug. He declined. There was no toast, just a fast glance into each other's eyes, a raising of the glasses, and a smooth tasting.

"Did I ever tell you my mother always told me my uncle had a drinking problem?" Doug set his glass softly in front of him. "I went over to his house one day when he was…oh…seventy five. He was chopping wood and then we went fishing. He rowed his boat maybe for forty-five minutes, and then we fished. Caught something. He rowed back. We drank a few glasses of something strong and bullshitted for a while, then I had to go. He went back to chopping firewood. So, I get home and my mother is on to me about how much he drinks, and all I can say is what brand is it?"

Greg smiled. For Doug drinking was a lifestyle, and he talked about it like hunters talk about killing animals.

There was a long nervous pause. Doug stared at the unopened brown folder. He flipped open the cover and read the first page then lifted and read the next several pages. These were four separate and detailed itineraries of Archbishop John Riley. The nice smile and cheery eyes faded. Doug's face was pinched now and his eyes focused, no longer shifting and taking in things and events around him.

The brown folder contained maps and floor plans and a photograph of John Riley was stapled to the inside. Detailed itineraries listing where the archbishop would be and who would meet him on three different occasions. Doug flipped the file closed and took another drink from his scotch.

"Where did you get these itineraries? It's pretty good."

"The archbishop's former secretary. Don't underestimate what people can do when they have to suffer injustice at their jobs."

Doug sipped again and went back to shifting his eyes left to right.

"Why him?"

"You mean Riley?" Greg stared at his drink. He paused and looked Doug in the eyes. "It's a job, right?"

Doug raised his eyebrows and then slowly shook his head. His eyes shifted again, lighting up. "You still have that same butt ugly jersey, Greg."

"You got one memorized?" Greg pointed at the folder.

Doug wagged his head and opened the folder again. He stared intensely at a page neither of the other men could see, slapped the folder shut, and nodded. Greg removed all of the items in the folder and sent them through a silent portable paper shredder. He put the empty file back on the table.

Greg knew better than to ask which occasion had been chosen. He knew it would be done. Doug never objected. It was strange that, this time, he even asked why Riley. Never did that before.

Greg saved his life, but no one ever did this purely out of loyalty.

"Will two hundred and fifty thousand do?" Greg asked.

"Yeah, that's a nice round number." Doug eyed the envelope. "Unmarked, right?"

Greg nodded. "The cell number I was using was rented. I don't know who it was rented from. So don't use it anymore. I'll know when you're done. The news will be sufficient notice." Doug shrugged and readied to leave the motel room. "You didn't call from home, right?"

Doug looked over his shoulder. "Two bucks and a quarter is a lot of cash. I'm sure you're getting something tidy. Who's paying?"

"My client."

Greg smiled and Doug nodded slowly.

Chapter 14

Greg received a text message with two letters. HM. Having memorized the itineraries of the archbishop, he knew immediately Doug had chosen the high mass where Riley would officiate for the gathering of the Opus Dei members. "Excellent choice, Doug." He called to see if Harry was in town yet and he was. "It's time. You should come over to my place. It will be over soon."

Harry arrived at Greg's cabin by mid-morning. Greg was alone in the cabin, sitting comfortably in the easy chair sipping a scotch. Harry wondered about people who could precisely calculate the death of another human being and carry on so causally. He sat on the overstuffed couch.

"So, your fellow is off and running? Isn't it a little early to start drinking?"

Greg shrugged.

"Does he need help with this?"

Greg looked at Harry and frowned slightly. "No, he doesn't need help."

Harry was confused now. "When is he going to do it?"

"Do what?" Greg set his glass down hard. "Look. The less you know now, the better. You're not like the other bishops I knew. They'd start to hear about one of their priests doing all sorts of crazy wrong things, and they would shut their ears. The less they knew, the better."

"I just like to be aware of the details, to think the problem through."

"Don't think about it. You thinking gets me in trouble. When we do exactly what we were trained to do, we succeed. I have no idea right now when the best time will be. I won't even know when it's right. He will. He makes those decisions, sometimes during the planning, sometimes in the field. He was trained right and will do the job he is being paid to do." His tone was cool and soft.

Greg stood and reached for the decanter, pouring the glasses full again.

"How do we know we can trust him?

Greg looked at Harry quickly, scowled, and then focused back on the computer screen. Harry almost apologized. He paced around the kitchen, moving pots and pans, opening the refrigerator, rinsing glasses in the sink. Greg slammed his hand flat on his desk. Harry smiled nervously and went out on the front porch to stare at the Tetons.

Greg and Doug had worked so well together, communicating silently, knowing what the other was thinking. Harry felt left out, like an alien. He didn't understand violence, and he had convinced two highly skilled men to wreck death on a man who had no idea it was coming. Harry needed to stop men like John Riley. But death?

And simply sliding five thousand dollars in cash across a table—for materials and travel expenses, not knowing when or where the services would be rendered—bothered him. It wasn't the money. It was the lack of knowledge, of control.

Was it really better this way? Greg giving Doug accurate information, and Doug picking the time and place.

Greg had assured Harry it would then be difficult to connect any of them completely, especially if the hand off
was clean. Secret agent, cloak and dagger stuff. Harry
never understood the attraction. What he had wanted all
along was immediate satisfaction; stand up to the bully,
smack him in the face, give him a bloody nose, and be
done with it. But this was so sanitized. All the passion
and emotion Harry had felt, leading up to this moment,
was boiling inside him.

Harry tried to visualize John Riley in his mind. He
wanted to see John Riley alive in front of him, tell him
what he hated about his methods and policies. He wanted
to change John Riley, not kill him.

And Greg was being so smooth, so on top of everything. His answers came out like syrup. How could any
man just go in that smoothly and kill someone?

Harry noticed himself scowling and crossing his arms,
his heart racing, and he was sweating. It wasn't too early
for a second drink today. He went inside and poured out a
large tumbler full, gulping down half of the first glass.

Greg laughed as he saved his work and turned the
computer off. "Wait up."

"If I think about this anymore, I'll do something stupid. Keep me under until it's over. The fucker deserves it,
and I just want it over with."

Harry was wide-eyed and pale. Greg recognized the
symptoms and patted him on the back. He poured himself
a drink. This was how operations failed or never really
succeeded. When untrained people gave orders to kill,
they thought the process was going to be like having a
subordinate fired. Quick and painless execution of an order and the worst that would happen was some financial
discomfort. But killing someone was not like firing an
employee.

"You get good and drunk there, Harry. By the time

you sober up and get rid of the hang over, John Riley may have already met his maker."

Harry gulped another half glass of scotch. "I didn't know it would be like this."

"Harry, you should have thought about this before. It's the same as when a bunch of civilians order troops in, and they start to see dead bodies on the news. Then they feel it. Right now death is very real, isn't it?" Greg kept his left eye trained on Harry. He was bracing himself against the side board. "For me, it is a routine operation. Very soon John Riley will be dead, and I will get on with my work."

Harry stared at him. Greg immediately realized this might end up where he didn't want it—a security breach. He would talk to Harry when he was sober again, convince him of the stupidity of talking to anyone about this.

"Why don't you sit in the living room, Harry, put on some music, and we'll get blasted together. I'll be the designated half-drunk, and you can just swim away into the ether world. Just forget what is happening."

Harry nodded and plodded listlessly away. The music was a bit loud, but Greg understood. He carried the half gallon and topped off Harry's glass. Babysitting again. He would keep the news on, CNN probably. No sound. At first, there would be no film. Maybe a grainy photograph. Then in an hour or so after it happened, film of the aftermath repeated over and over.

Harry would not want to watch at first. He'd be a blubbering baby when he saw the pictures for the first time. But watching the images would be a way of convincing him everything was okay. Just watch the images over and over and realize that he was fine. The world carried on. Soon, he wouldn't feel a thing. He would sober up and not want to talk about that night ever again. But he would be fine.

Greg's job now was to make sure Harry really was fine. His own life depended on it.

ℰↄℰↄ

Doug arrived in Puerto Vallarta two days before the high mass was scheduled in the cathedral where Archbishop John Riley would officiate. He walked the paved sidewalk along the beach, stopping occasionally to drop some coins into the begging hands of crippled old women. He saw the cathedral with the cast iron dome from the beach and walked toward it. It was noon and the regular mass of the day was in progress. He sat in the back, reciting in Spanish the prayers of the Eucharist.

The odd mix of architectures told a story of shifting interests and control of the cathedral. The result was something that, at the very least, was confusing but he guessed the Church did not teach history of architecture in their grade school catechism. He left before the part of the mass where everyone shook hands. He would be passed off as a curious tourist, many of whom wandered into the mass and were exposed, perhaps for the first time, not only to a Catholic service, but one in Spanish, giving it even more novelty.

After a late dinner in an excellent German restaurant full of German ex-pats drinking themselves into hilarity, he wandered back toward the cathedral. Earlier in the day, he noticed an alley to the left side of the main entrance and a service door with an old and useless lock. It was locked but a gentle tug to one side opened it. He let the door swing open and waited for an alarm. He had not seen any motion detectors during the day and guessed, correctly, there was no security system in place. He walked toward the main altar and noticed it was hollow under the marble flooring. A crawl space. They had made it all too easy over the centuries, as one interest held sway over another, and no one ever gave even the slightest attention to security detail. He would return in time to set in motion the mission for which he had been chosen.

He had left the door ajar the previous night and found it exactly as he had left it. No one had checked it the next day. He walked over the marble on the main altar and found the trap door—one piece of marble with a hole drilled in it. He lifted it and shone his flashlight into the crawl space under the altar. There was nothing but a series of wooden beams, the wood flooring under the marble, and the stone face on the sides. He was done setting the bomb in place in less than fifteen minutes. A drunk had entered through the open door and Doug ignored him until he was resting comfortably in a pew, almost immediately asleep. Doug left quietly.

The next day at ten-forty in the morning Doug stood behind a thin pillar in the choir loft among the singing members of the choir. The man he hired, to stand in the dark of the side aisle in the black leather jacket, moved precisely on time from the front to the back of the church. He exited at precisely the agreed-upon time, when Bishop John Riley was holding the large, flat host in the air, transubstantiation in progress, small bells rung by an altar boy. Doug pressed the button as the host reached the highest point in the ceremony. It was easy to walk away amid the screaming and confusion. Everyone saw him and no one would remember him. They would remember the man in the black leather jacket.

❧❦❧

CNN finally reported the explosion at 3:30 p.m. The shots of the debris and bodies being carried to the ambulances came sooner than Greg had expected. Harry had passed out, unable to maintain consciousness with Greg in custody of the scotch bottle. Greg was satisfied with the reporting. It was a big enough event to warrant uninterrupted coverage through the night and into the morning news, but not large enough to eclipse the minor wars and another shooting at a high school in Florida. Just right.

Part 5
Present Day Again

Chapter 15

On the fourth day of the investigation, no group or individual had yet claimed responsibility. Captain Moro escorted Grady to the cathedral.

The work of scraping marble debris was done quietly, almost reverentially, so as not to disturb the faithful who had been allowed into the first ten pews just at the main entrance. Conversations between investigating officers were carried out in hushed tones. The police nodded silently as Captain Moro walked with Grady past the barriers. They stopped to view the work as they would a corpse at an open funeral, spent the appropriate amount of time looking, and then moved on. There was nothing to see.

The residue was plastique, the same kind used by most European-based terrorists. The manner in which the explosives were set and the triggering device were unique. Moro already knew this. She nodded her approval to the nervous officers. Grady saw Moro shake her head slightly as she walked away.

Security was not an issue. In such a large and ancient facility, there was little hope of completely securing the premises at night, especially when custodians were not warned to watch for terrorists planting bombs. Anyone could have found their way in without being detected. And not since Romero had any Catholic prelate been assassinated, so no one gave security a second thought. Grady stood in the small chapel above the main altar and looked down. It could have been detonated from there. They summoned one of the officers and Captain Moro asked if the area had been sealed off for the high mass. The answer was yes. An usher had cleared out all tourists an hour before the mass and stood faithfully at the entrance until the explosion. Moro watched from a distance as Grady closed his eyes and saw nothing. She turned to look at the massive stained glass windows in the apse, her back to Grady.

They walked slowly over to the baptistery, a hundred feet away with a clear line of vision of the main altar. Grady closed his eyes. A form. A man. He saw a man holding something. Grady opened his eyes, aware Captain Moro was staring at him.

"Do you, well, see anything?" Captain Moro stood to the side, leaning against a massive column.

Grady smiled. He had what he wanted. "I need to see the crime scene photos."

"All five hundred of them?"

"Yes. And the photos and video taken by the eye witnesses."

Captain Moro turned away to answer her cell phone. "Si." Her face was strained and she motioned Grady to follow. The other officers faced their work but followed the two of them with their eyes.

"There is a threat. It was sent to the email address associated with the general Vatican Internet webpage. There will be a copy on my desk when we get back to my office."

Inspector Juarez greeted them in the foyer of Captain Moro's office, holding a dark green envelope used for secure internal communications. Captain Moro took the envelope with a polite nod and broke the wax seal as she entered her office.

She read slowly, memorizing the message, and then slowly offered the single page to Grady.

Grady showed more interest in the first email address listed at the top. "The person who owns this first address doesn't know it is being used. That person most likely did not send the message."

"Do you see who they are threatening and when?"

"Yes. The pope. This is not a real threat. Someone has masked themselves behind this person, this one here, and it's just an effort to throw us off the real track. They will put security on him, but nothing will happen."

"Is this something you knew already?" Moro asked, waving her hand above her head, glaring at Grady.

Grady was silent.

"We will receive news of the arrest of this individual. Much will be made of a breakthrough, and your FBI and CIA will be here, wanting to exchange information. They know we have something, my department is not above leaking information. Then I will have to deal with them about this trigger."

Grady stood and looked out the window at the ever-flowing traffic. "And you lose all hope of finding who invented it and planted it. They will bury this."

"It's my evidence. It stays here."

"They will get it from you. Your government will order you to turn it over. I know. I used to do that."

Moro was silent.

"If they know you have something, news of US origin, you will never see it again. A few of these assholes probably know who invented it, and it is in their best interests to keep that silent whether we ever solve this or not. These people are not above counting the dead archbishop as collateral damage in their own personal little wars. I know this."

Captain Moro leaned back in her high-backed leather chair. "How certain are you they have the wrong man."

"Not a hundred percent. Just ninety-nine percent" Grady shifted uncomfortably. "I just know how this is done. I used to do it. I still do it when I deem it necessary. Nobody who knows the first thing about email would ever send a message like this straight from their own computer. They would have to be a complete idiot."

Moro did not respond.

Grady breathed in deep. "If whoever really sent this is involved with the triggering device and he's friendly with the covert types, they'll arrest this guy and the real perpetrator gets away. Give me a couple of days."

"A couple of days?" Moro yelled. "They'll be here tomorrow. They won't leave until I give them everything about the trigger. You have one day. I need a definitive answer in twenty-four hours."

∾

Grady watched restlessly as CNN repeated over and over the scenes of Father Thomas Jurevics being arrested and the FBI surrounding his apartment. The effect of the shy, wide-eyed Father Jurevics staring helplessly into the camera said it all. The words added weight to the video clip—a threatening message, which took responsibility for the bombing death of Archbishop Riley of Seattle, was sent from his computer. The message also threatened the life of the holy father.

By midnight, it was reported Father Jurevics was under investigation by officials of the Archdiocese of Seattle and the Seattle Police, regarding allegations he had been involved in a group of activists who had recently begun to advocate violence against higher-level Church authorities. An angry letter written to Archbishop Riley by Father Jurevics attacked the archbishop for "unholy acts of spiritual violence" and went on to accuse the archbishop of oppressive treatment because of Father Jurevic's sympathetic stand toward the ordination of women.

Grady snapped the television off. He slept for six hours and was awakened by Inspector Juarez knocking loudly at his bedroom door. Grady hastily slid into his black jeans and opened the door. Juarez stared uncomfortably at his bare chest. Grady invited him in as he found his shirt.

Juarez's arms were crossed. "I came to see if you wanted coffee. I've been waiting for you, and you slept right through the free breakfast we arranged for you."

Grady recognized the sense of justice and correct living he saw in most police and intelligence officers. Breakfast time was for breakfast. *If the breakfast is paid for, get up and eat it. Letting it go to waste was something the assholes would do. We are different.*

Grady placed a hand on Juarez's shoulder and smiled weakly. "Sorry."

"Harold Brown returned your call. He called at three-thirty this morning. He wants you to call." Inspector Juarez walked ahead of him. "Don't you own a cell phone?"

"Yeah, but I turn it off and I left your number as a backup."

"Thanks. I appreciate that."

"I have his home number. Maybe I'll wait until I'm sure he's in bed and call him. Now, about that coffee."

Grady remembered to sit before ordering. He asked for a hard roll as well. "A little late in the morning for that, but, yes, they have a few left, but like I said breakfast was hours ago."

"I'll get it right one of these days."

"What?"

"How you order coffee in this country. It's such a ritual."

Inspector Juarez looked at him, puzzled. "It's just coffee."

Grady smiled to hide the humiliation.

The café was full of French and German ex-patriots. Older, dressed in white shorts and brightly colored shirts, they read newspapers, stirred coffee. They had nothing better to do than drink coffee, gossip about each other, and read their newspapers. Mostly older men, they offered a sharp contrast to the young Mexicans working the café.

"I need a few cups to get, hum, well, things moving. You don't mind. I'm such a jerk if I don't take care of things in the morning."

Between the tone of his voice and the subject matter, Inspector Juarez was both shocked and entertained. "Fine." He reached into his bag. "This is Captain Moro's son. This was taken a month before he disappeared. He was fourteen."

Grady saw the resemblance immediately. "This is why she's so interested in the altar boy."

"Yes. Crimes against children have become her primary focus. Not everyone is happy she spends so much time on that, but who is going to try and stop her?"

Grady slipped the photograph into his own folio. "Let's see what we can do."

"Did you find anything in the cathedral yesterday?"

Grady hesitated as he sipped his second coffee. "I sensed something the first day I got here. I am certain Ignacio saw something. A man. Not certain of the age. Calm, and he put something in a coat pocket. It's eighty-five degrees outside, and he's wearing a jacket. That's it.

That's why the D'Angelo boy looked, and it's why he's afraid. God. I need to work on that. Don't tell the captain yet. I want to see the crime scene photos, and then I need to interview the D'Angelo boy again, even hypnotize him."

Juarez nodded slowly. "Why the boy? Why not other people who were attending the mass?"

"He has a stronger connection to the event. The terror he experienced made him more acutely aware of the details. He will recall things now under hypnosis that no one would have noticed. And he looked right at the guy, caught his eye."

Inspector Juarez frowned and looked away. "My orders are to keep you away from the boy."

Grady nodded. "As well as observe me. Your eyes, every time you ask about what I know."

Inspector Juarez shrugged and answered his cell phone. "Yes, Captain, immediately." He looked at Grady. "Very odd. The captain wants to meet us at a graveyard. The last place they saw her son."

They drove through the crowded tourist hotel district. "The two goons in the blue Toyota following us—they really should get a bigger car. They're stuffed in there like sardines. By the way, tell the driver that police stake outs in the States usually do not include tequila. Our cops have a thing for doughnuts."

Inspector Juarez raised his eyebrows and smiled. "I will mention that to them." He parked the car in front of a large mausoleum. "Okay we walk from here."

Grady waved at the tail as it rolled through the parking lot toward the exit.

Beyond the mausoleum was one of the oldest cemeteries in Puerto Vallarta. Grady noticed some of the tombstones dated back to the late fifteen hundreds, some were recent.

"The grave sites you see that are new have been in families for five or six hundred years. Eight or nine generations can be buried together within thirty feet."

Grady stood in front of a bronze statue marking the grave of a young man, probably fifteen or sixteen—handsome, dressed in tight Levis and a T-shirt, artfully well endowed. "They obviously loved their son. But, hey, can anyone that age be that, uhm, big?"

Inspector Juarez smiled and shrugged. "The Moro boy came to the cemetery to visit his grandmother's grave. He did not tell his mother or the officer usually assigned to follow him. He was seen in front of her grave at eleven in the morning, arranging flowers and picking dead leaves away from the azalea shrub. Two maintenance workers spoke with him briefly, and he asked if they had a bag for the dead leaves. They told him to leave them and they would get them later. They saw him kneel down, and take out his rosary so they left him in his privacy. They came back not five minutes later and he was gone."

Grady stood by the grave and looked around in a full circle. Juarez glanced at him then turned his back and started walking slowly. He glanced back again. Grady's eyes were closed. Juarez turned away quickly. A rabbit sprang from under a bush, paused on the gravel walkway, and then sprinted toward a hole in the fence and then the grassy field.

"Russians. My bet is Captain Moro killed one of them. How active are the Russians around here?"

Inspector Juarez looked at him. "We've only begun to notice their involvement here in Mexico in the past few years. We've been following larger numbers of them here in Jalisco. Why do you say Russians?"

"They do this sort of thing. They follow people to macabre places where they snatch them. Were any graves being dug the day he disappeared?"

"I don't recall in any of the reports of a grave being opened or dug. I could be wrong."

"Let's walk around anyway."

Inspector Juarez's cell phone screamed. "*Si...si.*" He slapped it shut and slid it into his pocket. "Captain Moro. She isn't coming. We need to go back. Something about Harold Brown?" They walked quickly toward the car. "I will need to tell the captain. What you said about the Russians. And, yes, she did kill one of them, but let her tell you that officially."

"Yes, good."

"She will be very angry."

"I was aware the Russians have been here for quite some time, but my sources told me they were silent partners, not interfering."

"Until recently. I'll update later."

⁊⊃⁊⊃

Captain Moro jumped from talking about the email threat to yelling at Juarez for working on another inspector's case without first asking permission. She repeated, like a quiet curse, the words "golden medallion" ten times. She paced back and forth to the windows, stared silently, and then tried to talk about the email threat.

"I have a name of someone who might be able to help us, does email forensics for a police department, I think Jackson Hole, Wyoming. He is an Internet expert and he has assisted this and other police departments with very reliable information. This guy, Chief Grieg, trusts him and uses him occasionally. I cannot order you—" She looked quickly at Grady then stared at Juarez. "—even if I thought ordering would do any good. But this man...uhm...Greg Lucas, is waiting for us to call. If we can be sure the priest they arrested in Seattle is not the man who sent the email message, I can keep the FBI out of this a while longer, and I will not have to turn over any information regarding the trigger. I think it would serve our interests if you call him and see what he has to offer."

"I'm not sure what the need is here. I can check out an email and its origins the same as anyone else."

"I have no doubt. However, we need results fast, or we lose this and turn the evidence over to your FBI or some other agency that will just sweep this away and blame it on the drug cartels."

"I understand the pressure. How again did you find this guy…uhm…Lucas was his name?"

"The same way you found your way to me. Harold Brown. Brown knows Grieg, how I do not know. Just call him and see if we can't speed things up with another expert."

Captain Moro sat hard in her chair. "You want to talk to the boy again. Fine. Anything to get this thing solved. Sorry I was not able to join you at the cemetery. Inspector Juarez told you that was the last place they saw my son."

Grady looked away and then back. "It's been my experience that the Russian mob uses places like that—" He saw her close her eyes and stopped speaking.

After a long silence, Moro leaned forward on the desk and laughed lightly. "Russians, you say? I wish Captain Novarres would follow the leads I have given him." She hesitated again. "Do you understand I do not want to believe my son is dead?" She stood and walked toward the window. "I dream my son is alive. But then my dreams are not psychic, are they?" She rubbed both hands through her thick hair. "I suggest you call this man Lucas. There is a free desk down the hall. The desk clerk will give you an access code for the telephone and the entrance. Inspector Juarez, please remain here."

Grady stood to leave then hesitated. His eyes were

narrow and hard. "I can help you, then you can help me. I am not using your son."

"I know, I know. You have just touched a nerve, and I am feeling pressured. I just got a call from the governor. He wants a reason to keep this case here and to not give anything over to the Americans or the Vatican. I can't tell you exactly why, that's what you call top secret, but the pressure is on to track down the truth about this, no matter what."

"I understand. I'll call him. The archbishop's laptop, that's still mine to work with, correct?"

"Yes. No one but his assistant knows we have that, and I don't want anyone else to know. They may ask for it, and I need a reason to hang on to it."

"The Russians have been active in the past few years, sharing information on private chat rooms and forums that they think have been totally secured. More like bragging rooms. I can show this captain working on your son's case a few places to look, if you want."

Captain Moro paused and stared at Grady. "Perhaps."

Chapter 16

Officer Jerry Garcia had never believed the opinions about climate change until the past several years living in Jackson Hole. It was February and the town should have been buried in snow, but it was dry, in the high sixties. Even the trees had begun to bud. He approached Greg Lucas from behind. "Company leave?"

Greg flinched. "What?"

Jerry looked at Greg for a moment. "Your company. You had a guest. Did he leave?"

"Yes. A week ago." Greg stared at Jerry. "You sure do have your ears to the track."

"Hey, I think I found a fourth for the poker games. We are going to start them back up, right?"

Greg placed four quarters into the parking meter. "I assume so. Who is it?"

"New guy, LA movie money. I clobbered him in cribbage over at Emil's. Talks real fast, growing a cell phone out of his ear. Lots of dough."

Greg smiled. "Jerry, you're setting this guy up. You're a cop."

"Hey, a fair game of poker is legal, and I have two children and a mortgage. Now that you went and threw old Jim into the clinker, I've got to make it up somehow."

"How's little Jimmy doing?"

"He's with his own kind. He has no computer access, so he's safe from committing more crime." Jerry held his citation book on his knee as he rested his right foot on the bumper of a Chevy Suburban.

"Jerry, that's Bill Harlan's truck. He's local."

"Yeah, I know. I bought a snowmobile from him last year. Swell guy. He's also neglected to put enough money in the meter." Jerry signed the ticket and smiled at Greg. "You and your friend didn't go anywhere the whole time he was here. Drove by a few times and you hadn't moved your truck."

Greg looked at Jerrys smiling face. "No."

"Oh, yeah, call the chief. He has some work for you." Jerry smiled as Greg walked away.

An interesting reaction, that flinching. Lucas, the hero of children and skilled in guerrilla warfare, flinches when you talk behind him. Something. He's got something.

Jerry laughed softly and slapped his ticket book against his free hand.

⌘

Chief Grieg was slow to respond and his voice sounded like he was talking with gravel in his throat. Greg had seen him go into a cocktail lounge the night before and surmised the rest. "Yeah, some guy, an old rich man called. I used to know him up in Seattle, a long time ago. He's got high up connections with the Church, the Catholic Church. Donates a lot of money to them. Asked if I knew of anyone who knew the Internet, and I told him about your little trick with Jim Burns. Seemed convinced. Then another guy called and left a message. A captain in the Mexican police somewhere. Same case I think, but I was drunk when they both called so I don't know much. I called the captain back and gave her your cell phone number."

"Thanks."

"Yeah. You know that tourist you smacked? See the *Los Angeles Times*?"

"No. I read the *New York Times*."

"Yeah, right. But look. It's your fat boy, hunched over, his arms cuffed behind his back. Arson and insurance fraud. FBI trying to connect him with five arsons in California, all of the buildings owned by his estranged wife who has been in constant contact with him since their highly publicized and contentious divorce. The divorce appears to be a cover, since they both had in their possession plane tickets and hotel reservations in Bolivia." Chief Grieg rubbed his aching head. "Wish we'd got him. That would have been a nice arrest."

Greg's cell phone vibrated in his coat pocket. He walked out of the restaurant to respond.

"Greg Lucas, please."

"That's me."

"Good. The police chief in Jackson Hole, a former client of mine, referred you when I asked if he knew of any private citizens with Internet expertise and a history of assisting in police investigations."

"He said a rich old guy or a female police captain would call. Who are you?"

"Okay. An individual, I won't name, retained me to investigate a murder here in Mexico. The case is extremely sensitive. They have arrested a man who, I believe, is completely innocent. My proof of this requires extensive expertise in email technology, and Chief Grieg says you have that."

"Yeah? Who am I working for?"

"Well, after I check you out and you smell good, I'll tell you."

"Fair enough. Do you have a pencil?"

"A tape recorder and it's already on."

"I like you. What do they call you?"

"Grady."

"You got a last name?" Greg caught the waiter's eye to assure him he had not run out.

"I don't use it. I was with army intelligence, and I've heard all the jokes, so spare me. I can dig deep. Real deep. What am I going to find?"

Greg recited the usual sins.

"Okay, Mr. Lucas. Let me smell your butt for a few hours, then we'll talk at six your time. Here's a cell phone number of a certain Inspector Juarez, my babysitter here in Mexico. He's competent, so be nice."

"I can manage that." Greg hesitated. "Are you calling me because you don't have these skills?"

"No. I need you up in Seattle to track some email headers down. Get physical locations and users. I would do it but I need to stay in Puerto Vallarta."

❧❧❧

Grady called Sandy to update her and to express his doubt about Greg Lucas. "I have a social security number for him. Is it worth spending the money for a financial check?"

"It's only a hundred dollars. How uncertain are you?"

"Gut instinct tells me to watch this guy. The contacts I have seem like plants, like I was supposed to find them."

"You know what happens where there are too many moving parts. You said Olivia was feeling pressure to solve this to keep it out of the hands of the FBI. Pressure causes mistakes. You know that."

"Yeah, you're so right."

"What do you have control of here, anything? The less

control you have of the moving parts, the more danger you are in. This is what always makes me nervous when you do this. Get control of the moving parts. I'll run the credit check today and will have something later. You're ahead two hours so call me at seven your time."

Grady spoke to two of Greg's former commanders. The first refused to speak but Colonel Daniels, talking with a cigar in his mouth, suggested something else. "After what he did with Doug Dorn in Guatemala, if I had just one battalion of Greg Lucases, I'd march them right up to Pee-king, shoot the lock off the fucking door, and free those bastard Chinks. Then I'd let Lucas date my daughter. The guy just doesn't have the instincts to stay in at a higher level. Hates politics."

"Then I may actually like him."

"What?"

೮ာ೮ာ

Sandy got more than she wanted or expected in the credit check. Greg Lucas was five months behind on his mortgage on the cabin in Jackson Hole. Two credit cards had been charged off. There was no known regular income or employer. "Desperation. Period."

Grady paused. "Yeah, good call. I can't leave my wallet out, that's for sure. Why is everyone all fired up for this guy when he is nothing more than a bum?"

"You need to call Harold. You know histories like this always leads to disaster."

"I'll call him now."

Harold did not answer and Grady left a message. "Harold, doing due diligence on this guy Lucas and his credit stinks, real bad. Sandy found he's almost in foreclosure on his cabin in Jackson Hole and no regular income. I've got a desk in the police department, just call this number back. I want to talk with you. I'm going to go ahead and get this email to Lucas, but let's keep our eyes on the checkbook here."

❧❧

Greg sat on the front porch of the cabin watching the late winter sun bake the Tetons. "So how does my pedigree check out."

"Colonel Daniels sure has a hard on for you. Wants you to date his daughter, too."

"Yeah, he mentioned that once. Showed me a picture. I laughed and he got real pissed off at me. She's a cow."

"Sounded to me like you two were almost married."

"Who, me and the Colonel or his daughter?"

Grady cleared his throat. "I can tell you about the case a bit. I was hired to run an independent investigation into the death of the Archbishop of Seattle. What I need from you—"

Greg dropped his cell phone arm to his side and smiled.

"Hello? Hello. You still there?"

"Yeah, sorry, I was distracted. The Archbishop of Seattle?"

"Right. It seems to me someone is using an email address to send threats to the pope, but I don't think the person who really owns the address sent the threats. Can you track that?"

"Yes. I need a copy of the email, and I can track it down in a few days."

"I need it faster than that. The FBI has caught wind of a piece of evidence the Jalisco police are holding, something that I think suggests American involvement and not the usual terrorists. I am working closely with the Mexicans, and we do not want to turn the evidence over and then have it disappear."

"What's the evidence?" Greg guessed he would not be told.

"My lips are as tight on that one for now. Wanna try?"

Greg laughed. "No."

"My employer, Harold Brown is paying your fees. The same he pays me, three hundred a day and expenses."

"Is he good for it?"

"Yes, and then some. I want to send this email over to you. Give me an address."

Greg forgot his new, neutral email address, and had to fish for a card on his desk. He repeated it twice. In less than five minutes, a copy of his original email, threatening the life of the holy father and claiming responsibility for the death of Archbishop Riley, rolled smoothly out of his copier.

His heart racing, he returned to the front porch and dialed Harry's number. "Returning the call, Harry."

Harry was quiet and despondent. "My mother is not well. I don't think she's going to make it. I need to be with her."

"Okay." Greg hesitated, sweating a bit in his palms. "I'm sorry to hear this. If you need any—"

He had killed the archbishop. More thrilling to Greg now was the prospect of entering the game more fully. How sweet was the game that allowed him to do the good and the evil at the same time. Something like having sex while you confessed your sins to the priest.

"I don't need anything, thank you. My brother and sister are here. I need to lay low and take care of this. I'll call you."

"Right, Harry." Greg disconnected.

He sat staring at the mountains as they slowly faded into the dark, silhouetted against a moonlit sky, jagged and frightening at night, beautiful and assuring in the daylight.

He was neither pleased nor anxious about his life. His word would be ambivalent. He wasn't even moved by the fact he had set in motion the mechanics that not only killed an archbishop but got him directly involved in the investigation.

Chapter 17

The password to Archbishop Riley's laptop was not what he excepted of an Catholic prelate. It was four words connected as one. *ILiveALie*. It took little more than five minutes for the password cracker to reveal it in plain text. Grady smiled—another careless computer user who had no real understanding of the need for password complexity. A quick scan of folders, Internet temp files, cache, and a few other places most people don't think of thankfully did not reveal any pornography viewed or stored. What Grady did find gave him pause. There were two simple Excel spreadsheets with deposit and withdrawal dates. At the top of both sheets were the same Italian phone number and two different account numbers.

He opened the Internet browser and scanned through an extensive history list, many of them linking to the Institute of Works of Religion. Grady knew this is what was casually referred to as the Vatican Bank. Once at the site, he found a simple log in and then copied and pasted an account number from the excel spreadsheets and the same password. This one was a personal account for the archbishop, and Grady guessed immediately this was very normal. What was surprising was the short time between the creation of the account and the explosion, and even more surprising was the size of the personal account—seven million Euros.

He logged in to the second account for the Family Research Council of the Archdiocese of Seattle and immediately knew it was serious. The deposits came from three Mexican-based banks, and the total amount deposited in less than a month was in excess of fifty million Euros. There was one withdrawal of one hundred thousand Euros and marked as "Operations." There was nothing in the account information about where the rest of the millions were to be sent or how they were to be used. This was a classic, if also sloppy, money laundering operation. Grady logged into his home server and copied the entire contents of the hard drive remotely. He dialed Sandy's number.

"Got another one for you. I just dropped some excel spreadsheets on the server in a folder titled Vatican Bank. This is widening up to be something far more than I thought."

"Let me open them." Sandy accessed the shared drive and found the folder. "Which one first?"

"Doesn't matter."

She was silent for a few minutes. "Classic money laundering from Mexico to the Vatican Bank. Careless, too. Did you notice the account numbers and the contact information in Mexico?"

"No, I didn't. Where was that?"

"The Family Research Council spreadsheet has nine sheets. It's all on the last one with contact notes. That's a lot of money in both accounts. Be careful with this." Sandy was silent again. "Yeah, the passwords are all right there, and you could log in and move money at will. This is very careless. It's almost like a trap."

"Or maybe we're thinking they are a whole lot smarter

than they really are. These guys are not really trained in the money business."

"Yeah, but, Grady, keep your eyes open. This one is just too fishy for my comfort. Much more of this, and I'm going to pull your plug and get you back here."

"I hear you. I'll call you back on this. If you find anything more you don't like in there, call me right away."

❧❦❧

The police crime scene photos were neatly cataloged in six books. Grady scanned them all quickly then looked at each one carefully. He knew the cathedral had been cleared when these had been taken and gave up, instead looking at the photos and videos provided by people attending the mass at the time of the explosion. These were not well lighted or focused, but they did show what Grady was looking for—the people in the cathedral immediately before and after the explosion.

Inspector Juarez carried a laptop. He inserted a flash drive and opened a video clip of the actual explosion caught by a member of Opus Dei during the mass. Grady was not interested. It showed nothing but a loud snap. The camera was dropped in the shock and was not well focused on the event. Whoever was operating the camera was trying to film and run out of the cathedral at the same time. Juarez opened another. The person shooting the second clip was a little cooler headed. This one panned away from the altar after the explosion, recording the chaos and violence as frenzied mass attendees scratched and clawed their way toward the exit doors. His heart jumped when he saw him. It showed a man in a leather jacket, holding a cell phone, leaving the cathedral.

"Stop. Back up. Okay, there. Hold it. That's him. Get a print out of that frame."

"What?"

"The man in the leather jacket. It's hotter than hell outside, and this guy is wearing a leather jacket. That's him."

"Who?"

"He's involved somehow. Now play it. Look how he isn't panicking."

"Maybe he's deaf. Or just so scared he can't move—"

"No, look. Those aren't the manners of a frightened man. He's so damn calm. There, the cell phone goes into his pocket, and now he's walking away. Radio activated trigger from a modified cell phone. Let's get this printed out and see if he's on the other tape."

He was not. The print out was grainy, but clear enough to see facial features. Copies were distributed to uniformed officers, and they began canvassing the area around the cathedral to see if anyone recognized him. Many of the people asked were tourists, always so plentiful in late February.

Grady watched the tape several times, bothered by something but unable to name it.

Inspector Juarez answered his cell phone and then slapped it shut. "Captain Moro wants us."

◈◈◈

Captain Moro waited, tapping her foot on the floor, crossing and then uncrossing her arms. She stood in the covered entrance of a small building that had served as a classroom for a Russian Orthodox grade school, a rarity in Mexico. Some words in Russian were engraved above the battered wooden door. The officers who accompanied Moro stood to the side, smoking. They glanced occasionally at the pacing captain, careful to avoid her nervous wrath, but making sure they did not miss a command.

The rare February heat was heavy and oppressive. The air did not move and the smell of diesel exhaust was thick and chokingly sweet. They were waiting for Grady and the priest who currently was in charge of the school. Grady arrived first.

The small building was sandwiched between a church built in the fifteenth century and a row of shops and up-stairs apartments built in the late nineteenth century. There was no back entrance or any windows on the sides. Grady walked around the church, and then back along the row of shops. Moro said nothing, watching him carefully, arms crossed.

A nervous older man in a long black cassock arrived, jangling keys and apologizing loudly. Moro pushed the door open and walked around the empty class room. It had subsequently served as storage for some of the shop keepers. Moro asked quickly if any of these shop keepers were immigrants, Honduran or Nicaraguan. The man nodded, having a hard time remembering which shop it was, and they were now gone.

Grady stood in the middle of the room. He smelled the odor of mold and wet stone. Captain Novarres arrived with two uniformed officers. This was his investigation, but he always allowed Moro the latitude to follow leads and be present at any suspected scene associated with finding her son. Grady introduced himself, nodded at Mo-ro, and walked out of the room. Moro followed him.

" Why this place?" Grady asked in a very low tone

"When you said the Russians, I chilled. I will explain more later, but I made some calls and got this tip. Where do you think my son is?"

"Under the floor. That's what they do."

Moro walked back into the room and spoke quickly with Novarres. They argued for several minutes about ripping the entire floor up on what evidence? A suspicion? Novarres pleaded with Moro that doing this would utilize valuable human and financial resources, and what if they do not find the boy? Moro accepted full responsibility. Captain Novarres left the scene, glaring at Grady.

"Novarres is going to make this difficult, so we're going to have to wait for any construction people to show up. Have you looked at the archbishop's laptop?"

Grady glanced casually at the other officers. "How safe are we here to talk?"

"Let's take a short walk."

"Okay, an American archbishop, newly appointed, two accounts in the Vatican Bank of several million Euros. Both accounts opened within the last month. The source of the funds? Three different Mexican and Central American regional banks. Destination of the funds? A newly revived Catholic charity in Seattle got a tiny fraction of the money and the archbishop took a sizeable personal withdrawal."

"Laundering."

"Looks that way."

"I need to report this. That's a federal issue now. Did you see anything that would link the archbishop's death to the laundering?"

"No. It was all too new. Nothing in his documents, email, or Internet browsing history showed me anything like that. They had a cooperative person in a high-level office who had worked throughout Central America. They don't throw contacts like that away unless he threatened them, and I saw nothing like that either. He could have taken more money if he had wanted, so he wasn't on the run." Grady hesitated. "But there is more. If you ever have the misfortune of auditing a computer, it's like sticking your head very deep into a garbage can."

"I don't want to hear about any sex stuff, that's not my department."

"Well, it's not what you think. I found some very odd emails between the archbishop and my employer, Harold Brown. I've always wondered if Harold is not a bit…let's say…senile maybe? I don't know. My dad became obsessed with certain things in his old age, and this thing Harold has with homosexuals is more than an obsession. He was part of the effort to shut down any services for gays and lesbians and then to build up an organization to promote traditional marriage."

"Normal politics in your country as I understand."

"Well, several of the emails alluded to a conspiracy, an organized effort to harm leaders in the hierarchy of the Church. And you know what they say about paranoia. Just because you are paranoid doesn't mean someone isn't following you."

"Names. Did they name any names?"

"Former Bishop Harry Boyle was a very angry man and Harold connected him with a few very wealthy gays and lesbians and some very sympathetic and radical homosexual priests. When Harold contacted me, he expressed some theories I found to be extreme but the emails where he fleshes these out with the archbishop are lucid and coherent. I'm just wondering if he was on to something and really didn't know it."

"Interesting. No connection between any organized group and the bomb. Make that connection, and we have something." Captain Moro kicked the gravel. "I'm going to have to give up the laptop to the federales."

"I have a copy of everything."

Captain Moro smiled. "Yes, I would suspect that of you." A large truck stopped in front of the abandoned school and a crew slowly climbed out, unloading a jack hammer and shovels.

They did not find the boy's body but did find his clothes and a gold crucifix on a necklace in the pocket. A gift from her to him on his thirteenth birthday and something he rarely took off. Captain Moro knew it was a sign, a message. She looked away and cursed. "I suppose this might mean he is still alive. Is that your experience with the Russians?"

Grady shrugged politely. She ordered the arrest of five known Russian bosses in the State of Jalisco.

Hysterical news reporters wrote and spoke at length about the controversial methods used to find the boy's clothing, how an American clairvoyant was able to do a better job than the police.

Grady was not happy his photograph appeared on the front page of four national newspapers. Inspector Juarez had all four papers in his car when he picked him up the next morning. He carried the papers into the coffee bar and tried to read the text. Juarez translated for him. People passed by, recognizing him and congratulating him.

They left the coffee bar, instinctively looking around, making mental notes of who was near, who was watching from a distance, and who was approaching.

"How did you know the Russians were involved? And are you clairvoyant like the papers say?"

"I can say I don't know. Let me be more emphatic. I am not a seer, or a clairvoyant. Let's walk a bit. I'm feeling the effects of no exercise."

Shopkeepers were manually rolling up the metal shutters that protected their stores by night. Some rolled effortlessly. Others, from age, creaked and groaned.

"The first time I admitted I could do it was when I was seventeen. It was probably the hundredth time it happened to me. I just finally said to myself I know what some people are thinking. It was my girlfriend then. She wanted to break up with me for another guy. I just knew it plain as day. She said it was because I always finished her sentences. Then I pick up on them having sex, in my car that she borrowed. I just held that image in my mind for a second. It struck me. I never knew how her diamond broach got into the back seat. Then I just told her she could pick up her diamond broach. And that was it. She was history, and I knew I had this, like, skill. I took a test when I went into the army, and the next thing I knew, I was out of basic and being treated like a king, studying remote viewing."

"Can you tell what I'm thinking?"

"Not yet."

"What triggers it?"

"I get it strongest when someone is trying to hide something. Those are the most clear."

"Then I should have nothing to worry about." Juarez stepped up to the car, unlocked the door, and Grady got in—silent, smiling. They drove quickly out of the neighborhood. Grady glanced over at the high walls surrounding the large luxury hotels. "Who would stay in a hotel that's all walled in like that?"

Juarez smiled. "Rich little girls. They come down here to drink and take drugs and they are afraid someone will kidnap them so they stay behind the walls. Whatever."

Chapter 18

Grady did not see the truck accelerate and then enter their lane. He never saw the wheels of the truck climb over the hood of the car, effortlessly crushing the roof, and then drive away. He lived only because his seat broke away as the weight of the truck crushed down on him. He lay flat back, not aware of what was happening, his head severely cut. Inspector Juarez was keenly aware, so much so he was able to remember the license of the truck.

It took Juarez most of the rest of the day to contact Sandy. At first, she did not believe him and was angry for what she thought was yet another fictitious account of her husband's death. He finally convinced her, and she told him she would call back when she had made plans to fly to Puerto Vallarta.

Sandy sat quietly in the kitchen, waiting for Grady Junior to return from school. She told him in the same matter-of-fact language she had always told him anything about his father. Grady's years behind enemy lines as a communications specialist with the army rangers provided many opportunities to prepare Grady Jr. for what they all thought would be the inevitable. At fourteen, he was almost as tall as her now. His backpack remained on him while his mother explained what happened and the fact that his father was still alive. She would go to Puerto Vallarta immediately, and he would stay with Sandy's mother and then they would decide later if he would fly down as well.

Sandy had never met Harold Brown personally, and she was suspicious of his offer to put her in first class on any flight she wanted. She couldn't call Grady and get the truth right then, so she had to trust. She called the airline and expressed her suspicions and they assured her there was an open first class ticket in her name and it was purchased by Harold Brown. She only needed to check in and pick the flight she wanted.

Her mother took the news stoically. Her first husband, Sandy's father, died early in the Vietnam conflict, and she warned Sandy against marrying a military man. Sandy married Grady just before his second deployment. That was the first of the secret deployments—one day working the garden, that night slipping away in the dark very late at night so as not to be seen or heard from for three months, maybe longer. After the last deployment, just before Nine/Eleven happened, Grady was planning his retirement. He and Sandy had set the programming shop up in their free time, and his plan was to run it full time and then sell out at some point and permanently retire.

"I have no idea how long I will stay down there, or even if I can fly you down to see your father. I'll call you as soon as I see him. You focus on school. He's alive and, knowing him, I'll be wasting a trip down there."

Sandy kissed her mother and son and drove home to pack. She was not able to catch a flight until the next morning when the majority of Mexico-bound flights were scheduled, placing vacationers in their respective resorts up and down Mexico in the early to late afternoons.

She slept badly.

Grady had postponed retirement for a deployment to Afghanistan in November 2001, which lasted a full eighteen months, and he was able to talk to Sandy and Grady Jr. regularly for the duration. He finally decided it was time to let the younger professional soldiers take over and do their very best. He had given more than anyone had ever asked and in the spring of 2003, he was done with the rangers.

Their client list grew rapidly and included work for everyone from MomandPop.com to Microsoft. The work load was so heavy by 2010, they had to make a choice of moving to a new building and doubling the size of their programming engineers, outsource the work overseas, or sell. Grady put his foot down on the outsourcing. Not one single job he had created was going overseas. The offer to buy him out was lucrative enough it was an easy decision. He handed the keys and the passwords over on a bright Sunday morning and walked away rich. Sandy was going to dedicate her time to charity, and Grady decided he was going to sit back and relax. That, Sandy recalled as she dodged traffic to the airport, lasted all of a week.

He found himself advising covert ranger operations, involving complex communications systems. When he was on the military payroll, he wrote the code. Now as a consultant, he stood in front of a white board and told the staff programmers what to code, and he drove home for dinner.

SeaTac Airport was usually busy with long security lines, but that early morning Sandy walked up to the scanner and was through it and out to the gate within minutes of checking in. She chose a direct flight and settled into the first-class section as the long line of tourists with huge suitcases stumbled to the back of the plane. There was something about the sound of jets that calmed her and, fifteen minutes into the flight, she was catching up on the sleep she had lost the night before. A little over four hours later, she was sitting upright and preparing to land in Puerto Vallarta. As the door was unlocked and opened, she could smell the balmy warm ocean air. She immediately regretted not bringing Grady Junior.

The customs check was quick and effortless, and they barely looked at her bags. Outside the small, single-story airport was a line of buses and a few cars. A young, uniformed police officer held a sign with her name on it.

"I'm Sandy Marcs." He bowed politely, took her bags, and walked her to the waiting white SUV. "Who sent you to pick me up?"

"The police captain here. Captain Moro. She instructed me to take you directly to the hospital, and she will meet you later."

"The police captain? What happened here?"

"I am not so sure, Mrs. Marcs. But your husband, Mr. Marcs, he has uncovered some important information, and he was in the newspaper for helping to solve the murder of the captain's son. That is all I know."

She and Grady had been to Puerto Vallarta many years earlier over an extended leave. They only spent a few days in town, actually. Tourists' tastes dictated menu choices she did not like. The streets were loud and a little dangerous then with drunken Americans and Europeans wandering from one bar to the next, often fighting with the local police who were merely trying to clear the streets.

They drove out to a small village called San Sebastian where the food and atmosphere was more authentically Mexican.

The hospital was not far from the airport, and Sandy was inside asking for her husband with the assistance of the English-speaking officer. When they found the room, she thanked him and shook his hand. He tipped his hat and left silently.

Grady was on his back, tubes in his nose, and a mask over his face helping him breathe. She moved a chair next to the bed and sat down, holding back her tears. She touched his hand and then held it. There was a twitch. She wasn't sure if it was recognition of her or just a physical reaction.

"If you can hear me, I am happy you are alive and want you to know we all love you. Now, that being said, this is the last time you walk into enemy territory. I am going to lock you in your office, and you are going to write tawdry novels about love affairs on military bases." She did not see Captain Moro standing behind her.

"I'll buy them. Sounds like good reading." Sandy was a little embarrassed. "I'm Captain Olivia Moro. You're Mrs. Marcs?"

"Call me Sandy. What happened?"

"Well, what we know happened is a large truck drove over the car Grady and Officer Juarez were driving in, and your husband was crushed. There were a few minor bone fractures, one rib, and a severe laceration on his head. He has not regained consciousness since. The doctor can give you more specifics. They don't seem very worried, but I am happy you were able to come right away."

"Do you know a man named Harold Brown, and why he would pay for a first class ticket to come here?"

Captain Moro smiled. "I've known Harold Brown longer than your husband, but he hired Grady to investigate the murder of the Catholic Archbishop of Seattle. Didn't Grady mention what he was up to down here?"

Sandy nodded her head. "We just talked about the new guy, Greg Lucas, and then the spreadsheets. The money laundering. I told him to keep his wits and get out because there were too many moving parts he had no control over. But I married a military man, a secret military man. I find out what I need to know."

"I was aware of the spreadsheets, and they have been handed p over to the federales. They have special units to investigate that. What about Mr. Lucas?"

"When Grady was doing his due diligence, I ran his credit and his history is terrible. They are about to foreclose on his home, he's had credit cards discharged, and he has no known employer."

Olivia nodded silently for a moment. "I see. Money problems. My instinct told me there was something wrong." She paused again. "Do you know if Grady told Harold Brown?"

"He said he was going to call him."

"I see, yes. Well, Mr. Brown is legitimate and seemingly on the good side here, but he has become something of a nuisance. And now this with Mr. Lucas, I don't know if he is back in Puerto Vallarta or not, but when you do meet him, you will completely understand what I am talking about. Have you eaten? The food in the cafeteria is excellent."

The captain was right. From the chile relleno to the shrimp rolled in white fish, the food was as good as any restaurant. Sandy sat back in the chair. "Why the royal welcome?"

"I am glad you are here, first of all. I hope it will help Grady recover faster. However, he helped identify people who might have been involved in the death of my son. These are Russian nationals who are doing business with local cartels. My suspicions are the truck that, as I consider it, was sent to attempt the murder of your husband was hired or actually driven by one of these men. I am slightly in fear for your safety." Captain Moro turned and waved slightly. Three uniformed officers, one of whom was the driver from the airport, appeared from around the corner of the cafeteria. "These officers have been assigned as your security escort as long as you are here in Puerto Vallarta, and I have taken the liberty of placing you in a hotel just two blocks from here under an assumed name. I hope you are okay with this."

Sandy breathed deeply. "There are many enemies out there just waiting for Grady to drop his guard, and it looks like one got through. Your efforts are appreciated. And what I said earlier about the tawdry novels? I meant it. This is it. We have a fourteen-year-old son who needs to see his father as an old man."

Chapter 19

Death might be as certain as taxes, but it never arrives in the same manner. Harry Boyle Sr., Harry's father, died instantly of a heart attack. He just slumped over at the dinner table, and it was over in three minutes. Harry Jr. was even able to finish his dinner before the reality of his father's death sank in.

It did seem odd that Harry's mother, who faced the imminence of death, appeared to be waiting for something. Harry mentioned this to his brother Peter, who made note of the fact that her mother, two brothers, and three sisters had all died in the month of March. It was February twenty seventh. Eunice Boyle would hold out until March.

Harry found it interesting that the stroke that had set the dying in motion was so debilitating she could no longer speak. She was the one who always spoke. Harry Sr. would nod, look at his three children, and motion for them to do as she had said. She was the one who dispensed advice, wanted or not. She was the one who talked to the teachers, to the rector of the seminary when Harry Jr. first announced his interest in becoming a priest. Eunice Boyle dealt with the plumbers, carpenters, car mechanics, and the neighbors. If there was an issue, it was Eunice who spoke long and untiring until everyone agreed with her. She was president of various parish service clubs and the most vocal supporter or detractor of whichever priest the local bishop sent. Harry's sister Mary laughed as he recounted these memorable details.

"When Mother and Aunt Mary Beth lived together in the nursing home, they were both chatter boxes, just making everyone around them feel so good. When Aunt Mary Beth died, Mother continued to talk just as much as the two of them had talked."

Harry stroked her head gently. Now she lay silent, tubes protruding from her nose and mouth, intravenous feeding tubes in her arm. There was only the difficulty breathing that was so noticeable when someone was approaching death. He had seen this so many times, administering the rites, knowing that death was so near, the families all praying futilely for a different outcome.

Harry had always wondered why we had the inherent will to live when life could be so wretched. He knew it had to do something with not really knowing what was on the other side, after death. No matter what they told us in catechism classes, and even when studying Theology, they really didn't know, and when people were old and vulnerable, they often lost the conviction of their faith and feared the moment.

Each hour as they waited for Eunice to die, the three Boyle children told more stories, celebrating her life. Hers was a life of goodness, even if it was peppered with an occasional nosy intrusiveness. The siblings did not have secrets or shameful skeletons, until now. They had always been peaceful and close, supportive of each other. Peter and Mary had been there when Harry was ordained, when he was installed as a bishop, and when he was removed from his office. And they had always treated him as a loving and cherished brother.

What would they think now?

At three thirty-five a.m. March first, Eunice Boyle died. Harry asked the nurses to remove the tubes and monitoring devices and allow her to lie peacefully for him and his siblings to observe before the body was removed from the room. For half an hour, they silently looked at her, all three crying occasionally as they recalled one memory or another. Their mother was dead. It was a shock when their father died, but now they felt very much alone in the world. They saw it in each other's eyes.

"You were right, Peter. It's March. All of them except their father died in March. Explain that."

"You're the priest."

"I don't think God had much to do with that. I think they just decided to die in the same month."

"What about us?"

"I think it will be August. The three of us always had so much fun at the lake together in August. We didn't have friends, we had each other, especially in August." Mary sat on the edge of the bed and held her mother's hand. "Let's all die in August, okay? And let's agree to take the ashes up to the lake and all three of us will be in the lake. Okay, guys?"

Eunice's body was cremated. Harry had explained to her several years earlier the Church had approved of it, so Eunice decided to have it done. She did not believe in having her ashes strewn to the wind, only to have beasts and non-Christians defile the ground where she lay. Harry bought her a place in the mausoleum. He was granted special permission to celebrate her funeral mass on the fourth of March. In his sermon, he spoke of the value of life and how precious every life was. He saw this so clearly in the impact his mother had made on so many people.

Their tears that day were tears of genuine sadness at the passing of such a special life.

Harry hanged himself the morning of March the sixth, meaning he died in the same month as his mother and her siblings. He decided not to wait until August. He used fresh, stiff rope tied to a tree in his back yard. Father Carol went looking for him when he missed a weekly tennis match, did not answer the phone, and, from the looks of the car parked in front and the lights glowing throughout the house, he did not appear to be away. Father Carol walked around the house and saw him hanging, lifeless, hands limp to his side. Father Carol did nothing to the body. The police would want to see it first. He prayed for a few minutes then went inside the bishop's house to phone the police. Prominent on the dining room table was a lengthy, neatly typed suicide note. He wanted to read the note, but knew he must not touch it with his bare hands. He carefully turned each page using two dinner knives.

He read out loud. "'One. This is the story of the passion and death of our Lord Jesus Christ according to the defrocked Bishop of Newark, New Jersey. This will also serve as an explanation of why I have taken my own life, and I will further detail how Archbishop Riley was murdered and who was involved. For the record, I want to say the people of Newark, New Jersey, are among the finest I have ever met, and I miss serving them very much. The result of a passionate life is normally heartache. The joy we experience in life is heartache's companion. The passions of our Lord were deep and exciting and lead him to Jerusalem. How could such a passionate man stay away? Jerusalem is a city, strongly compact. It is there the tribes went up...to be passionate? They went to believe, to pray, to sacrifice.

"'It is there they met other passionate men and women

who believed and felt as they did. Jerusalem is a holy city, an historical city, a violent city where anything can happen. Even death. What did Jesus know about his eventual demise in Jerusalem and when did he know it? Did he know these passionate people would have him killed? That the drama the hungry masses would succeed in whipping up their passion into a crazed frenzy? Our Lord, a passionate man himself, in spite of his predicament, must have at least appreciated the smell of this electric passion in action.

"'I am always amazed that one day these people wildly cheer his entry into Jerusalem and lay down palm branches like the red carpet for him to walk on. Then they turn on him and have him killed. Pontius Pilate was a master of manipulation. He got the crowd to dictate the fate of Jesus and then washed his hands. He set the standard for ambitious, cunning, hypocritical, and evasive politicians and Church leaders. Many have dutifully followed his example. The passionate Jews got what they wanted, and they hauled this fiery-eyed little man off to jail, then off the Golgatha, the place of death. Jesus must have been partially swept up in the sheer energy of this madness. But here's where it all falls apart.

"'The Jews can shout a good line, but they can't deliver. The rules of their religion do not permit it. They hauled passionate Jesus up to the gate of Golgotha and stopped. A religious principle prevented them from completing the task they had so passionately yelled for earlier in the day. Maybe they just didn't have the stomach for it. What is crucial here is that the early Christians learned a valuable lesson—religious principle used to motivate extreme action. So, Jesus is hauled to the gate and the impartial Roman soldiers finish the job. Jesus died pretty much alone.

"'His closest followers, the fathers of this magnificent

Church, abandoned him. Two. The night before he was hauled up to Golgotha, Jesus called his followers together, just before he was arrested, and they scattered like bunny rabbits. He had them in a large room and he said, 'Before we go on, let's eat.' Now, I've said it a thousand times myself, eating is a sacred moment and Jesus used this sacredness to comment on the world as we know it today. 'Before I die, I want to eat with you and pour my passion out as only good food and wine will allow us to do. In the exciting heat of this moment, my Disciples, know that among you is a traitor whose passionate love for money will best him and in his passionate greed will be tempted to kiss me, not out of love, how sad, but out of unbridled greed. I don't want to mention any names, but I knew who were by the scent of the wine on your breath, now my blood, and the crumbs of this bread in your beard, now my body, when you kissed me, you carnivorous greedy bastard, Judas. You dropped a dime on me you stinking lousy son of a bitch. Pilate set the standard for popes and presidents and you have done the same for sniveling, lying, duplicitous, and avaricious money grubbers. You are the lord of the money grubbers. You love your money more than you do the very breath of your mother. Judas, your kiss is soft but it tears holes in my heart. Give my regards to your mother, Judas, and thank her for the lovely sandals. I have to ask, Judas, what will you do with all of the money now that your soul is stone dead?'

"'Now, let's finish up. I hope you can all make the crucifixion. I hope you're all as real as you are loud. Three. The Jews did not have AIDS, but they did have leprosy. And lots of hypocrisy. Just because Jesus loved the sick, demented, weak, broken, sinful, poor, angry, hostile, lost, forlorn, and did not fit the corporate mold and did not lay the groundwork for the rise of the prosperous middle class, they tied a beam to his shoulders and marched him. And the Jews stopped at the gate. It was impure to cross over. They could spit, cuss, yell, and insult this man, but they could not go into the place of death, Golgotha. The newly formed band of followers, the earliest Christians, took this notion of hypocrisy in action and perfected every aspect of it. Pretty good idea, this spiritual justification for selectivity and license to condemn.

"'These Christians easily followed the soldiers up to Golgotha. They were renouncing their Jewish heritage and the transfer was symbolic. It was their show now. What happened at Golgotha was all Jimmy and Tammy Faye Baker needed to justify weeping into the cameras and bilking millions from unsuspecting old ladies. Jesus saw it all coming. He kept talking about feeding the hungry, clothing the naked, comforting the afflicted, and they nodded approvingly, not understanding any of it. They were off thinking about capitalizing on this man's popularity and building a religion the size of which no one had to date ever even imagined. They saw it becoming so wealthy and powerful the weak and poor would have to ask permission to join. The churches would be sumptuous temples, adorned with art work and controlled by rich and influential old men. They would employ 'principles' to decide who could enter the churches and who would be forever damned.

"'These good Christians waited at the base of the cross. In just a while, it would all be theirs. They barely heard the last words; "My God, my God, why have you forsaken me by giving me these people more interested in money, principles and domination than they are in feeding my sheep?" Having received no answer to his lament, Jesus died. (All kneel) Then sky went dark, as if to remind the poor, defenseless Friends Of Jesus the party was over. Old white men were now in charge and the rest of you could all just go suck. Four. I find it interesting when I reflect on the fact that the resurrected Jesus purportedly showed himself first to a prostitute. Perhaps to underscore his message that you have one chance to live a passionate existence. I find it more interesting that the followers, who later were called disciples, who were then later called the apostles, who became the de facto first cardinals, or the highest and loftiest members of this new world religion, saw this resurrected Jesus just after this prostitute.

""I guess we know what Jesus really thought of pompous old men and powerful organizations. This is how I feel about the powerful old men and the monstrous organization that led me, and me alone, to plan and incite the murder of Archbishop Riley. With funds stolen from the AIDS assistance office, I retained the services of one Greg Lucas to plan and organize this murder. Others may be involved, but I am not aware of the names. I give these names here and now because I was wrong and should have let him live. I only intended to satisfy my own need for immediate retribution. I wholly regret what I have done.'""

Father Carol removed the last page. He folded it neatly in his coat pocket and left the house. He walked back to his car, drove to a nearby grocery store plaza, where he anonymously telephoned the police reporting the potential death of Bishop Harry Boyle.

The suicide note was entered as evidence. It was carefully noted the pages were numbered and the text ended abruptly on page two. One or more pages were missing and an separate investigation was launched to determine who had tampered with the evidence. The death was quickly ruled a suicide, and the suicide note was given to the task force in the Seattle Police Department investigating the murder of Archbishop Riley. Captain Terrance Cooke took possession of the evidence and, after logging it correctly, locked it in his filing cabinet. Requests to release the suicide note to the press were met with his usual silent stare.

Chapter 20

"Lucas here."

"Mr. Lucas, this is Harold Brown. You spoke with a gentleman who works with me, Grady."

"Yes. I've started working on the Internet message and I have some interesting results."

"Good, good. The reason I am calling, however, is there has been a rather terrible accident. Well, not quite an accident. It appears to have been quite intentional. The gentleman who contacted you, Grady, originally regarding the investigation into the death of the Archbishop of Seattle, has been severely hurt. All of this we think is related to another investigation he was engaged in that was not related to Archbishop Riley."

"Is he going to be okay?"

"We're not sure. His memory is, well, he has none right now."

Greg Lucas smiled. He anticipated more to come out of Harold Brown's mouth. He waited.

"As you can well imagine, we are very sorry this happened to him. We are also committed to getting on with the investigation. You have begun working for us already—"

"Yes. As I said I've made some interesting progress."

"Yes. You said that. Are you available to meet me in Seattle? I want to talk with you about leading my private investigation. You need to be here tomorrow evening to meet with me and Cardinal Day."

"Okay—"

"I assumed you would consent and you will receive a ticket today by express delivery. There are instructions about where you will meet with us. A driver will pick you up at the airport. I look forward to meeting you."

❧❧❧

The limousine dropped Greg at the front door of the Olympic Four Seasons. He was waved away and assured his baggage would be taken care of. He had been thoughtful enough to stuff several five dollar bills into his pocket. Harold was paying the way, but wasn't there to tip.

Harold greeted him in the lobby. Greg remembered a story Harry Boyle had told about being greeted in the lobby of a Hilton Hotel by John Riley and escorted to see Cardinal Day. He guessed the French Cardinal Richelieu would have approved.

Cardinal Day appeared just as Greg had remembered. He was taller than Greg, white-haired, and quiet. His piercing blue eyes flashed from Harold to Greg, not necessarily following the conversation. Greg recognized the same charismatic quality in this Church leader that he had seen in the generals he had known. Whether it was a natural characteristic or something acquired through training, he appeared to be above the fray, ready to stop the conversation or direct it in any way he wanted at will.

Greg held out his hand and gripped the cardinal's firmly. "We've met."

"Yes, I remember something about an incident at

Mateo Ricci high school." Cardinal Day nodded and sat down, looking away from Greg.

Harold took over. "Are you certain the Internet message came from Father Jurevic's computer?"

Greg nodded his head slightly. He had always been a convincing liar. "He may not have written the message. I cannot tell you that. But I traced the message twice, and it definitely came from that computer."

Harold nodded, scowling slightly. "It might make sense that he did not write the message. He lives with two other priests. One of them is Father Joe Carol. Are you aware of what happened here in Seattle when Archbishop Riley was installed?" Greg shook his head. Harold glanced at the cardinal, who nodded slightly, and Harold looked back at Greg. "I did not tell Grady this, and perhaps I should have."

Greg enjoyed conspiracy theories. He watched television programs about the paranormal and read well written espionage novels.

But, none of this, not even his career in the special forces, had prepared him for Harold Brown.

What intrigued him most was the theory regarding a group of homosexuals. It confirmed what Genelle had told him, but Harold's take on it was mildly entertaining if not also grossly incorrect. "The electronic message you are examining we believe comes from a group of disgruntled radical homosexuals who have clearly stated their intent to wreck violence on the revered leaders of the Roman Catholic Church."

Greg corrected him in his mind on the topic of certain revered leaders.

Harold spoke with an unusually clear and angry vice. "This latest message is an indication that not only are the violent and corrupt elements of the homosexual community involved in this, but, and God help them, former priests as well. This Jurevics character is not alone, I am certain."

And it wasn't just the gays, Greg reflected to himself. It was every free thinking Catholic in Seattle.

Harold emphasized this last point by thrusting his right index finger into the air and speaking more loudly. He slowly placed his hand back on to his lap. His eyes were wide and angry.

Cardinal Day breathed deeply and glanced at Greg. "We intend to expose this and to show the world who these people really are."

Harold nodded slowly. "Let me ask you something, Mr. Lucas. I want you to be straightforward with me. Are you a homosexual?"

Greg laughed but realized Harold was serious. "No. I've never married, but I definitely like women. Why do you ask."

"Are you promiscuous?"

"This is going beyond a normal job interview."

"We need to know these things."

"No, I am usually not very lucky."

Harold proceeded to ask a few more intensely personal questions and then explained why. To fight the most corrupt elements of society, it was necessary to begin with incorruptible people. Harold pulled a three page report Grady had written on Greg Lucas. Everything Greg would allow to be known about himself was there.

"The extreme measures you took on that boy, well, that is regrettable. But your courage to act for what is right, now that we admire greatly. You are well known for your strong beliefs. My dear friend Grady is a very good investigator, but I have often wondered about his motivations. What has happened to him is terrible, but Divine Providence often works in ways we do not understand. I think it is evident we need someone of your timber involved more directly in this, and we should act on this providential opportunity."

Greg said nothing. He looked at the cardinal, then back at Harold. These men were serious. He smiled internally. If they were convinced radical homosexuals killed Archbishop Riley and were threatening the life of the pope, then he would help them prove this. Greg decided then that life was very good, indeed.

"I am certain of the involvement of a radical element of the homosexual community, and I am also aware that this must be proven beyond a reasonable doubt to the court of public opinion. We will find what we suspect is happening." Harold hesitated and glanced at both men.

Cardinal Day raised his eyebrows. "Do you understand, Mr. Lucas, how seriously we consider this matter? What would you do if you begin to discover these homosexuals aren't really involved and this…uhm…proof Mr. Brown is talking about, is debunked? What happens then?"

"First I would wonder if they are good at covering and evading."

The cardinal squinted. "They are. I am certain, Mr. Lucas, you will find that theory to be consistent with the truth. Your efforts will begin to reverse the world-wide trend of sympathizing with the homosexual agenda."

After a long silence, the cardinal stood and gazed out the window at the Seattle skyline. He crossed his arms and breathed deeply for a few moments. "I cannot sanction anything. You are acting independent of the Roman Catholic Church. Any claim otherwise will be swiftly and absolutely denied. Is that clear?"

"As I expected, Eminence. It is not our intent to receive publicity. In fact, we will wish to remain totally anonymous, and this will be a condition of our agreement with Mr. Lucas," Harold said smoothly.

"What you men do with your time and money is out of my control. Is that clear?"

"Yes, Eminence."

"This is a job that should have been done years ago. I'd really like to **see** the cards turned on these guys, especially here in Seattle." Cardinal Day sat back in his chair. "Thank you, Mr. Brown." He held out his hand.

Harold rose quickly and shook his hand. "No, thank you Eminence." He bowed slightly and turned to leave.

"I would like to speak with Mr. Lucas, alone, if I may. Just for a few minutes."

Harold nodded with some hesitation, but silently left the room.

The cardinal sat back down in his chair with authority and grace. "Where are you originally from, Mr. Lucas?"

"California. San Louis Obispo." No reason to lie right now.

"Do you know why Harold Brown is such an ardent supporter of the Church? He's strong on that, more than I have ever seen. Harold Brown has been a member of Opus Dei for many, many years. What you saw here has been a lifelong crusade. He has given hundreds of thousands of dollars to the Church in its efforts to promulgate the need for strong families. He's the real McCoy. My contacts in the Knights of Malta and Rome confirm that he's got connections, everywhere." The cardinal hesitated. "Officially, I don't know anything about him or you, and it's going to remain that way. I know what he's proposing, and I don't want to be associated with it. I think I will like the outcome, but I will deny knowing anything about him or the works of Opus Dei."

Once outside the cardinal's office, Greg noticed Harold appeared noticeably distressed.

"Some interesting news." Harold whispered. "It seems a man living here in Seattle, used to be a bishop in Newark, Harry Boyle. He killed himself and left a suicide note that may have information about the murder of Archbishop Riley. My source tells me the note is incomplete, though. A page, maybe two pages are missing. There is some reference to the murder, suggesting those involved will be implicated."

Greg showed no reaction, but internally he smiled. *Good thing Harry paid in advance. Imagine collecting hit money from a dead man's estate.*

"I am told the suicide note is very long. I would like to get that to see if it supports my theories."

Greg squinted. "Are they suppressing the note."

"Well, they're not releasing it. Do you know who this man is?"

Greg shook his head convincingly.

"He was a bishop in New Jersey who was removed from his office and came here to Seattle ostensibly to care for his aging mother," Harold continued. "But under the liberal leadership of Archbishop Schwartz, he was allowed to work among the priests as sort of spiritual instigator. He even started the program that gave assistance to homosexuals with AIDS." Harold paused and then acted as if he needed to spit. "And he advocated for women priests and even married priests. Imagine."

Greg saw Harold's face contort the more he spoke. "Grady told me the Mexican police had a piece of evidence," Grady said. "Something they were not talking about, very conclusive stuff. Did he ever share that with you?"

"No. Why?" Harold motioned for Greg to follow as other visitors came to see the cardinal.

"We need to see the note, and we need something to trade for it."

Harold was quiet all the way to the parking garage. He leaned against his Mercedes and looked at the cement floor. Greg could see the worry lines on Harold's forehead deepen.

"Mr. Lucas, you go to Puerto Vallarta and see if you can't make this trade. I'll contact friends close to the Seattle Chief of Police and let him know what we are doing. I am certain they do not want publicity, and a silent broker would be beneficial to both sides." Harold slid quietly into the car and started the engine. He rolled the window down. "Mr. Lucas, it seems you have a problem with your creditors and this concerns some people. You can't hurt me, so I suggest if you have any ideas of obtaining money from me through anything but legitimate for hire work, you think otherwise. I don't know if you realize how well connected I am, and I doubt, even with your past military skills, you would want to find out. Don't embarrass me. Am I clear?"

"Very."

Greg watched Harold drive slowly and cautiously out of the garage. He did not like the idea of a suicide note. This could easily spiral out of control, especially if Boyle was stupid enough to mention anything significant about the operation. It was time for Greg to set up diversions, point away from the note. Discredit Boyle as a man pushed over the *edge*. Then blame the homosexuals. Make the connection. Doug?

☙❧

Entering the hospital in Puerto Vallarta, Greg passed through a wall dating back to the Roman Empire, through a variety of architectures. He always admired the way Mexicans could blend so nicely the various stages of their art and design. A tall, attractive woman in a police uniform met him outside the room where Grady lay unconscious.

Two armed police observed him dispassionately. Inspector Juarez was inside the room.

"Greg Lucas. Your captain sent me here."

"Inspector Juarez. Captain Moro told me you would be coming." He looked at Greg. "You sure you want to get in the middle of this?

"Would you like to get something to eat while we talk?"

Juarez hesitated. "Yes, I haven't eaten for a while."

"Is there a nice restaurant—"

"I like the cafeteria."

"Hospital food?"

The food was good and very cheap. The sauces were stove cooked, not from a can. The mole was fresh. The tortillas as good as any restaurant would serve. And the small bottles of the local beer capped off Greg's first meal in Mexico.

"You heal faster if you eat well. Something your American hospitals should learn."

"You know I have been retained to replace Grady for Mr. Harold Brown."

Juarez sipped his beer slowly. "And how does that affect us?"

Greg stared blankly. Juarez looked at him squarely, without expression. "I would hope to be able to work closely with you, perhaps exchange information that would be useful to your investigation."

"Do you have anything?"

"At the moment, no. I need to pick up where Grady left off, perhaps you can help."

"We'll complete this conversation in Captain Moro's presence."

Captain Moro did not stand as Greg followed Inspector Juarez into her office.

"I am sorry we did not have a chance to talk when you

first arrived, Mr. Lucas. I have a few very pressing investigations on going."

Greg offered his hand and Moro instead picked up a brown file.

"Special forces. Honorable discharge. Some trouble in a high school in Los Angeles. Unusual level of violence inflicted on a teenage boy as discipline."

"He was a risk to himself and others."

Moro looked at him then back to the file. "Special commendations from the Jackson Hole Police Department. You caught a few Internet crooks." Moro paused. "One of my investigations is into the murder of my fourteen-year-old son. Another investigation is into the murder of a sixteen-year-old boy and the physical harm that was inflicted on his fifteen-year-old brother. Excuse me if I do not applaud your record of disciplining teenage boys with bodily harm, Mr. Lucas." Moro stood and walked behind Greg's chair. "What can you do for us."

"I'll be honest. A man in Seattle, a former bishop, committed suicide. He left a note connecting himself to the murder. Mr. Brown and I would like to see the note. Grady told me that you have a piece of evidence that might be of interest to the American police agencies involved. I want to make a trade. You get the suicide note, they get what you have."

"Did Grady tell you what our evidence is?"

"No."

Moro considered this answer. "Maybe you see some value in the suicide note. I am not sure what it can do for us. I doubt this bishop…who?"

"Boyle, Harry Boyle."

"Yes. Boyle. You see, I know several bishops and none of them are capable of building, placing, and detonating a bomb. I will look for the person who did this on Mexican soil and abroad if I need to. If I learn this Boyle was in Puerto Vallarta at the time, I might then have more interest in his suicide. Until you can do that for me, Mr. Lucas, I am not sure what I can do to help you." Moro walked behind her desk, sat, and leaned back in the chair. She stared at Greg. "Your friend Grady has helped us, me, in many ways. He is not dead and will recover. Before I spread this investigation out too thin with too many players, I want to wait a bit and see when he can return. You understand, don't you?"

"Yes. I had presumed your close relationship with Mr. Brown and Opus Dei would have…well, motivated you to be more willing to assist Mr. Brown."

Moro smiled. "Sometimes I think Mr. Brown is a bit extreme."

"You know him?"

Captain Moro smiled and did not respond.

Greg guessed this was his cue to leave.

He nodded politely, thanking the captain and Inspector Juarez. He asked directions to his hotel and Juarez gave them as they walked out of the office. Greg thanked him again and walked out of the station. He flagged down a taxi and gave the driver the address of the hotel. The ride was fast and the city unfamiliar. Greg was lost in the thought of what would be necessary to move the evidence in the direction he wanted. Maybe someone else had to die, and the evidence would be so similar, they would have no choice but to work with him. The taxi dropped him off across the street from the entrance to his hotel. He walked in, bought a calling card from a kiosk, and entered a room with several public phones. He dialed an access number for the phone card, then Doug Dorn's number.

Chapter 21

Olivia liked a show of force, even though she quietly admitted the subtle approach was often more effective. Fighting the cartels required negotiations, undercover investigations, and silent arrests. The repercussions, however severe, had not until now resulted in a manageable, respectful co-existence. They were a different customer from earlier gangs. In appearances, the leaders were like any international business person. Kind, professional, generous, and polite. Their methods of persuasion, however, were blunt and crude. There was no negotiating with them. Moro's treatment of them brought disapproving comments from her superiors and local politicians. She always responded with a greater force, equally blunt and crude. Her objective was to find them and shut them down.

The last time she was involved in an investigation of the cartel's organized crime syndicate in Puerto Vallarta, it cost her one very good man, shot in cold blood from behind in a ruthless ambush. When Roberto, the shooter, surrendered with a wide smirk on his face, Moro did not arrest him.

She simply pulled her revolver out and held it on the man's head between his eyes. He wet himself and she laughed. She holstered the gun and told him it was lucky that other police officers were present. She knew they would retaliate.

She expected to lose another officer, a judge, or maybe a local politician. Killing her son raised the stakes to an all-time high.

Moro was not in on the arrest, but she would watch the interrogations. She would not be allowed to get near the five men. She would watch as the best interrogator cajoled, convinced, threatened, slapped, trapped, beat, and otherwise got the necessary information.

An officer knocked lightly at her door and entered. Inspector Adolfo Hernandez. Six-foot-seven, barrel chested, smoking. He apologized and looked for an ashtray. Moro waved off concern for the cigarette.

Moro held up the golden crucifix. "You've come for this."

"Yes, captain." His voice was kind and soft, unlike his role during interrogations. "Do we have photographs of Hektor wearing this?"

Moro slowly handed the crucifix to Hernandez. "Novarres has the file."

It was unspoken that the crucifix belonged to Moro and was on loan only for the interrogations and never as evidence.

"Captain, they did this and we know it. Today, one of them will whisper to me, a confession, a tearful plea for mercy. We will solve this today and they will pay. Your son's honor is my foremost thought today, Captain."

Moro nodded and started to dial her telephone, waving Inspector Hernandez out of her office. She talked to her boyfriend at length, not about the interrogations, but about their plans for the weekend if she could get time away from the case.

Inspector Juarez reminded Moro the interrogations

were about to begin in five separate rooms. Moro nodded, waving him away, pretending to work. Captain Novarres walked into her office, motioning at his watch, shrugging. Moro smiled and pointed at the open files on her desk. Novarres left, and Moro leaned back in the privacy of her office. She waited for another fifteen minutes then walked slowly, purposefully, into the first room and watched from behind the one way glass.

Inspector Hernandez carried on in a loud drone, repeating questions and shaking his head at the expected answers. Moro would rather have been at home cooking than watching these interrogations.

"The gold crucifix. Don't tell me you didn't know. Hektor owned this, a gift from his mother. His own mother and he died wearing it didn't he? It was always around the neck of a fourteen-year-old boy you killed in retaliation. Now we find it buried in the floor of your church school."

"I have never seen this crucifix. It is very nice. You tell your captain to wear it in good health. I am sure her son treasured it very much, and it must be a very sentimental reminder of her beloved son."

Moro smiled. Novarres shook his head and went into the interrogation room, whispered something into Hernandez's ear, and disappeared.

"Here. Here is Hektor wearing this. See? The same crucifix. You took the crucifix off him, along with his clothes, and buried them. His beautiful shoes he loved so much."

"Please tell your captain she has a good eye for jewelry—"

"Captain Moro is watching behind that glass. Remember what she did to your predecessor? I am getting tired of this, and I need to go home to my family. We would like to take our vacation, and you are getting in my way. I think I would like to let Captain Moro talk with you. Would you like that?"

Roberto did not smile, but rather wagged his head, saying nothing.

"You enjoy your time with Captain Moro." Inspector Hernandez opened the door and started out.

"Wait. Let me see your pictures again." Hernandez hesitated. "Maybe I can remember something," Roberto pleaded.

"I've shown you the pictures five times. What can you remember now?"

"I don't know, maybe something small, unimportant."

Inspector Hernandez grabbed Roberto by the short collars, ripping the shirt, and standing the obese man on his feet. His right hand cocked back and slammed hard against the whimpering face, sending him sprawling across the room. Hernandez grabbed him again and slapped him down hard on the floor.

"Now you remember, you pig. You killed a mother's son. You tortured him. Did you screw him, too?"

"You stop that. I am not like that. You insult my family—"

Hernandez grabbed him again, slapped him hard, sending the man against the opposite wall. Blood dripped down his face onto his torn white shirt.

"You screwed him, didn't you, you slimy pig?" Hernandez grabbed him again and slammed him against the wall, thumping his head hard.

Captain Novarres abruptly entered the room again, placing a gentle hand on Hernandez's shoulder. "Inspector Hernandez, what is this? You may step outside and allow Inspector Juarez to take over from here. We do not interview suspects in this manner."

A bespeckled Juarez sat calmly at the interrogation table and smiled.

"But, Captain, we are so close. He has almost admitted more than just murder—"

Novarres scowled. "Inspector Hernandez, now."

Hernandez bowed slightly and obediently left the room. He winked at Moro as he proceeded to the next interrogation room.

Captain Novarres held the gold medallion and looked at Roberto. "Some officers become so emotional. When a captain's son is murdered, obviously out of revenge—" He set the medallion on the table in front of him. "You understand, no?"

Roberto sat expressionless.

Captain Novarres set a Rolex watch on the table. "Speaking of fine jewelry. We know about your associate Colonel Dmitriov. He was wearing this the day Captain Moro shot him. You were with Dmitriov that day, am I correct?"

Roberto smiled, saying nothing. He leaned forward on the table and smiled at Novarres. Moro walked out of the viewing booth and down to the next interrogation room. The second suspect was sprawled on the floor, holding his face.

"Filthy pigs. You are a disgrace to your people. You shame your heritage, you beast," Inspector Hernandez yelled, grabbing him by the shirt collars, picking him up off the floor, and slamming him back on the table. "I'll make you swallow my fist unless you tell me who ordered the hit."

The man clutched his chest and rolled off the table. Hernandez eyed him carefully for a moment and, seeing he was in no real danger, grabbed him again. "You have a weak heart? How about your stomach. Maybe you should not be in this business. Maybe you should be a street vendor. Did you see what they did to the boy?"

The man was white faced. He sat at the table, holding

his head in his hands, weeping. "I will die if I say any-thing."

"You will die if they convict you, I'll make certain of that. You cooperate or you get convicted."

"I saw only a little bit."

Hernandez grabbed him again. "You lying sack of—"

"No, please. I have seen everything. I will tell you. Just don't hit me anymore."

Moro watched dispassionately. She would have just shot this man dead. Captain Novarres allowed them to live, to suffer the consequences of telling, knowing they would eventually die at the hands of their own. He would stop when the first man cracked, get a statement, implicate the others, then bring the statement to them. The case would be solved and the one who told would die. Hernandez made sure of this. Moro approved of this definitive and decisive application of justice almost as much as her own.

Captain Moro was about to join Hernandez in the room as the broken cartel mobster was about to retell the story from his extremely subjective point of view when Inspector Juarez approached her.

"They have struck again. Cathédral Metropolitana de la Asunción de Maria. The cardinal is hurt, not seriously, but he is in hospital undergoing examinations. This was received only moments before the explosion, not allowing most people time to evacuate."

He handed Captain Moro a copy of an email. She turned on the television in her office.

They cycled through the limited footage they had of ambulances screaming away from the cathedral square, city and federal police out in force, surrounding the cathedral.

༄༅༄

The report said a bomb threat was received. The cardinal insisted on making sure all other people were out, and he followed the last of them slowly. The explosion was small, the plastique located in the arch behind and above the main altar. The shock waves pushed the cardinal face down on the altar, pieces of stone hitting him on the back of the head. He had remained conscious throughout, but stumbled to the floor because of shock and old age. His attendants, bleeding and dirty, rushed to his side. They calmed him and waited for the desperate moments as the police cleared the cathedral and escorted the medics to the cardinal.

The email message Captain Moro was holding called it a warning shot. She nodded silently and found Captain Novarres. "There was an explosion in the cathedral in Mexico City. The cardinal is hurt, but probably will survive. I am certain these are not related. However, Mexico City might be related to money laundering. We found some things on the archbishop's computer and turned them over to the federales. Vatican Bank, money from Mexican banks deposited in the name of the archbishop and a charity he ran. The cardinal went on record last month opposing the cartels and that made him a target. I doubt he had anything to do with the laundering, and that's why they picked Archbishop Riley. I now know he had a history in Central America, made connections with nefarious types, just got promoted."

Captain Novarres nodded. "You want to know what they can tell us about the laundering. We're about to crack your son's murder, and you want us to pressure them for this?"

"I know who killed my son. Now we need to give the federales something more on the laundering."

"Okay, I can do that. But how are you so certain these two acts of terrorism are not related?"

"The archbishop was doing the laundering, the cardinal expressed public opposition. The archbishop has other skeletons, and if we are distracted by the money laundering, we will never find the truth. If the federales take on the laundering leads, they will leave us alone."

"I see. Good thinking. I will let you know if we find anything. You don't mind if I promise some forgiveness on your son's murder."

"Not at all. The prosecutor will never agree to your promise, and they will all receive the punishment they deserve."

Hernandez approached carefully from behind and motioned to Olivia. She stepped away from the conversation about the new explosion and gave Hernandez her full attention. "We know where his body is. I will go there now and direct the excavation. You are most certainly welcome—"

"Where?"

"In a shallow grave, not far from your husband's, in the cemetery."

"You are certain?"

"Two of them said this. We are taking the older one with us."

She stood silent. Everyone in the room knew instinctively what she had just been told. They looked away out of respect, most of them about to burst into tears. Strong men capable of beating ruthless crooks senseless crying over the death of a fourteen-year-old boy.

Olivia breathed in deeply, shook her head, and sighed. "Please keep me informed."

Chapter 22

You are brought on to the case to help a private citizen discover who was really sending Internet electronic messages and now we have another incident." Captain Moro would not sit at her desk. She stood, facing Greg Lucas.

"No matter who you bring in to look at these, Captain, they will see what I see," he said. "The messages originated from the same computer as the first threat. And whoever has access to that computer sent this message. I need to trade information with the Seattle Police and determine how much this fellow Boyle was involved and now, obviously, who else was involved." Greg leaned back and savored the silent moments that followed.

"I'm not computer literate, Mr. Lucas. But let me ask you this. Isn't there a way to use someone else's email address? Hasn't this been done for some time?"

"Oh, yes. I am familiar with this technology. There are identifiable marks left on this list of servers the email passes through that would red flag that this did not come from what is seen here as the source. If you don't know what those marks are, let me assure you I can do this and show you the difference between this email and one that is using an emulation software to hide behind another user." Greg tracked both what he was revealing about himself and how he was pushing the evidence in the right direction. He caught Moro staring at him.

Captain Moro always and immediately thought the worst when she felt her hands were being forced. She looked from Greg to the ceiling, determined to ask someone else about this. "We will get back to you, Mr. Lucas." She walked out of her office and waited in the hallway for Greg to follow.

Greg politely shook the captain's hand. He visualized killing her.

Moro watched him walk away and out of the station. She had no hard evidence to suspect Greg Lucas. She just did. She had lived too long in a world where best friends would watch your family have their throats slit for a million pesos. She also had no reason to immediately trust Grady, but she did. Instinct?

She walked silently through the hospital hallway leading to Grady's room, Inspector Juarez at her side. She had said nothing to him other than indicating she needed to talk to Grady. They stood by the bed, Grady still not conscious from his last operation. He would be fine, the doctor assured them, in a few weeks.

Moro did not have a few weeks. "When he is conscious, call me immediately. It is extremely important that he calls me." She turned to leave and spoke to Juarez over his shoulder. "Call Harold Brown. I want to see him here in Mexico City tomorrow, day after at the latest. Get a helicopter lined up for me." Moro walked alone away from the hospital, a habit when she needed space for thinking.

She knew two officers were assigned to follow, and they did so without interrupting her.

Captain Moro first met Harold Brown as a college student doing poorly in her studies. Harold was a guest lecturer in Economics. The young Olivia Moro approached him to ask a few questions about the American economy and how it was being affected by their participation in the Vietnam War. Harold noticed the crucifix hanging around Olivia Moro's neck and inquired about her religion.

Their many subsequent conversations convinced Olivia to accept Harold's offer to move to the United States and study Economics. She would work for Harold in Opus Dei. At first, Moro was the most dedicated young member, attending mass every day and living by the very strict moral code that forbade drinking, sex outside of marriage, and anything else a young woman might find entertaining on Saturday night. Her work for Opus Dei was focused on providing information about the Catholic Church to other young people and operating a poorly attended Catholic social club in New York.

When her studies were finished, she prepared to move back to Mexico. Harold convinced her to plan on joining the chapter in her home city of Guadalajara, and she agreed but never followed through. She accepted an offer to apply to the academy and was enrolled. She finished near the top of her cadet class and was immediately assigned to financial fraud upon graduation. It was here she made friends in the federal police force, and it was then Harold stopped trying to convince her to stay on in Opus Dei.

As she rose in ranks of the police, Harold Brown contacted her more and more. At first, he occasionally inquired about a certain case. Out of a sense of loyalty, Moro would give him more than she would ordinarily give anyone else. When she moved out of fraud and into vice and then murder, Harold stopped calling her. When she was elevated to rank of captain, Harold asked her pointedly to investigate a Greek banker living in Mexico City.

When Moro asked what he was looking for, Harold sneered and said the man was given to having sex with young men. Moro asked if they were too young, perhaps this man was engaging in illegal activity. No, Harold was certain they were not that young, and probably of adult age.

Captain Moro politely told Harold Brown she would not investigate. Harold openly asked Captain Olivia Moro if she was still faithful to the Church or had her success in life corrupted her.

Moro did not speak to Harold for three years. She grudgingly accepted a telephone call when Harold was visiting Puerto Vallarta with his wife and daughter. They ate together and Harold was careful not to mention their last conversation. Since that visit, they had spoken on three occasions, each time Harold asking for direct assistance in some of his Opus Dei work and each time Moro politely refusing.

She compromised by allowing Harold's private investigators access to her office and some case files. She found herself freely extending this to Grady, but was reluctant now to work that way with Greg Lucas.

"What are you looking for, Harold? Why are you so anxious to have this man Lucas involved?"

Harold usually enjoyed controlling every conversation. This was not possible with Captain Moro. "Olivia, I do the work of God while you do the work of the State."

Moro rolled her eyes. "Doesn't your constitution separate those? Perhaps you should, too."

"The work of God does not recognize boundaries."

"I am being respectful, Harold. You were a good friend to me many years ago, and so I treat you with respect. I have allowed you great latitude over the years. You have used my office, my rank, to carry out your work, and I have not objected. I do not do your work for you, but I have accepted and assisted the people you have hired to work for you. You know this. But I do not trust your man Lucas. I need to draw the line."

Harold set his coffee cup down hard. Moro noticed how he had aged since he last saw him.

"Olivia, this is important. This is not an investigation into the sleazy depraved lifestyle of a wealthy banker. A bishop has been murdered—"

"And we are conducting a thorough investigation."

"You are being stifled in this effort because your government and my government are not co-operating. There is the suicide note—"

"Harold, I know how to conduct an investigation where there is little or no co-operation. I have worked with your government before, and I have my contacts. When I need the information, I will get it without your private investigators."

The two sat silent for several minutes. Harold offered to pay for the lunch, but the waiter refused. Moro smiled at him. "I know the owner, Harold. I told them in advance to hold the check and I will pay it later." She stood.

Harold rose slowly and stiffly. "It's unusually hot here hot here for this time of year."

"Yes, I would prefer to be at the beach myself, but here I am investigating terrorism in Mexico City." For Harold's benefit, they walked in the shade to the office provided for Moro to use while she was in the city.

"Olivia, what can I do to convince you to use the professional services Mr. Lucas can provide."

"Harold, I don't know if he can do anything."

"If he brought you the suicide note from Seattle, implicating Bishop Boyle, would you allow him to have access to your investigation?"

"Tell him to bring the note and then I will talk with him. I will not promise anything more than that." Moro sat hard in her chair. "What are you digging for here, Harold?"

"I will bring you the suicide note and other evidence that will convince you my efforts are legitimate and necessary for the safety of the Mother Church." Harold jabbed his index finger into the air.

Moro smiled.

Harold called Greg early in the morning and asked him to meet the next day in Puerto Vallarta. Greg spent some time walking around, peeking in the windows of the small tourist shops. They weren't offering anything on sale. He stepped into a shop offering expensive leathers, marveling at the atmosphere—loud conversation and bone-thin women flitting in and out of fitting rooms. A fashionably clad young man motioned him into the elevator and served as his personal escort through the men's section. Greg gasped when the man converted the pesos in his head for a sweater Greg liked. He smiled and motioned he wanted to leave.

"Si, si," the young man said kindly as Greg walked away and two middle aged men entered the elevator.

Greg decided a little cycling would help pass the time. The address of a bicycle shop was written in the back of his passport. He thought it would stick out more, be more noticeable. It was tucked between two other businesses, the exterior old and gritty, the interior a testament to a lack of architectural design. He didn't know which was more fun to look at—the gleaming new bicycles or the interior of the store.

"Americano? You want a bike to buy?"

Greg nodded and ran his fingers lightly over the frame of the first bike he approached.

"You like?"

"You knew I was an American."

"You face…uhm…and you hat. Ad Bulls."

"Oh, yeah. Can I buy this here, ride it while I am in Puerto Vallarta, and then have you ship it to my home?"

The slender young man waved his hand and laughed. "Not good English. Moment." He reappeared with an older man, in his fifties, wiping grease from his fingers. "You want to ride the bicycle here and then have us ship it?"

"Yes, if that's possible."

"Possible, but very expensive. You call this man, and he will ship it for your cheap. He sends many things to the United States."

Greg was determined to buy one, and the older man knew it. He spoke in rapid Spanish to the younger man and disappeared into the shop.

"I want to ride."

"Not this one. This one here. Same. But it for people to ride here."

Greg remembered five minutes into his test ride what joy was. The deep satisfaction that came with the really valuable things in life. Some people got this feeling when they were with their children, others when they drew. Pure simple pleasures. So many people clouded their lives with greed and violence and never felt this. He wheeled the bike into the shop and nodded at the young man.

"Where you ride tomorrow?"

"Around."

The young man shook his head and laughed. "You want?"

Greg nodded and, after a few quick measurements of his legs and torso, the young man pointed at a frame hanging from the ceiling.

"But I wanted it today," Greg protested.

"Yeah, sure, in one hour it look like this one."

Greg smiled and nodded.

He bought a new set of cycling clothes right down to the short socks and yellow shoes.

The young man wagged an index finger in his face as he left. "No *cyclo* the coast. Other way, *el norte, bueno.*"

He pointed to a map indicating a well-marked bicycle trail loping along the highway. Greg calculated the ride to be thirty miles or so. He nodded his thanks.

He returned to the hotel where Harold had put him up and flipped through his telephone book. He dialed the number of Major Jeff Patton in San Diego.

"Jeff, you're in. Lucas here."

"Lucas, you sad sack of pig crap, how the hell are you?"

"Fine, fine. I'm in Puerto Vallarta…uh…some private investigative work. I'm going to bicycle around a bit while I am here tomorrow—"

"No, you idiot. Not here. No one bicycles around here. You stay there. I've got some business I can take care of tomorrow down there. Where you staying?"

"The Hyatt."

"Noon."

Greg fingered through his wallet and found the number for the escort service in Puerto Vallarta given to him by Mike Gerard. He called from a payphone. The woman spoke excellent English and cheerfully told Greg his escort would meet him at his hotel in an hour. Greg made sure the woman understood he wanted more than the usual. Was his escort willing to enjoy some bondage? Of course. It would cost a bit more, but Angelica specialized in that. Greg walked back to the hotel to get ready.

At four, he walked to the bicycle shop and saw his bike standing next to a glass showcase. Two spandex clad cyclists admired it. They acknowledged him.

"*Militare?*"

"No." Greg was aware how passionately most Mexicans felt about the presence of an American air force member in their country, especially considering their recent behavior. Knowing he was an American tourist just visiting got a nod and a smile from them.

In the morning, he wheeled carefully through the city until he reached the canal and then enjoyed uninterrupted bliss as he worked his way over easy rolling hills into the Lombard country side, the humidity much less oppressive next to the water. The large eighteenth-century villas of the wealthy merchants who built Puerto Vallarta into the financial powerhouse of Jalisco invited him to stop and absorb. He stopped at a small taco shop and ordered the special. He gazed at the villas, thinking about his anger, his ever present companion. Wealth had passed him by. That made him angry. He really hated Doug Dorn. Doug made him angry. Why? *Admit it. You don't need a reason to hate. It's just always there, a permanent condition, right next to love.* He returned to the hotel in time to shower before Jeff Patton arrived. The telephone rang and Jeff Patton was waiting in the lobby.

"Greg Lucas, you look like a dying dog. Haven't seen you since you went candy ass on us after a little work in Guatemala. What's this business you're here on?"

"I'm involved in an investigation in Puerto Vallarta. Private. Wealthy former banker looking into the murder of Archbishop Riley."

"Yeah. Press down here didn't make much of it. More space on the dead altar boys. There was another guy in on that…uhm…former ranger."

"He checked me out so now I'm checking him out. You know anyone connected to that office here?"

"Maybe. We get briefings from them intelligence types all the time. There's a guy who's been here for years, I'm sure he knows your dude."

They ate quickly in the hotel restaurant and sat in

Greg's room, talking about their time in Central America. Jeff Patton was a born politician and was never bothered by what they were really doing there. Even if he did not have a direct stake in exchanging arms for hostages and selling drugs to finance that, he was along for the ride. He loved the game and made no secret of it. "Before I go, let me call this guy maybe you two can connect. He's not in Mexico, officially. He does a lot of military intelligence in flowered shirts. Fits in at all the tourist spots."

After talking briefly then waiting, Jeff Patton talked quickly and loudly, explaining what he wanted. He stopped and handed the phone to Greg.

"Captain Michael Healy. Can I help you?"

"Major Patton thought you might know someone I'm working with. Fella by the name of Grady. Doesn't use a last name."

"That's correct. I do know his last name, and I know him very well. Why am I helping you?"

"I have to work with him. He checked me out so now I'm returning the favor."

"Where are you?"

"Puerto Vallarta."

"I am in Guadalajara, and I will meet you there this evening at seven. I really want to talk with you" The words were quiet, measured, and cold.

Captain Healy hung up after saying them. Greg stared blankly.

ⓔⓢⓔⓢ

Captain Michael Healy looked like he had walked out of a recruiting poster. He was regulation to the length of his finger nails. He stood erect, hands held neatly behind his back. He could not hide this under the shorts and ugly beach shirts. He was an hour late.

"Captain Michael Healy. Army Intelligence. My apologies."

Greg offered to walk instead of going to his room. Captain Healy nodded efficiently. The evening was very warm, but still pleasant as people moved quickly, energetically home for supper. Greg sensed Healy was not given to humor so didn't try. He was also aware that there must have been a special reason for army intelligence to drive from five hours to Puerto Vallarta at the mention of Grady's name.

"You knew this guy, Grady?"

"That was my job. Yes, I knew him. Very well. His personal life became a concern to the force. He was dating a model, and she was pretty typical of that kind. Very beautiful but excessively thin, and for good reason. She used, shall we say, certain recreational drugs to make sure she stayed thin. It was my job to report this. He claimed he didn't know." Healy stopped talking and stood almost at attention. "You knew Doug Dorn." Healy wasn't smiling now.

"Yes. I saved his life in Guatemala.'

"Really? Quite a debt he owes you."

"Debt? I'm not sure what you mean."

"The ultimate price is death, right? What would we pay to fool old man death?"

What did Healy want from this? Where did Doug Dorn come from? Greg's mind raced quickly through the sequence of events. No paper trail, no credit card trail, Doug Dorn would not speak. He owed Greg and promised. He trafficked drugs. Caught red handed. Who would believe him? Doug knew all of this. And, of course, there were the photographs Doug took of the Chairman of the Foreign Relations Committee and the colonel at lunch with Estobar. The United States government, the United States Army, and the drug lord, smiling, casually planning a next move. Who would not kill to destroy that evidence?

"You knew Dorn well. Ever think he might be savvy to some really sensitive information. Something he may have seen in Central America?"

"I don't know what you are talking about." Greg smiled inside, comforted by Healy's obvious incompetence.

"Maybe in the heat of battle, when you were saving his life, he told you something, thinking he was going to die. A confession of sorts."

"Doug was an incorrigible brat the whole time. Kept whining about how much it hurt. Confession? Doug Dorn isn't sorry about anything."

"Yes, well. You wanted to know something about Grady. Ask him about Dennis Hofburg. An East German national."

"Good friends, bum pals, what?"

"We'd like to know where he is. Maybe Grady knows."

"Is there a clear connection?"

"He supplied drugs to Grady's girlfriend. He was also a fairly important link in our information chain regarding the Russian Mafia. When I discovered what may have been a breach of security, that is Grady's girlfriend receiving drugs from Mr. Hofburg, Grady resigned his commission. Very soon after Mr. Hofburg was not seen again. I've given you a lot of information, Mr. Lucas. I hope maybe you can convince Grady to tell us if he knows anything about Mr. Hofburg."

"Captain Healy, I appreciate your time. If I find anything out, I will let you know."

"If you see Doug Dorn, tell him to call me sometime. It might save his life."

"Yeah, sure. By the way, what is active army intelligence doing in Guadalajara?"

"Need to know." Healy smiled and walked away.

Chapter 23

Harold was tired from the sweltering heat. He dispensed with the suit coat and wore an open-collar, short-sleeve shirt. They sat in the coolness of the air-conditioned bar in the Grand Hotel.

"So, Captain Moro has been cooperative with you all these years because you paid her way through college, but now she has decided to cut you loose?"

"It's not that simple, Greg. Olivia has had some terrible experiences, and I think it has shaken her faith. I pray for her. But I think she is reluctant to think of her work with me as the work of God. I think she is losing contact with God."

Greg was well into his second scotch and soda. His own theories of God would send poor Harold into cardiac arrest. "How do we get the information we need from her?"

"You go back to Seattle. You talk to this man." Harold handed him a small card with a name and phone number neatly written on it. "He will help you convince the Seattle Police to make available the suicide note. Then you come back here when you get it, and you talk with Captain Moro."

"Just like that?" Greg laughed. "It appears your contacts are not as co-operative as I would like them to be."

"You need to make the best use of them and get the information we need."

Greg finished his scotch. "How is Grady holding up?"

"He has unfortunately slipped into a coma-like state. They're not sure what to make of it."

Greg nodded. "I sure wish he had told us what evidence these local guys have."

"He was about to tell me, but then he was hurt." Harold wiped his face with his left hand. "The ticket here, though, is the missing pages. Someone got to that suicide note, and we need to find them."

Greg could not agree more. Harold had a firm grip of the obvious. It was time to see if Genelle didn't know who had the pages.

Harold rose slowly. "I need to rest, then I need to fly to Rome. I am meeting with some cardinals interested in this investigation. You will be greeted at the airport in Seattle and will be given a cellular telephone. I will contact you on it and, that way, will be apprised of your progress. Good luck, Mr. Lucas."

Greg stumbled happily back to the hotel. He had decided the evidence Moro had was not substantial. She was either bluffing, or she had no idea what it was she had.

≈≈≈

Greg scrounged for the bottle he had hidden in his suitcase. Mid-range scotch, with a little water, not bad. Greg would bet his right pinky it was Doug's trigger, something new they had never seen before. Knowing this for certain would lift the pressure from Greg. He could pin it on Doug with that alone. Good to have insurance. He decided this game was a lot more fun than paying Riley back. Just getting control of it was the biggest thing. Once he had the evidence from Moro, who would need Grady? Terrible things could happen in hospitals. *What is the objective here? Revenge? No.* He had had that. *It's a game. Just a game. To win, someone else is fingered, convicted.* Winning was all now. Everything that could happen to a man had happened to Greg Lucas. What was left was winning. He had never really won before. He won and Riley lost. He didn't give a hoot about the files of AIDS patients. The nuns in Guatemala, that just set the bar a bit higher. He got Riley, period. Game set match. And now, for no particular reason other than it would be easy, he would watch the end of Doug Dorn and walk away from the Riley game a free man. Just like the old days.

Greg called and left instructions in a voice message to have Doug meet him in two days in Seattle at the W Hotel.

An hour later, Doug got home, listened to his voice messages, and swore softly. He got the first from Greg setting up the meeting at the W Hotel. It was the second message that stopped him cold. It was from Father Carol, claiming he had a page from the suicide note. He sat on the edge of the bed running his fingers through his hair. He called Father Carol's number and the priest answered.

"Where did this come from?" Doug asked.

"An angel."

"Who?"

"We have a mutual friend who indicated you would be interested in this." Father Carol coughed lightly. "I can't talk for long. Just tell me how you want to get the page."

"Don't be stupid. My life depends on this." Doug lay back on the bed. "Tell me."

Father Carol paused and then said lightly, "I had talked with Harry several times about taking dramatic action against the Church, pay-back for centuries of hypocrisy and persecution. Not just for gays, but for all repressed peoples. They were close enough that I had made some suggestions for action, but Boyle decided to act alone. If I had not been there the day after Boyle's suicide, who else might have found the note?"

Doug sighed and covered his face with his hands. "But I don't understand something. This guy Boyle, he was not the killing type."

"Did he tell you about Denise and Genelle?"

"Lucas told me something about some money for retirement."

"More than that. More like revenge money"

"You knew about this. What else is there?"

"I really can't say much. Do you want the page?"

"Why do I get the suicide note and how do I know there isn't a copy?"

"If you want the page please tell me how best to get it to you."

Doug grunted.

"I understand through our mutual friend that Boyle was introduced to Lucas because he had the kind of angry edge that would see this through," Father Carol continued.

"Did you know I was involved in that?"

"I was told that Lucas saved your life and could depend on you."

"For saving my life?" Doug snorted. "Not very likely. Lucas knows something that could cost me my life. I saw something in Guatemala, saw who did it, got the evidence hidden, and Lucas knew about it the whole time. If I tell what I know, it interrupts the flow of cocaine into the United States."

"This is all very interesting, but I need to go, and if you want this page—walk away from this."

"Can't. Either I play the card or it gets played on me, thanks to Lucas."

"Does it end if Lucas is dead?"

"I don't know."

"Well, like I say, I need to get going."

"Fine, scan it if you can and text it to me, to this number. I can get a print out if I need to."

Doug undressed and slid into bed. He had never really wanted to hurt anyone. He was trained not to think of his work in terms of harm. He followed orders, placing explosives when and where he was told. He did not read any of the damage reports. He knew he had succeeded. He simply went on to the next job.

Does one pay for taking so many lives? What could he possibly do to make recompense? All those women now widowed, all those children in the way at the wrong time. *What kind of monster blows up children?*

Doug had once advised a group engaged in religious terrorism on the finer points of triggering devices, ones that would be set off by sound, a certain high-pitched frequency usually heard only when children are playing. They used it to advance their religious agenda. He once received orders to take down a bridge at a specific time. He set the explosives and the timer and walked away, off to drink at a bar. He was in the middle of a long, boring story about his years as a high school quarterback when the first news of the explosion hit the village. Three children had been playing on the bridge, a search party was forming to find them in the ravine.

Even though he was trained not to think about it, he did. People thought about their actions and whether they received formal religious instruction or not, somehow they used whatever inherent sense of right and wrong they possessed, and they reflected on them. Some, like Doug, became obsessed with them.

He did not keep notebooks. Information such as wiring diagrams, chemical formulas, dates, times, locations, who was killed, and anything else related to his work was kept in his head. It might have been easier had he written it down. He could leave it in a locked drawer, maybe just symbolically walking away from it. But as it swam around in his head, this pool of information was ever present to him, ever available both for his work and to remind him.

Is anyone ever really forgiven their sins? Who forgives us? Who has the power to forgive? Who is in a place or position to presume this role? God? That might satisfy the faithful, but what about everyone else? Where does their forgiveness come from? From the person who loves me today? From love itself? Doug often wondered why he ever first committed an evil act. What was it about evil that drew him so, sucking him in with little concern for the consequences. He saw it in others and abhorred it, but ignored his own, like when he couldn't smell his own defecation. Atheists did not believe in the devil, the evil one. Doug did. To be evil was to have a relationship with him, to suck his saliva and taste the sweetness of evil. Evil was always more intoxicating than any liquor Doug ever tasted.

He decided he could not pay for the evil. He didn't have enough of anything that would equal in value what he had taken. He could only stop evil in himself. That would be enough. He would do it through love.

He poured a few ounces more. He long ago stopped eying what amount remained in the bottle. He just poured out small amounts and sipped until he slept. *When does it start to change? When does love start to do its job?*

The bottle dropped on to the hardwood floor. Ramone stirred and looked at him. "What happened?"

"I dropped the bottle. I didn't mean to wake you."

"That's okay. Always nice to see you."

"Drunk?"

"Do you really want to know? What are you drinking tonight?"

"Turpentine."

"No ice? Do you want some ice? I won't have to do much with your body until morning if I pack it full of ice tonight."

"No."

"Spill and you die. I just had the comforter cleaned."

Chapter 24

When accompanied by an official of the Institute for Works of Religion, a United States citizen did not require a passport to enter the Vatican City. In fact, no one needed a passport but the Swiss guards would make certain you did not wander where you were not allowed. How did one know where they were allowed? Take a walk down a hallway sometime and you would find out.

Harold Brown, while not employed in any manner in the Vatican, passed freely anywhere he wished. He smiled at one of the guards and walked through the hushed hallways, nodding at this cardinal and then that one. He slowly walked up a stair case and past the guarded hallway leading to the pope's private residence.

A long hallway with tall arched windows afforded him a view few other lay persons would ever see—the Pope's back yard where he took his daily walk. Harold stood at the door of George McGurdy's office, knocked lightly, then just opened the door.

"Harold, thanks for coming on such short notice. This stuff is really getting awful in Mexico. Any word on Riley, who really did this?"

"I'm getting close."

"I'm worried about any information Riley may have lying around. Laptops, cell phones, and those palm pilot things these days, you know how easy those are to crack."

"I have a good man working on all that," Harold lied. He had not, until this very instance, thought about any financial information Riley may have left and the implications it might have. "Is this what Mexico City is all about? By the way, how is the cardinal?"

"They say he will be fine. The Mexican nuncio is on his way here. I will be meeting with him and the holy father tomorrow on the future of our plans there. We groomed Riley and had him set up, and it was going to work fabulously and now all this." George sat back in his chair, picked up a cigar, lit it, and savored the flavor. "Do you know how long we have been watching Riley? Fifteen years, ever since he was assigned to Honduras." He puffed hard and long. "You want one?"

"No thank you, George, I don't smoke."

"Neither did I until I met that Cuban archbishop. Turned me on to the finest smoke you will ever know."

"George, you know what I do, how I operate, and I know what you do. Normally, we have nothing in common, our paths do not cross. On this rare occasion we were working our particular interests with the same man. Why did you bring me here? I have nothing to do with Vatican money. I have my own."

George hesitated, puffing more on the cigar, and then smiled. He shoved a file across the desk toward Harold. Harold picked it up and read the name on the label. Bishop James Sanders. He opened the file and found the standard Vatican background information. He flipped through the pages. Harold nodded when he read his history with Opus Dei. His own work first in Central America and then back in Madison, Wisconsin, as a young, newly minted bishop was even more militant than John Riley. A Jesuit rewarded with a bishop's chair for his work in South America. "We are fortunate enough to have a backup. The holy father plans on replacing Riley with this guy. The word will go out that he's temporary, as the holy father does a rigorous search for a proper fit to replace Archbishop Riley. But he's the guy. He's completely loyal and, in fact, will be in my meeting with the holy father tomorrow. You know him?"

"In passing, a few events. He spent most of his time in Central America and then teaching in a seminary in Mexico City, as I recall. Worked quite a bit with John Riley."

"Would you mind getting to know him over there in Seattle, call me every once in a while, tell me what you think? He'll be expecting you."

Harold closed the file. He knew about various missions of the Mother Church, and financing the right organizations with the correct causes played a central role in the life of most modern popes. There had been exceptions. But the financing did not grow on trees. "George, you know I typically steer away from the Institute's works. I have provided generously when asked to do so, you know that. I have my own mission."

"I need to know how he is with money. Does he like expensive watches, does he have a mistress, is he a gambler? It looks like he came from money, and my bet is he learned a long time ago how not to show the colors."

"I have an investigation I need to—"

"The holy father is going to ask you personally tonight at dinner so I thought I would give you a chance to think up some clever positive response."

Harold smiled. "Dinner, with the Holy Father."

"Yes, in his private residence."

"Well, I see. It's not very easy to deny the holy father a personal request to serve the Mother Church."

"I told him I figured that would be your response. You ever meet him?"

"When he was a cardinal."

"Funny what the white robe does to a man. Changes him. I've known four of them now. John Paul the Second was my favorite, but this guy seems to understand money better than the others. Reminds me of what I read about Pius after the war."

෮෨෮෨

Harold was not disappointed. The dinner was simple fare, served by older men with impeccable manners. As he motioned for a cab back to his hotel, he reflected on the evening. The holy father never mentioned the source of the money, or what happened after it was used ostensibly to fund charitable organizations. Harold knew all too well. High-interest loans secured by easily sold real estate always of greater value to cover the cost of the charity and the stipend. The original investor could easily see a ten-to-fifteen-percent annual return and the Institute would enjoy the rest.

The holy father delighted in showing pictures of hospitals and schools funded by these gracious donations around the world. Universities, seminaries, grade schools. He was especially cheerful when talking about Archbishop Riley's chosen charity; an organization advancing the cause of the traditional family and fighting the legal process and local electorate that insisted on the normalization of hedonistic same-sex relationships. On this Harold agreed.

He admitted he began to see the providential wisdom of the current works of the Institute. When he told the holy father his opinion of who may have perpetrated the death of Archbishop Riley, the holy father appeared genuinely surprised and became acutely interested in Harold's theories of an organized cartel of hedonistic homosexuals set on the harm and even death of some of the most trusted and highly placed servants of the Holy Mother Church. That is all he talked about for the duration of the dinner and was called away before they could pour coffee.

Back in his hotel, Harold calculated the time in Seattle. Roughly one in the afternoon. He dialed the cell phone he had given Greg Lucas. He listened quietly to an account of the frustrating process of trying to get the suicide letter and then the even more frustrating Captain Olivia Moro.

"We'll deal with this in good time," Harold said. "I have something more important. Find out what Archbishop Riley used when he travelled, a laptop, a palm pilot, one of those tablets. There might be some sensitive information on whatever he was carrying. Financial information. Don't push too hard, just nose around a bit."

"Anything specific I am looking for?"

"A charity in Seattle, advancing the cause of the traditional family. Call the archbishop's office and see if his assistant can help."

⁊ↄᥱↄ

Greg Lucas hung up and called Genelle. Yes, Riley had shot down all services to what traditional Catholics referred to as being on the fringe and revived an organization with long political tentacles reaching into State politics to protect traditional marriage. Greg knew what it was immediately. He knew how the Church funded organizations like that directly from Rome and not locally from donations. The people who fronted the money were often the ones hired to carry out the more silent operations. Funding a political fight for traditional marriage was the mild, public face of the Institute for Works of Religion. He made the connection immediately to the cartels and the need to launder cash, lots of it, and for a fee an international organization like the Institute for Works of Religion might be very willing to assist. Greg wasn't so sure now that he wanted to be involved.

Chapter 25

reg's previous visits to Seattle had been summertime fair-weather events. He had always enjoyed the abundant sunshine. As he walked slowly off the plane, the cold rain of March spattered loudly on the covered walkway. The rain water sprayed off the roof, splashing baggage handlers wrapped in rubber rain gear.

He spotted his name scrawled on a large card, his last name spelled "Lukas." The man behind the placard was sixtyish, heavy, with large, sausage like fingers. Greg held out his hand.

"Lucas. A different guy this time."

"Captain Sam Pillsbury. Yeah, I've heard it before. I'm what you look like if you eat too many cut-and-bake cinnamon rolls."

"Captain?"

"Retired. Seattle Police Department."

"You have a retirement. Why are you driving a limo?"

"Limo? You're not that good looking, buddy. Ha. I work for Harold. I do fine on my retirement with the free-lance work I do for Harold. Limo. Shit."

Sam Pillsbury's racing green Jaguar XKE fired up with a gentle roar. He eased it into reverse, then first and rumbled out of the parking lot. The rain had mysteriously stopped as they sped with ease north on Interstate 5.

"It was raining a minute ago."

"Does that. Starts up like a cow pissing on a flat rock, then cow's done, and it clears up. Should be a nice afternoon." Sam wove in one lane then another, averaging seventy-five in heavy traffic. "I told Harold not to send you. I had an angle on this, and I think you will be staying for a very short time."

"You have access to Boyle's suicide note?"

"The little jerk holding it is a career kiss ass. I've talked with the current chief. Nice guy, old school like me, but the department is so bogged down with politics. Chief has to watch his back all the fucking time. We're working on an angle to…uhm…negotiate with Captain High-and-Frickin-Mighty."

"What is he holding it for? Hasn't the press requested it?"

"The press here are a bunch of liberal dumbasses. The only thing they want is the goods on Republicans and rich folks. Catch a Microsoft exec on tape wanting to crush the competition, and it's front page news. Look into the extreme and potentially dangerous political affiliations of a liberal Catholic bishop and, yawn. Not interested."

The Jag roared off an exit, into the jaws of a thriving and anxious city. Pillsbury cursed the long waits at lights, often lasting three red, green, yellow cycles. Traffic in Seattle ground forward. Even Puerto Vallarta moved faster than this. It took longer to travel fifteen blocks than it did to drive from the airport to the downtown section. Pillsbury commented that if he had become mayor as he hand once hoped, things would be different. Greg decided not to ask how.

"I called Bishop Boyle's brother and asked if he could call the chief and the captain to see if he could get a copy of the note. Harold offered him fifteen thousand dollars and since the guy's mother just died leaving absolutely nothing, he bit. We're meeting him in the bar at the Four Seasons."

The retired captain huffed and wheezed as they rode the escalator from the parking garage to the main lobby. "We're early. Thought I would fill you in a bit on Harold Brown and give you some of what motivates the old boy." He sat with an aching grunt in a deep, overstuffed chair, his hand diving immediately into a bowl of cashews. "Double Dewar's, rocks. Lucas, what are you having."

Greg pondered the choices one might have in a four-star hotel bar. "The same." He reached for his money clip.

"I expense it. Harold treats me well. Hey, you working with that Mexican Captain…uhm…Moro."

"Moro. yes, That's why I'm here. She has evidence she's not sharing. If I can spring the suicide note free, I think I can get what she's got."

"Right. Careful with her. She's not as friendly to the cause as you and I are."

"The cause? I'm working as a private investigator on behalf of Harold Brown. I'm not with any cause."

Pillsbury rolled forward in the chair to take the first sip of his drink. "When you work for Harold Brown, you are."

Greg smiled. "And what cause might that be?"

"Harold believes, and I agree with him, the homosexuals in this country are about to turn terrorist, in fact, we believe they already have. In retaliation for a few extremist incidents like the bombing of a gay bar in Atlanta and they found a bomb in a gay bar up here in Seattle a few years ago, they have organized an underground terrorist cell that makes that dead sand sucker in Libya look like a choir boy. They are targeting legitimate and peaceful leaders of church and government institutions."

"This is the first I've heard of this. Of course the CIA, FBI, and all other intelligence gathering organizations know about this, right?" Greg winked as a way of both thanking Gene Pillsbury for the drink and the amusing information.

Pillsbury gulped and shook his head. "The thing is, it's too hot. All those m-effing PC a-holes in the press are just waiting to hear the government is keeping an eye on those light loafer types. That's where I come in. I liaison with the various agencies and give them what we find. That's where you and the ex-ranger fit in. Only I was getting vibes from that boy he was just in it for the paycheck. Now, you fit in nicely because you have a history of serving good causes. I know about what you did to your poker player buddy. Good work." Pillsbury gabbed another handful of cashews and shoved them into his mouth, a few spilling out and rolling down his shirt. "Do you know anything about Opus Dei, Mr. Lucas?"

Greg shook his head.

"Good. If you're not going to join and devote your entire life to it as Harold Brown and I have done, then its better you don't know. Let me assure you that, between us and the Knights of Malta, we are connected to every major European, South American, North American, and many Asian government leaders, financiers, businessmen, and statesmen. The Catholic Church has more than one billion members, about one sixth of the world's population, and we are devoted to making sure outside influences do not infiltrate and corrupt the essential message of the Gospel and the work of the holy father. Our number one enemy is the homosexual community. Their insistence that their perverted lifestyles are accepted and blessed by God is an absolute abomination.

"They are very clever, Mr. Lucas. By cozying up to

the press with contrived stories of persecution and heinous lies about priests molesting boys, they have turned
the tide of public opinion against the Church. I am here to
make sure it stops." Pillsbury belched and held up his
empty glass. "Excuse me. I get worked up over this, as
you can see." He caught his breath. "You have confirmed
that the email messages that came from the computer be-
longing to Father Juravics did not come from any other
computer?"

For sport, Greg nodded.

"Right. We know that a priest who lived with Father
Juravics—" Pillsbury smiled and rolled his eyes. "—was
just fired from a program that gave money to guys with
AIDS. Freeloaders, most of them. Bar buddies, you
know? Well, the little angel has fallen. That's what we
call these gay boy priests when they run off with their
man stud. Fallen Angels. We don't know where he is.
I've got two other investigators out looking for him.
We'll nail his sorry ass, and my bet is we find him in the
lap of homosexual luxury, rewarded for his part in the
murder of Archbishop Riley, and now the near murder of
the holy father—" A cell phone interrupted Pillsbury.
"Captain Pillsbury here. Right, Harold. He's here." He
handed the phone to Greg.

Greg covered a few details and ended the conversation. They would talk again in two hours. "Have you
found anything other than the email messages that link
these people…uhm…the gays, to the explosions."

"The suicide note," Pillsbury bellowed. "Boyle was
their scout master. I want to know what that says, hand it
all over to the local prosecutor who will do absolutely
nothing about it, then give it all to the press and embarrass the bastard. That gets the old colon excited enough to
ward off political constipation."

Greg saw an opportunity. The hand off to Doug Dorn

was clean enough to protect him. Boyle was dead. "How large is your organization."

"Opus Dei?"

"No. Your efforts, the investigations that are financed by Harold Brown."

"Like I say, Mr. Lucas—"

"Call me Greg."

"Fine, Greg. Like I say, we have contacts. Mr. Brown has been involved with Opus Dei for forty-eight years. He has been a very successful and influential international banker and has met with numerous—"

"Are you tied to Opus Dei directly or is Harold working on his own?"

"Mr. Brown works independently. The fact that he uses his contacts and the fact that they agree with the work he does is purely coincidental."

Greg declined a second drink as Pillsbury ordered a third. "Where are you in all of this, Pillsbury? El presidente, cabin boy, what?"

Pillsbury smiled. "Let's focus on what you are for us, okay?" He shoved more cashews into this mouth and talked around them. "I want to know if you believe these gay boys are out to kill Church leaders based on what you have seen."

"I've seen nothing. Moro has not cooperated with me at all. She trusts Grady."

"Yes, I know. You know he claims to be like psychic or something, Grady does."

"I didn't know that."

Sam Pillsbury stared at him. "A guy I worked with, Chief Greig, I think you know him."

Greg nodded.

"He and I worked a homicide desk for about ten years. He used this guy just before he took the chief position in Jackson Hole. We were looking for a little boy, presumed dead. Grady went to the last spot the boy was seen, had some kind of hallucination, described a place for us, and sure as it rains in Seattle, there was the boy. You can bet ole Grady went right to the top of my suspect list. I had rank then and grilled the living crap out of him. Nobody has those kinds of powers. Grieg tells me to back off and then actually finds the bad guy that did it, using Grady. I think to this day Grady is a lying sack of crap and rather than being psychic, had a connection to the murder. I'll find it."

"Then why did Harold hire him again."

"Harold doesn't believe me. Grady has done some pretty good work for Harold, and so he likes him. Harold thinks he's got the devil in him or some goddam thing and—" Pillsbury gulped hard from his glass. "So, when Harold needs something like this, he calls Grady and sends him out into the field."

A slight, doleful man walked slowly up to Captain Pillsbury and handed him a handful of paper. "I was able to get them."

"Mr. Boyle. Well done. This is Mr. Lucas. He is working for Harold Brown and has some keen interest in this. How are you holding up?"

"Not so good. I finished going through my mother's things, and now I've just got started on my brother's."

Greg was flipping through the pages of his copy. "Have you read this?"

"Yes. It is very strange. I almost did not give it to you. I think it reflects that my brother was experiencing some very serious problems. And, of course, part of it is missing. You do know he was removed from his office as Bishop of Newark, New Jersey?"

Pillsbury grunted.

"I don't think it will be of much help to you," Peter Boyle continued.

Greg glared at Boyle. "Missing? Part of it is missing?"

"Yes. They've started an investigation into evidence tampering. See, up at the top it says he will name the people involved in the murder of the archbishop. But one or more pages are missing."

Pillsbury and Greg read in silence, Boyle sat silently in a chair.

Pillsbury read fast, shaking his head. "Mother of Mercy. I hope this man prayed hard the minute before he died. I have never read such blasphemy. This is awful. I hope you're right about your brother being psycho, Mr. Boyle. I don't see God forgiving this otherwise."

❧❧

Greg set his copy on the table. "It does ring of someone undergoing great psychosocial stress. I doubt it would be given much credence, Mr. Boyle. I am sorry your brother appeared to suffer. Have the police found anything about the missing page?"

"Not that they would share."

Pillsbury's other cell phone rang and he had to dig for it in his coat. "Yeah. Hey, Chief Grieg. What? Really? Really? Okay, I'll do that." He snapped the phone closed. "That was the police chief in your little town of Jackson Hole. Says he has something for me, wouldn't tell me what. He's calling back in an hour."

Pillsbury leaned back in his chair. Greg's face was no longer professional. It was mean, gray, and angry. Pillsbury observed him for a few moments. "Mr. Lucas, do you need another drink?"

Greg nodded. He listened to the endless, if often humorous, stories of Pillsbury's work with Chief Grieg. This kind of information could be useful later, so he endured through a decent steak and very good coffee.

Greg left the table momentarily when Pillsbury took another call to confirm his flight to Puerto Vallarta in the morning.

Pillsbury wiped blueberry pie filling from his face. "You seem out of sorts, Greg."

"Jet lag."

They shook hands. Greg walked to the W Hotel and retired to his room. He sat in the chair, looking out at the electric Seattle skyline. He read through the suicide note again.

He should have seen it. At the camp. Boyle was not an operative. Greg wondered if there was a diary, notes, anything about that meeting and what Greg agreed to do. It could be said the death of his mother and the state of his career pushed him over, but that wasn't it.

Boyle had hired a hit and was not the kind of man to do that. He was a good and decent man who was broken by a system much larger and more powerful than him. When a man broke, he did funny things. Harry Boyle was no exception.

Forgiven? Yeah, Harry Boyle would be forgiven his sins. Greg was not certain of his own.

He replayed in his mind the stories of Chief Greig. A good cop. Good field operatives sting like bees and run like hell. Good cops grind slowly and thoroughly, missing very little, always arriving at the correct answer. Good cops do not let people slip through, they get them. Jerry Garcia was a good cop. There was a light knock at the door. Greg opened it and smiled at Doug Dorn.

"Doug. Serendipity."

Doug walked slowly into the hotel room. "Serendipity?"

"I walked backward into something larger than life."

"Is this why you told Ramone you wanted to meet with me?"

"I am usually not this careless, but this time, my ego got the best of me."

Doug shook his head. "You been drinking?"

"Not yet. Remember what we saw in Central America? Remember what turned us off so much about our military service? Remember how we always thought it was those awful cartels in charge of all the drug flow, and when we found the truth, we were all shocked and we held those secrets and still hold those secrets?"

"I think about that every day and wonder when they will find out what I know."

"Right. So do I. Now I know even more than I ever wanted. Riley, the archbishop in Puerto Vallarta, he was the new banker."

"For who? The Vatican?"

"Yes. I did not know the tie when I agreed to take this on."

Doug stared out the window and then back at Greg. "This is a shit mess. I am out of it."

"No, you're not. Boyle committed suicide and left a note and part of it is missing. I know Ramone is connected with some of the fairy queens—"

"No, Lucas, we are done. Permanently. You are in as much trouble as I ever was, and I am now free of this. We are done."

"We're done when I say we are."

Doug shook his head and walked out of the room and down the hall.

Chapter 26

Officer Jerry Garcia was not a doughnut man. He preferred the buttery crisp croissant, instead. No almond paste or raspberry jam slopped in the middle—just a good, plain croissant and dark, rich coffee. Not out of a one gallon can, coffee freshly ground and made in a French press.

His favorite stop was Emils, a coffee shop in the bohemian tradition where the children of the wealthy of Jackson Hole could sit all night, drink espresso, and play broad games. Jerry Garcia would appear at any hour of the day or night, talk with the local teens, nibble a croissant, and drink some good coffee. On slow nights, he could be found playing cribbage with his two children or sitting in a deep, over-stuffed chair reading. In spite of the fact that Emil loved having a police man in his coffee shop and offered to give Jerry anything he wanted, Jerry always insisted on paying.

One night as he sat reading a stray copy of *The New Yorker*, two men walked in and approached the girl at the cash register. They pulled a gun and demanded all of the money. Jerry watched casually as the girl laughed and told the men it was certainly not their luckiest night. She pointed at Jerry who had by then stood, drawn his gun, and was reaching for his cuffs. The man holding the gun shook his head and set the gun gently on the floor and stepped away. While they waited for another cruiser to arrive, Jerry allowed the men a cappuccino each, paying for them both. They thanked him, cooperatively got into the two cruisers, and rode to jail.

Officer Garcia would always take time out for mass on Sunday morning if he happened to be on duty. Dressed in his uniform and wearing his gun, he would join his wife and children. One bright May morning, a drunk entered the church and started shouting violent curses at the priest. Jerry finished reciting the credo and then escorted the man to his car, locking him inside. He returned to the church and, when mass was over, drove the man to jail.

Jerry kept a small, black, three-ring binder in his cruiser. The pages were filled with observations. They usually did not amount to anything right then, but it did help him develop an understanding of character. Over time, he would notice behavioral changes, newly ac-quired trucks or skis, when someone would stop saying hello to him, usually right after he had written them a speeding ticket. He particularly liked knowing who had what kind of guests, how long certain tourists would be in town, and where they would stay.

He observed one tattered motorhome three times in the same month, parked once at the south edge of town and then the other two times near the Travel Lodge. He looked back in his notes the third time and saw he had noted the fact the windows were covered. In the winter, this might help insulate a motorhome, something he had seen often, but this was September in the middle of the day. He figured tourists who paid all the money to drive up to Jackson Hole wanted to see it during the day. He stopped his cruiser in front of the motorhome and walked around it. He noticed the air vent on top of the home was open and occasionally white steam or a very light smoke would drift out of it. He knew immediately what it was—crystal meth in the production stage.

He radioed for back up and sat reading a novel until the other three officers and Chief Grieg arrived several minutes later with two state patrol officers. They placed themselves strategically around the motorhome and knocked on the door.

"Jackson Hole Police. Open the door please."

There was loud cursing and the motorhome began to rock. Two officers observed the byproducts of the crystal meth operation pour out of the sewage line and on to the street. Everyone stood back.

"Hey, Chief, they just flushed the drugs down the toilet, but you know what? The drain line isn't connected to anything. Brilliant. I'll get the haz-mat guys over here to clean this up."

One patrolman pried the door open with a crowbar while the other officers stood flat against the side of the motorhome. Fumes wafted out the open door and the officers covered their faces, ordering the occupants out. What emerged was almost laughable—two thirtyish men, globs of hair falling out, thin, pale, and sporting red pock-marked faces. Now Jerry had seen almost everything—a mobile meth lab serving the needs of Jackson Hole, Wyoming.

෨෬෬

Jerry was diligently writing case notes. "Have you heard anything from Lucas? What kind of case he's working on?"

The chief was wandering around the office. "Uh, no I haven't. I think it has to do with some archbishop dying over there. Some American archbishop. You're his poker buddy. Thought you would know."

"Yeah. Reminds me. Got a new guy now that our friend Jimmy is explaining why he screwed around with old ladies' money to a bunch of friendly family men in the pen."

The captain snapped his fingers. "Hey, on that—I got a call from a lady down in Laramie. We may be able to add to Jim's vacation time. She was contacted by someone on the Internet, and she thinks the guy used the name Ralph Crand, Esquire. She had just inherited a boat load and this caller was requesting repayment of a debt. Same MO. She sent him an email to get a copy of the contract he said he had, but then they got rid of the computer and bought a new one so they don't have a copy of the email. They use a service provider in Laramie, and it's worth checking out to see if they have a copy of the email in archive. If they do, we can get that over to the Laramie Police, and I can ask old Chief Buzzard Breath to give me some information on that trucker who decided to build a new freeway through George's gas station. He's got a rap sheet down there but that old bastard won't release some information on a similar case the driver was involved in." Chief Grieg was opening and slamming shut drawers and cabinet doors.

"What are you looking for?"

"My gun. I went out drinking last night, and I know I left it here, but I can't remember where."

He found it lying out in the open in the top of a filing cabinet. Without expression, he holstered the .38 and sat at his desk. "The guy drove down to Laramie and had a sweet rendezvous with the woman, which the woman says she agreed to and wanted, but unlucky for our friend Jimmy, she recorded the conversation. Can't use the recording, but if I can get the email exchange, I think that information is about as useful to Jimmy as windshield wipers on a goat's ass."

Jerry nodded. "I'll call her back, get the name of the service provider, and have an answer for you in an hour. You want me to go down there for any kind of statement?"

"No. I want you to embarrass that old fart they have for a chief down there by handing him a solved case he's ignored because he doesn't own a computer and has no idea what the Internet is and how these bad guys use it."

Jerry laughed, saved his notes, and set himself up to complete the research. "Do you know the name of the archbishop who was killed in Mexico?"

"Well, look at that. You ask me that question, and I am looking at the goddam piece of paper I wrote that down on when that captain called me. I was drunk on my ass and I could not for the life of me find that piece of paper. Archbishop John Riley. That's it. What's the interest?"

"Just curious what Lucas is up to."

"You watching him?"

"Always. The man has a sharp edge to him, and I get uncomfortable when I'm around him."

The chief nodded and left the office for some coffee. Jerry looked up the number for his priest and called.

"Archbishop Riley had just been installed in Seattle. I never knew him, but I watched the little news coverage they had. In Puerto Vallarta. That's where he was killed."

"Seattle." Jerry opened the notebook and wrote his thoughts on the subject of Greg Lucas and the coincidence that he knew a bishop in Seattle who committed suicide very soon after the newly installed archbishop of Seattle was killed by a bomb in Puerto Vallarta, Mexico, where Greg Lucas was now working as a private detective on that case. Coincidences like this, no matter how they appeared to add up to something, sometimes just fell apart and nothing ever came of them. Then, again, often they became the basis for full-blown investigations that ended in conviction of yet another criminal. Jerry slapped the notebook shut and dialed the number for the family in Laramie.

The line was busy. He pulled the national police directory from his desk drawer and looked up the Seattle Police Department. He reached a woman in homicide who said she knew the officers assigned to the Boyle suicide. Yes, she would take his name and number.

Jerry reached the woman in Laramie, got the name of the service provider, called them, and determined after several minutes they had an archive of the family's emails. Jerry wrote careful notes and called the Chief of the Laramie Police Department. After struggling through an abusive conversation where Jerry was accused of meddling in another department, the chief turned Jerry over to a detective who sighed and said nothing when Jerry commented on the old chief.

"Thanks for this. We'll take care of it from here. If you ever need anything, just ask."

"Well, my chief wants some file information on that trucker you guys tried to take down last year. Seems he remodeled a gas station up here, and the insurance company wants it all to go away, but we think the guy has something else going on."

"It's not my case, but I'll get what I can. Have your chief call me."

Jerry watched the phone all morning, anticipating a return call from Seattle. Nothing. Maybe it was all just coincidence. Jerry waved at the dispatch office and got into his cruiser. He drove to the south end of town where he could park and look at the mountains. He opened his binder and began reading his numerous observations of Greg Lucas from the very beginning one more time.

Chapter 27

It was difficult for anyone to feel good attending a funeral for a fourteen-year-old boy brutally tortured and murdered. But they came. Politicians, cardinals, the rank and file of the Puerto Vallarta and Jalisco State Police, and even some federales. There were also private citizens. The small neighborhood church was filled, people were turned away.

Inspector Juarez sat with his fellow officers. At least he could wear the new suit he had bought two years ago and never had occasion to wear. He received a communion and then drove to the hospital to visit Grady.

Grady was sleeping when he arrived. The nurses said Sandy had gone out to use her phone and would be back. Most of the bandages were off and Grady looked better. Juarez walked slowly, thoughtfully, to the cafeteria. His captain was a good officer who did not deserve to have her child tortured and murdered. But at least they found the boy. He shook his head and ordered a coffee. A well-dressed man walked up behind him and patted him on the shoulder. "So, you finally had the nerve to wear that ugly suit."

"Pedro. Thanks for meeting me here."

"Are we being discreet? A hospital cafeteria?"

"Oh, well, I am babysitting an American who was run over."

"I read about that. How is he doing?"

"Fine. We'll be back on the case in a few days."

The last time Juarez fell in love—okay he was admitting it to himself. Damn emotions anyway. But the last time, he moved back to Mexico and his lover would not follow. He stayed back in the states. Juarez's career was in Puerto Vallarta, under the careful guidance of Captain Moro, and he would enjoy success. So, no, he would not go back to the states if something happened. Find someone local, no matter the social stigma, and do the job well.

⌘

Grady was sitting up, watching a soccer game on television. He glanced over at Juarez and then back to the game.

"Grady?"

Grady looked at him again. "Who?"

"You. Grady."

"Is that my name? Do I know you?"

A nurse entered the room.

"Amnesia?" Juarez asked.

The nurse nodded and removed a tray of the mostly eaten lunch.

"I'm Inspector Juarez. Is your wife still here?"

"Who, Sandy? I should be so lucky to have a wife like that. She's back at her hotel." He sat looking at the game for a minute. "Hey, I saw you in a dream I just had last night. Did I tell you that already?"

Juarez shook his head. "Can you remember the dream?"

"Oh yeah. As soon as you walked in, it was like I had

just seen you." Grady looked back at the television.

"Can you tell me about it?"

Grady looked out the window for a few moments, blinking. "Yeah. I guess so. You and I were in this cemetery, and I was looking at a statue of a boy, and I made some comment about how, well, big he was, then you started telling me about another boy who had been there and then disappeared."

Juarez sat down.

"Then I said to you I knew where the boy was because I could see a gold medallion, of a horse. Then we were in this small room and I knew the boy was there, and they dug up the floor and there was his body, like I had these powers to see things or something." Grady paused and looked at Juarez. "Strange, huh?"

Juarez nodded.

"Then you were in this church, this huge church, and there was like holes all over the altar area, like a bomb or something had gone off. I think it was a funeral, yeah it was a funeral. It was for the boy. Then I saw a man in a dark coat standing by a pillar, watching the father of the boy. There was something in his pocket, though. It was like a garage door opener. And before you left the church, he left. Then the man was in a police station. I'm sorry, but some of the transitional details, like the time frame, are very fuzzy.

"But he is in a police station. And this garage door opener is like really important. I don't know why. But then you came into the hallway where a woman was and asked her if she needed anything and she said no. You started to leave and the woman took out the garage door opener—okay now it's clear, I see it very vividly, even better than in my dream, and she started pressing the button frantically.

"Then holy hell broke loose, like a bomb went off.

And this is weird. The father of the boy at the funeral, who was at the police station, was in a black suit. I don't know if he was with the police or what, but as soon as he came out of a room, this thing happened.

"Then you were running over to the man, but he was dead. Like he had just been to his own son's funeral and then he was dead.

"I think the strangest thing about it was I knew he wasn't supposed to be there, and this explosion was not supposed to kill anyone. The man in the dark coat didn't know the man was in the room. Then I woke up."

Juarez reached for the telephone next to the bed and dialed. "Is Moro still there?"

"No. She is with her boyfriend. They took the afternoon and are going up to the mountains for a late lunch."

"She's not going by the office, is she?"

"No. Not with her family for certain. I know she'll be back by seven tonight, and we have the briefing on the bombing case."

Grady turned the television off. "What is that all about?"

Inspector Juarez sat down again and took Grady's hand. "Half of what you told me from your dream kind of really happened. With your amnesia, you don't remember right now that you have some sort of gift that does allow you to visualize things. Like I say the first half of what you said is partly true, except for the fact you really just said something about the Russians, and Captain Moro sought out tips and got the truth. So much for that. But the second part of your dream, the man in the dark coat, that worries me. That hasn't happened, yet. I think I need to go right now and take care of something, to prevent the man in the black suit from going into her office."

ɷ

Captain Novarres listened, squinting his eyes and once shaking his head. "Do you believe this stuff?"

"What I saw with the Moro boy, leading us right to it—"

"That was just good police work. This guy Grady had good intel on some Russians, it clicks in Moro's head, and she reaches out and gets the information she needed. Like I said, good police work. What are you driving at with this dream and this man in a dark coat?" Novarres slouched in his chair and stared silently at Juarez for several minutes. "Well, Moro won't be back until this evening. Let me make a call, then I'll see if I can get the bomb sniffers over there later to take a look. Don't talk about this with anyone."

Juarez drove back to his station. He bought a dead sandwich in the concession room and ate it quickly. Modern Mexican life was forcing him to give up so many traditions, such as the long and peaceful mid-day meals and the naps that had followed. Now it was terrible food, wolfed down, and back to work.

Inspector Hernandez held three of the same sandwiches in his massive right hand and sat next to him. "I hear there is a pile up on the highway. Moro is turning around and coming back."

"What time?"

"Not sure. We are still meeting at one. Are you sitting in for Moro?"

Juarez rolled his eyes then noticed he had forty minutes before the meeting. He excused himself, went directly to the case files, and found the remaining color copies of the man in the dark coat. He walked up and down the street either way of the station asking local shopkeepers if they had seen the man recently. Two had, just that morning, at different times. Juarez gave all of the shopkeepers a copy of the photograph and his cell phone number. He walked into the meeting five minutes late. Inspector Hernandez stopped talking and waited for him to sit.

The meeting droned on until two, through minute details of recent murders, robberies, and anything connected to any organized crime. Coffee was brought in at two and, after a very brief break, they went back to examining the mountains of details. At three, Captain Moro opened the door, still dressed in a black funeral suit. She nodded graciously and started back out the door.

"Sir. Something urgent."

"Can it wait until after the meeting?" Hernandez removed his glasses for some kind of emphasis.

"No. Sir, I need to talk."

"Let's go to my office." Moro normally did not interrupt these meetings. However boring, they were the backbone of an inspector's work.

Moro approached her office.

"Don't go in, sir. Please."

Moro stopped and looked back at him. The tone of voice and his expression convinced her.

"It's Grady, I saw him this morning. He's got amnesia, but he had a dream, and he accurately described our meeting in the cemetery that lead to the discovery of your son. Then he described you, in that black suit, in the police station, and a bomb going off." Moro stood away from the door. Juarez glanced around and saw, at the far end of the hall, a short dark-haired man coming out of the stairwell. The door to Moro's office opened and one of the explosive experts appeared, smiling.

"Got it. Captain Novarres called us. Told to keep it quiet. I got here first and could see it wasn't anything big or complicated so we didn't evacuate. Pretty crude actually. It's all being entered as evidence now. Checking for prints and residue."

"Any idea what the source is, who makes these things."

"Local. Really simple little bomb I've seen popping up lately. It's intended for small, isolated effect. Had you opened the door, you would have been hurt badly, but you probably would have survived. These are usually for hire to scare people or as pay back. The guys who make these are usually young technical college kids looking for a few pesos. Definitely not pros. We take pictures of the various parts and the electronics instructors help us figure out where the parts were acquired. We'll find him."

After helping gather evidence at the station, Juarez went to the hospital and sat by Grady's bed. Grady could remember the dream, but still did not remember who Juarez was. Juarez told him the details as he could remember them. "Any more dreams?"

Grady shook his head but winked. "None that I can tell you. I don't know you."

"You still don't remember me?"

"I wish I did."

"I'll bet you've said that to all the nurses here."

"Just two."

"You remember that? The man you saw in your dream. Recognize him? Was something different about him in the dream?"

"Different? No. I can't say I would recognize him, even if I have ever seen him."

"The second part of the dream you told me about earlier. The guy in a dark coat in the police station planting a bomb. Something similar to that just happened. Can you go back and recall the dream?"

Grady looked at him with a sly smile. "You know, when I get my memory back, I'll forget everything I've said, right?"

"Amnesia affects people differently."

"The dream. What about the part in the cemetery? Was that true?"

"Kind of. You were telling me about some Russians who operated in a way you thought was similar to the MO in the abduction of Captain Moro's son. We told her, and she made the connection and realized she had been looking at Mexican nationals all along and not the Russians. She got some tips and here we are."

"And the second part of the dream, did that happen?"

"Not exactly as you told me, but a small bomb was planted in Captain Moro's office. Someone saw a man in a dark coat running from the station. He's the one they will do an artist's rendering of. I want to bring that to you and see if it jogs your memory."

"I see. Yes, if it helps, I would like to see the drawing."

"Of course." Inspector Juarez walked out of the room. "I need some coffee."

Chapter 28

Cops like Moro had good instincts, and the reason Greg would not be able to control the game now was because Moro didn't trust him, suspected him of something, maybe. The suicide note would be passed off as insanity. Until they found the last page. Then what?

Greg had fooled good cops before. Sometimes they ground so slowly people like Greg could craft the correct evidence and, when the answer came to them, Greg was safely gone.

He had done it before, he would do it again. He had to be in Puerto Vallarta now. The timing was not good to cut and run. Run now, they'd chase. Find someone to stick this on, fade away slowly, and just not be there if they ground thoroughly enough to find the truth.

Captain Moro sighed. "Mr. Lucas, this is the writing of a lunatic. A rambling idiot. This is evidence of nothing but insanity, however sad. I am appalled by it, I think it is sacrilegious, and I do not intend to use it in any way. And, furthermore, it is incomplete. Someone has tampered with this and this whole note is of absolutely no use to me here until that matter has been resolved. If you were thinking that you would trade this for any evidence I may have, you are wrongly mistaken." Moro watched

Greg shift in his chair. She stared for a few more minutes. "Do you have anything else for me?"

Greg stared Moro in the eye then glanced out the window. He looked around the room at the damage being repaired after the bomb. "You are aware what Harold Brown is up to, I'm sure?"

"He hunts down prominent government officials and business people who are queer and he leaks the information to the press. That's primarily what he does."

"Are you aware of his theories regarding these explosions?"

"Gay terrorists."

"His man in Seattle, Pillsbury—"

Moro interrupted with a laugh.

Greg smiled too. "Captain Pillsbury. My dinner with him was enlightening. At first, I thought this guy was just a fat old man who dislikes homosexuals. I could see, however, in the depths of his crude form of professionalism, there is a deep conviction. He is a Catholic before he is anything else, and a Catholic with pretty good police instincts and skills.

"After dinner, I started to think about it. I put together in my mind a few things. This priest in Seattle loses his job. A job where he is helping gay men. He's gay. I'll say that for argument. There have always been very vocal and somewhat militant groups of homosexuals. Act Up was one. They didn't engage in violence, but they were almost crazy enough to do it. The Catholic Church has really been pressuring gay groups, lots of public condemnation. What these extreme, if inexperienced, activists need is someone who can actually pull off a job like killing Archbishop Riley with a bomb."

"Like who?"

"Someone kicked out of the United States military, maybe, for being openly gay. Someone with very advanced skills. The military is dumb enough to piss these people off."

"If someone like this existed, why not retaliate against the military?"

Greg knew he had Moro's ear. The furrow between her brows deepened as he talked. "I don't know. I want to find a connection."

"You know someone who might be capable of doing this?

"Yes. And if he didn't do it, he might lead me to the person who did."

"What are his credentials."

"Explosives, period."

"Can I verify that?"

"Yes, a Captain Michael Healy, stationed in San Diego but working covertly here in Mexico. He knows of this guy, Doug Dorn."

"Dorn. Doug Dorn." Moro wrote quickly. "He homosexual?"

Greg nodded slowly. "Healy will confirm not only his extensive explosives background, but the fact he was kicked out for being gay. I knew him well, and I want to find him. I want you to keep this under your hat for a bit. Don't go to Healy just yet. Before you do, let me find Dorn."

Moro shrugged. "You can do anything you like. I'm not sure I buy your theory, and I have a larger concern to devote my time to. Your man may be targeting church people, but I've got a different game going on here. You noticed how my office has been forcefully remodeled." She stood and walked toward the window. "Would you be familiar with the type of explosives this man Dorn used?"

"Oh, yes. But since we worked together, he's been a freelancer. He invents things, experiments."

Moro turned around fast and glared at him. "Triggers?"

"His specialty. If you have scraped anything together—" Greg had done it. It was Doug's trigger, that was the evidence.

"We've got something. This one in here in my office was the Russians. The first one that killed the archbishop. Well, now, that was a work of art."

"Russians?" *Very creative, Doug.*

"So, you see, I've got to focus my time on saving my own hide from these Russian thugs. You've got time. I'm not going to show you anything specific, but if it's triggers this guy does, and if you are familiar with his work, you'll know when you see it."

⇜⇝

Harold's face puckered and he shook with anger as Greg laid out the same scenario of a disillusioned former military explosives expert meeting up with gay activists and targeting the Church, specifically because the Church decided to get out of the business of supporting people financially who were leading lives that the Church found repugnant.

"I want to know if there is a connection," Harold hissed. "You find this out. You say he was removed from the military for his public display of homosexuality."

"Yes." Lies bought valuable time needed to fix the evidence and disappear. This was rule number one for field operations of any government. This allowed for time to correct Greg's own evidence.

Harold sipped his coffee slowly. The American-style breakfast—bacon and all—gurgled in his stomach. "I think it is a good time to let Grady go completely. If he regains his memory, I will tell him. You are in full charge of my efforts. How did Captain Moro take the news?"

"She seems to be busy, something about the Russians who set the bomb off in her office."

"Yes, she has her hands full. I don't think you will need access to her office anymore. I think you should start in Seattle and, before you talk with this Dorn character, work with Captain Pillsbury again. He is a good policeman. If you're going to undertake this work, you should get to know him better. You haven't talked to this Dorn guy recently, have you?"

"No, Doug and I have been distant for many years. As for Pillsbury, I'd rather do this alone."

Harold studied Greg. He had faced many men in his life. Enemies across a field firing weapons at each other, men who wanted to steal business from him, men who pretended to be friends who ultimately crossed him. It was one thing to check a man's history, but when he was dealing with such clever men, he ultimately depended on his ability to judge a man's character through discourse and the study of his mouth and eyes. Shifting eyes perhaps indicated guilt in the weak and stupid, not the experienced and intelligent. These men had learned how to use their eyes to fool you. Well, fool the weak and stupid who were fleeced of their money and wondered how it all happened.

A discerning eye could catch inconsistencies, not through some sham surprise, but during ordinary discourse when the other guy was trying to impress you. They forgot to focus their eyes just so, and in a flicker, you saw it. Maybe it was fear, guilt, sadness, or something, but he saw it. They remembered and covered it up again, but he'd seen it. What he saw in Greg Lucas's eyes was either the passion of the Lord Jesus Christ Himself, or the rage of the Devil. The moment the eyes were bared, flashing what was inside this Greg Lucas, the upper lip curled, and the face was something from the point in the circle of life where extreme good and evil met. How different was a man who preyed on children, abused them, and killed them from a man who killed abortion doctors and went to church the next day? Not very different at all. The continuum of good and evil was not a straight line with polarized opposites. It was a circle and the two met at some point. Harold decided this man Greg Lucas had been trained to live at this point, where most mortals would not survive, even a few seconds. The products of these encounters wandered the streets, singing, babbling, unwashed, certain they had seen both God and the Devil in the same room and they had. Greg Lucas was perfectly capable of being either being a child killer or the extreme child protector.

"I don't fear you, Mr. Lucas. I know your type."

Greg squinted and examined the impassive old face. "I'm sorry, Harold, I must have missed something."

"Mr. Lucas, your kind is useful to many different and conflicting causes. You don't live where the rest of us live. You come from the other side. You are capable of both loving and hating me at the same time. Very few people can do that." Harold placed a pile of pesos on the table to pay the bill. "I have lived through the most extreme conditions this human existence has to offer, and I have met the hardest, meanest, most broken people you can imagine. But you are superior to them in this. I have also met the kindest, most God-fearing people you can imagine, and they are not capable of loving as deeply as you are. The Gospel says you cannot serve two masters. That is true for most people—not for you."

Few people had ever before correctly analyzed Greg. He hoped his face did not reveal his own fear and amazement. This was worse than being found out as a player in the death of Archbishop Riley. This was Greg's key to his very survival—to live one moment in the world of either extreme and then the other, back and forth, as needed—and this old man saw it. How? "I'm not sure what you are talking about, Harold."

"Yes you do. But, it is not my concern where you live psychologically. I need you and now that I have seen what I just saw, I am confident you will have no trouble completing your mission, even if it is different from the one I want you to complete. Your work will serve my purposes, even if it serves your own as well. These things I know, Mr. Lucas."

Chapter 29

Captain Moro lifted the phone to call home and then set it down again as Inspector Juarez entered her office. "You're in a good mood."

Juarez smiled as he sat in one of the chairs. "His memory is back. I walked in and he starts talking about his theories of the case."

Moro did not smile. Juarez was disappointed. "This is good news, for sure," she said, "but I am informed by Harold Brown that Lucas will be working for him and Grady has no business here in Puerto Vallarta. Harold has asked me to inform Grady that he has no official role as an investigator and can go home."

Juarez looked away, nodding. "It sounds like you don't want that to happen."

"No. I would like him to stay. I have approval to retain him here working for us in a discreet capacity. I want these outside influences gone. I want Greg Lucas watched very carefully, if he ever comes back here. I'll handle Harold Brown."

"What's your read on Lucas?"

Moro sighed deeply. "I am very concerned about this Lucas character, so I want Grady first to find a man by the name of Doug Dorn. Lucas dropped the name on me too easily. He was associated with Lucas, and Lucas drops his name as a possible perpetrator. Maybe I smell Lucas instead of Dorn here." She stood and scratched the back of her head. "You should go with Grady, as a…well…representative of my office. That's okay with you, isn't it?"

"Whatever you say, sir."

"You haven't called me sir in a long time." She smiled. "If I wasn't a crazy old captain, I'd say you were probably hoping to be sent."

"Yes, sir."

"Good. At least there will be two people in this department who like each other and can work together. The paperwork is waiting in accounting. Make sure it's filled out right and then get it to me to sign." Moro sat back down. "You'll tell him about Brown."

Juarez nodded.

"And ask him if he wants to do this for me."

"Yes, sir. How is the trace going on the truck that hit us?"

"Abandoned, no plates, identity number scraped off. Mercedes, the type so typical throughout Mexico. Interesting, though, the fibers in the seat. Very expensive Italian slacks. Very expensive, not many Mexicans can afford them. Mostly for the very rich. That troubles me. Who can afford those slacks and would also take on the lowly work of assassinating a private investigator?"

"Your friends in the cartel. The Russians?"

Moro shrugged. "It is not wise to jump so hastily to conclusions. Inspector Hernandez is pulling fibers from chairs where Russians sat most recently. We'll compare them."

Juarez nodded and rose to leave.

Moro held up a hand. "You know this Riley case is my case, and I am focusing my attention on the cartel, for obvious reasons. Keep me informed, but carry on as you see fit. I'll answer for you if there is any reason to, just give me the right answers." She waved him out.

⁓✇⁓

The nurse told Grady that Harold Brown had made sure the hospital expenses would be covered, so he had only to dress and leave. Sandy had insisted Grady return home with her, but he insisted he was going to stay and finish in Puerto Vallarta, then he would retire to that life of researching and writing tawdry romance novels. Maybe he would stick to just the research part.

His walks around the hospital had not been enough to totally revive his strength. "I need to take a couple of days to get my strength back. You'll train with me?" he asked Juarez. "And by the way, you talk to me using my first name. I'm going to use yours."

"How is everything?"

"Everything's fine."

"I mean…uhm…up there—"

"What's up?"

"We're going to Seattle. Moro suspects Lucas is involved both ways. She thinks he's connected to a conspiracy to kill the archbishop and Brown has unwittingly hired him, one of the conspirators, to replace you."

"Replace me? Why?"

"It didn't look good there for a few days. How are you feeling?"

"Well. Let's see. I got run over, then Brown fires me, hires Lucas, and you and I are looking for someone in Seattle when the real case is here. That's how I feel. " Grady stood to the side of the bed. "Let's get out of here."

The nurses insisted Juarez take Grady to the main entrance in a wheelchair, where he promptly stood and walked toward Juarez's car. The tickets to Seattle were waiting for them at the station. Their first stop would be Colonial Daniels in his barren office at Fort Lewis, Washington.

ↄ◑ↄ

"No, Doug Dorn was not removed from the military for being gay. Nobody knew it until a year after he was gone. We don't know who he was fiddling with, or even if he was. Some might have, but they would have been well advised not to tell me." Colonel Daniels always talked around a cigar, whether it was lit or not. "Doug was caught with a serious supply of cocaine and given the opportunity to leave. We know he had a drinking problem, so they added two and two together and got the wrong answer. Doug had nothing to do with the cocaine. He was set up."

"By who?"

"I've often wondered how that much cocaine could get into his satchel in DC."

"Greg Lucas?"

"Nah. I thought about that, but Lucas and he were close. Too close. For a while I thought they were dating each other, but Lucas left a string of broken female hearts, so I figured it was battle love."

Grady had never heard it described with those words. "Do you know where Doug Dorn is now?"

"Yeah. I've used him, quietly. He's the best damn explosives man I've ever known."

"Would he kill an archbishop?"

"Depends. Depends on if the Archbishop was in the wrong place at the right time."

"He's not a killer?"

"No. Killing bothers him. Would never talk about it

like he's supposed to. Bottles it up inside. I've seen his type go over the edge if they don't deal with it."

"Lucas saved his life. Is he a puppet now?"

"Happens too often. Hero calls in the chits over and over. But I'm talking chits, not murdering for someone else. This would be the most extreme case I have ever seen."

"Got an address, phone number?"

"Why?"

"I think we've got him linked to the murder of the Archbishop of Seattle."

"Doug?"

"Lucas, too. But I think Lucas is driving here and Doug was used."

The Colonel hesitated. "Lucas. Huh. I think you're right. If Doug is there, Lucas has him on the string. What links Doug? Trigger?"

"You're asking me?"

"He invents things. Creative fellow."

"We found something no one has ever seen before. It's only recently we linked Lucas and Dorn. Trying to get this thing buttoned down before our side finds it, hides it, and counts the archbishop as collateral."

"By our side, you mean the FBI? They do that all right. When you called me about Lucas, I had this funny feeling in my stomach. When you asked me the first time when you were checking him out for this guy Harold Brown, I meant it when I said he was one of the best damn soldiers I ever saw in my career. But I don't know what it is about him. Haven't really spoken to him recently, but when I did he was cold and hard. Guys like him get that way. They got it both, you know, the sweet and the bitter. One minute they love you, the next they're cutting your toes off. Happens when you go through what these guys got. Hey, if it turns out to be him, don't blame me for the reference." The Colonel actually lit the cigar he had been sucking on. "Doug lives with a guy by the name of Ramone, North Seattle. Always polite, and Doug always calls back."

"What do they do?"

"Ramone is a dentist. Doug? He hires out. I use him for property damage. Told me he wouldn't kill. Okay. He can blow up anything, and I pay him well for it." The Colonial wrote an address and phone number on a small slip of paper and gave it to Grady.

⌘

The house was a modest three-bedroom rambler set in what had been a working class neighborhood of North Seattle. It was an idyllic charmer with a white picket fence, flowers abundant in the garden. Grady found Doug in the back yard, rototilling a garden area. He flashed a quick look at Juarez, asking with his eyes if this was the man Juarez saw. He shook his head. Doug listened silently as Grady laid out what he knew and thought about the death of Archbishop John Riley. Grady got no reaction when he talked about how often one must serve the needs of someone who saves our lives. He wasn't looking for any particular external reaction. He wanted a mental picture. Anything. And he got it. Cocaine in a satchel. A man putting it in, not Doug Dorn. "Do you know a man with a purplish birthmark on his neck?" Grady asked.

"So, you've met Lucas. And?"

"No, I've never met Greg Lucas. I've spoken to him, but I have never personally met him. And besides, the birthmark is down lower on the neck, low enough to hide with any kind of shirt, right?"

Doug shrugged.

"He put the cocaine in your satchel."

"No, he didn't. I put it there. I bought it on the streets of Columbia, used someone's diplomatic pouch, and was going to meet a contact in DC, but I got busted. I'm just lucky they didn't throw my ass in jail."

"That's not how it went at all. Lucas put it in your satchel, and I can see vividly the look on your face when they open it and find it. Lucas set you up."

"No he didn't. Why would he? He could have gotten rid of me in Guatemala—"

"You are far more valuable to him alive than dead. And with you owing him your life, he's got free labor whenever he wants it."

Doug slouched in a metal lawn chair. "You don't know anything, Mr. former army intelligence. No, that's not how it went at all." He didn't look at Grady or Juarez.

"He's setting you up now. You're going to take the fall for the bombs in Puerto Vallarta and Mexico City. They have a trigger, something never seen before, the handiwork of someone as creative as you?"

"I didn't set them or ignite them."

"But you planned them. To the most minute detail, any teenager could set them up. Who did you use?"

Doug was silent.

"Lucas dropped your name to Captain Moro of the Jalisco state police. Moro played it off and sent me here to talk with you. She smells something on Lucas, and Lucas thinks we're chasing the cartel. I know how you guys work in the field. I respect it. Are you certain he's going to contact you in time to clean up your trail? Did you know he had already dropped your name?"

"He wouldn't do that."

"No? I know guys like Lucas. He would trade away his own mother to get what he wants. My next stop is Jackson Hole, and I walk with the captain out there. Lucas has been working for them, real effective. Found a guy chasing old ladies' money over the Internet. They think his shit doesn't stink. He's a local hero. He saved your life, he's used you, and now he's going to pin it on you."

Grady stopped abruptly and stared at Doug. "You know different, don't you?"

"No, it doesn't work that way. He needs—"

"Needs what?"

No answer.

"I can make you disappear long enough to let this blow over. I still have contacts and Inspector Juarez has a network of safe houses in Mexico. Take whoever you want. Six months, a year. We nail Lucas."

"What do you want from me?"

"Enough information to get the job done."

"I can do it myself."

Grady smiled. "I know that. And now, after sitting here with you, I think I also know why." Grady stood slowly and rubbed his fingers through his hair, looking across the well-kept yard at the Olympic Mountains in the distance. "You know about remote viewing?"

Doug nodded.

Grady smiled and pointed at his own head. "The photographs you took, in Guatemala, an incident involving US officials exchanging cash for seized cocaine. Those photographs you say you hid so well aren't where you hid them, are they? Lucas has wanted them so badly for so long because both you and he are in the pictures. You were at the heart of the exchange. I'm right on this, aren't I?"

"That's good. Very good." Doug smiled and looked away. "Indeed very good. But I can handle it."

Grady started to walk away. "You're special forces, right?"

Doug nodded without looking at him.

"If someone's trailing you, make a circle, come back on to your own tracks, and ambush the folks who intended to ambush you. Put your hatchet in the back of their head. Right?"

Doug nodded again, eyeing Grady carefully.

"And, let the enemy come until he's almost close enough to touch. Then let him have it and jump out and finish him up. Still on track here?"

Doug leaned on the fence. "When you're marching, walk far enough apart so one enemy shot can't go through two men."

"Good. You do your job, I'll do mine."

Grady was silent in the car for several minutes as Juarez drove. "I'd love to talk with that guy for a couple of days. He's got so much I can read. That's the strongest I've ever gotten it. I wonder what Lucas will be like." Grady leaned back in the seat. "If Doug insists he's going to handle this himself, we need to get to Jackson Hole."

Chapter 30

George McGurdy did not need a reason to show up anywhere he liked. As Assistant Director of the Institute for Works of Religion he could be in Rome on Sunday, Rio on Monday, and Moscow by Wednesday, and no one would ask. Sitting in the back of a mostly empty St. James cathedral in Seattle on a rainy Tuesday in March might have been a little odd if it were not for the mass celebrating the temporary installation of Bishop James Sanders to oversee the Archdiocese of Seattle until a replacement for Archbishop Riley had been chosen by the Vatican.

Harold Brown spotted him and nodded. A priest approached George from the side and motioned for him to follow. They disappeared behind the ornate apse and entered the vestibule where Bishop Sanders and Cardinal Day were ceremoniously putting on the various layers of robes and chords in preparation for mass.

"Bishop Sanders, what a great occasion this is. Truly, the holy father has chosen wisely in this time of need, and no one better than you to serve the Holy Mother Church." George offered his hand to shake.

"Mr. McGurdy, thank you for coming." The bishop kissed the stole and place it around his neck and prepared for the final gown. "Cardinal Day explained that we will be having lunch with you after mass."

"Yes, just yesterday morning as I prepared to fly here, the holy father himself asked me to offer his congratulations."

Bishop Sanders glanced wryly at a smiling Cardinal Day. "The holy father?"

❦

Bishop Sanders had not yet met the housekeeping staff in the archbishop's residence and was sitting down to a formal lunch being served by Mexican ladies in black and white uniforms. Cardinal Day was seated at the head of the table. He had been in the residence once, as a priest, many years earlier, and the decor had not changed. It was a turn-of-the-century Craftsman and the furnishings in the dining room dated and gaudy.

"You know, Archbishop Schwartz never lived here. He had a room over in the rectory adjacent to the cathedral and shared a kitchen with the priests. He became far too close to them, and I think the archdiocese suffered." Cardinal Day placed the pressed white napkin on his lap and accepted the soup course with a smile. "When I would visit, this place would be so empty, and he kept a minimal staff. John Riley got things back into proper order here, and now the residence is functioning as it should for an archbishop. The staff will give you a proper tour this afternoon if you like. Are your things in transport?"

"Yes, Cardinal. And thank you for such a fine welcome to Seattle. I actually did not get much to eat this morning as I was up late last night packing. This is quite an excellent meal."

"Yes, yes. Well, much work to do here in Seattle, and

I think we have chosen the right man for now, and the holy father has a weighty decision to make for a permanent replacement. Do you know who George McGurdy is?"

Bishop Sanders glanced at George, who was slurping his soup. "John spoke of you a bit. He was delighted you were assisting him in raising finances for his charity."

George nodded as the soup bowls were removed and a watercress salad was set in front of the three men. "I liked what I saw when he presented the idea to me. Focusing on promoting the traditional family, and I think he was going to expand his services to assist unfortunate young women find adoptive families, am I right, Cardinal?"

"Absolutely, and I know this is a cause so dear to the holy father's heart. We would like to see the work continue, much like you have been doing in Milwaukee."

Bishop Sanders smiled and pushed his glasses back up the bridge of his nose. "Well, I had it so much easier in Milwaukee. They were already receptive to such rightful causes, all I had to do was expand their efforts."

"What were your sources of funding?" George did not particularly like the salad and pushed it aside. It was taken away with silent proficiency.

"We had some good connections with United Way. They were sympathetic. We also did two or three special collections every year, then maintained a very minimal staff. Most of the funds went directly to the services. We had two nuns who traveled to the parishes in a modest motorhome. They would stay in a parish for a week and visit the regular catechism classes. That was our largest expense, but it had very good impact. They had a great program on the traditional family for all age levels, and we got great support from the parents and the parishes. We had two counseling offices in Milwaukee helping young pregnant women make wise choices, and we worked closely with Catholic Community Services in finding proper adoptive families." Bishop Sanders was sweating a little and his glasses had to be pushed back up his nose.

George didn't like the sweating. He knew inside every good man was a tiny little black box, and one day it would just open and the very best of men would become heinous criminals. He just didn't know enough to figure out what was in Sanders's little black box. George had asked but no one knew anything bad about James Sanders. No accusations of sex crimes, not even a whisper. He drove an old Buick his father had given him fifteen years earlier, in spite of numerous offers to get him into something more respectable, considering the office he held. It was the Central America years no one could really trace. The years he and John Riley worked together. That might have been a good source of information, but Riley was dead now, and no one had any other contacts from that time. George had to keep the operation fluid, or he would lose the benefactors in Mexico.

"My guess, Bishop, is that Seattle will not be so easy on your mission to promote a healthy idea of a traditional family and to counsel young women on wise family choices. You might need to look for funding outside of the archdiocese. Oh, I'm sure the parishioners will fork over a bit now and then. There are some very traditional parishes here as I understand. But, by and large, the damage done by Archbishop Schwartz will be long in repairing, am I right on this, Cardinal?"

Cardinal Day wiped his mouth and cleared his throat. "Yes, George, you are so right." He turned to Bishop Sanders. "I think you will enjoy the independence of outside sources that are not beholden to local politicians. Your political leaders here in Seattle will not eye your boldness and decisiveness on these issues as a virtue. I have asked George to meet you in order to consider other sources of funding."

Bishop Sanders smiled but his face turned red. "I wish I had met you in Milwaukee."

There's that sweating and the loose glasses again, George thought.

"Mr. McGurdy, I am more than willing to discuss options for raising funds for such righteous causes."

"Of course you are." George liked the salmon and risotto and cleaned his plate as he talked. "I represent the Institute for Works of Religion, and we operate out of the Vatican, as you most likely already know. Some people call us the Vatican Bank, but we think of ourselves as an institution for promoting the faith anywhere we see fit around the world. There are many…oh, shall we say?…very successful men and a few women of means who contact us on a regular basis and offer to channel funds through us to causes such as those Archbishop Riley established and that you seem to want to continue. Knowing how difficult it was for Archbishop Riley, we understood the need to offer some personal funds to maintain a status…shall we say?…in such a financially blessed area as Seattle. So along with funding your charities, we make a certain amount of the donated funds available to you and you can access them just as you would any bank on the Internet. I can show you how to set up an account later if you like."

"I think the salary and the home are sufficient compensation—"

"Bishop, excuse me, you drive a fifteen-year-old Buick with Mid-West rust around the wheel wells. Forgive me, but I think you will want to project a more polished presence here in Seattle."

Bishop Sanders wiped his mouth and took out a handkerchief to wipe his forehead. He pushed his glasses up again. "I see. May I ask what sort of numbers we are talking about here?"

George glared over at Cardinal Day and then back at Bishop Sanders. "How much would you like?"

"How much was Archbishop Riley receiving?"

"He felt he needed ten to eleven thousand a month, depending on what was available."

Bishop Sanders coughed into his napkin and held it over his mouth. George decided it was money inside that little black box. James Sanders never had any. He probably went into the seminary broke and was happy to get a free education and then the menial salary a priest got because his parents had nothing to offer him.

"Mr. McGurdy, that would be more than I need. Perhaps to save a little for the charities, we could cut that back."

"Not a problem, Bishop. No problem at all. Let's say we deposit seven thousand a month and see how that goes. Okay?"

"That would be fine. If you would please excuse me, I need to use the restroom."

One of the Mexican ladies motioned him toward the hallway. Cardinal Day and George stared silently at each other.

George smiled. "I like poor priests. There is something special about the day when they see real money. But, for now, I think he's perfect. I am sure academically he was probably at the top of his class, but when it comes to life, he's a complete simpleton, and I like that quality. He'll do exactly as he is told, am I correct, Cardinal?"

"Yes you are, George, yes you are. We all do what we are told."

Chapter 31

Greg did not want Doug Dorn to call, ever. It was always the other way. "Where the hell are you, buddy?"

"I'm at home, in Seattle." Doug's tone never changed.

"I'll fly out. We need to talk."

"No, I've got something else going on," Doug argued. "I'm out of commission until late next week. And unless you're ready to end this completely, don't bother."

"You know what I need to end this. You give me that, and this is over."

"That's it, huh? It's all over?"

"Over and you move on."

Doug hung up the phone and looked at Ramone. "We're driving to Wyoming, now."

∽∾∽∾

Ramone drove to Wyoming, changing out music almost like clockwork on the hour. Eighteen hours of driving. Time for gas and relief, munching anything within reach from the ice chest in the back seat.

They arrived at nine thirty Thursday night. The motel room was cheap, bland, and faceless. The television was so large your eyes focused on it and nothing else until it was snapped off.

Doug said he was going for a walk. Ramone did not ask when he would be back.

☙❦❧

Officer Jerry Garcia wanted to show off the local Italian style coffee at Emils. Inspector Juarez was curious why he was doing this but didn't ask.

"I was in Venice when I was eighteen," Jerry boasted. "Mid-winter, worked in a restaurant up in St. Moritz and spent a week down there. You've been there?"

Juarez shook his head.

"You really should try the croissants. Very good." Jerry shoved the plate across the table. "Here, you eat this one, and I'll buy another."

"When does the chief get in?" Grady asked.

"Hard to say. Sometimes seven, sometimes eight, sometimes nine, and when he's been drinking, maybe ten. Not much happens in Jackson Hole. Pretty quiet place. I was sitting right over there when the first robbery in five years happened. They pulled out a gun, and I watched it go down, then I got up and arrested them."

"Didn't they turn on you?"

"No. I knew the sister of one of them. He was just a doper, looking for some easy cash. Now these crystal meth people. Whew. Watch out for them. I busted two guys making the stuff in a motorhome. Real smart types, started flushing the drugs down the toilet in the motorhome, only thing was the motorhome was parked in the middle of the street and the sewage line wasn't hooked up to anything. Gosh, thank goodness crooks around here are not much smarter than the cops."

Jerry went on to extol the virtues of mountain living,

how his children would rather go skiing than with their mother down to the mall. "Don't find a lot of Garcias listed on the United States Ski Team. Well, little Jerry says he's going to change all that. Could be, he's got the moves."

Juarez really did like the croissant and bought two more, one for Grady. Jerry wandered around the coffee shop, acknowledging the locals. He sat down with a contented grin on his face.

"You know Greg Lucas?" Grady watched, but the grin remained.

"I do. Local guy. I play poker with him once in a while."

"He caught a guy in the act of on line mail fraud."

"His reputation travels, my goodness."

"You like him?"

"He's a friend."

"You ever watch him, keep surveillance."

"Life in Jackson Hole can be so slow, I even keep surveillance on the local birds."

"We think he was involved in the terrorist attack on a Roman Catholic archbishop."

"Really?" Jerry saw the chief walking across the street toward the coffee shop. "Well, he's early."

Jerry excused himself as the chief and Grady rehashed old case notes. He walked across the street to the station, smiling and talking to shop owners as they unlocked, swept, and braced themselves for a hot late summer day and a healthy gaggle of tourists.

A new Mercedes was parked in two spaces. Florida plates. He reached for his ticket book and started to write. A thin, black-haired man walked briskly to the car, unlocked it with a remote beeper, got in, and roared away. Jerry waved, determined to run the plates as soon as he could.

He checked for any messages and then returned to Emils. Chief Grieg slid his cell phone back into his belt. "Tell us what you know about Greg Lucas," he ordered.

Jerry smiled. "A bishop in Seattle commits suicide, and it doesn't get much press coverage. Some tourists leave behind a Seattle newspaper, and a week or so after the event, I find that newspaper in here. I read through. Not much to do in Jackson Hole. I see a picture of a man I recognize. I see he's a bishop, and I am amazed my friend Greg Lucas knows this bishop. I'm a good Catholic and I'm impressed. Now, how do I know they knew each other? I drive by Lucas's place and see his car is gone, but this man, the bishop, is standing outside on the deck. Sees the cruiser and almost jumps back inside. I drive by again, later, this time the door's shut, shades closed—sealed off, like. One night, I just sit across the street in my cousin's Jeep. Nothing. Lucas's car is gone and someone is inside. I make a few notes. Maybe a relative. But back to the newspaper article. I think maybe Greg wants to know something about his friend, so I see a woman, a mutual friend, and I ask her if I should call Greg. She acts not like I would expect, so I make a note of that. A good friend, not sure Greg would want to know that a guest who had been in his home only a week before commits suicide. And the timing got to me. Just a week after the Archbishop of Seattle is murdered in Puerto Vallarta. And Greg Lucas is then working as an investigator on the case. What do you think?"

Grady laughed lightly. "I think you've nailed the bastard."

"I would suggest we have a person of interest."

"Yeah. He's interesting all right." Grieg sat heavily back in his chair. "Is he back in town?"

"Late last night. I wanted to drive over there this morning, but we have guests."

Chief Greig grunted. "He doesn't leave, okay?"

"I figured you would say that, so I alerted the state patrol." Jerry looked Grady clearly in the eyes. "You know his back ground?"

"Yes. Special forces. Capable of many things."

"Indeed. I don't want to frighten anyone," the chief weighed in loudly. "This goes smoothly, and the peace is kept. Peaceful, okay?" He turned to the Mexican cop. "You, Juarez, make sure you have a gun. I don't care what the law says about foreign cops, carry a gun."

Grady nodded. "Are you still going to meet him?"

Jerry nodded. "Oh, yes, I will be the friend I have always been. What would you like?"

"Half an hour with him a while after you're done, with back up, then we watch him and see what he does."

❧❧❧

Jerry shut the door of the cruiser gently. Greg stood from his chair on the deck, sipping water, dressed for cycling.

"New bike?"

"Yeah. Bought it last week. Had it shipped back. Thought it would be longer before I got it. Out for a ride."

Jerry nodded graciously.

"Hey what's up with Jimmy?"

Jerry laughed. "Well, turns out there was a guy down in Cheyenne, a private investor, met him on the Internet. Fleeced him. I learned something from you, Lucas. I was able to help the guys down there find the evidence they needed to bring charges, and he'll stand trial for these new charges. I think we have not heard the last of this. The article ran front page in Cheyenne, and it turns out the chief down there was alerted to this but didn't react.

Didn't know much about the Internet and that kind of stuff, so he sat on his butt. Now there's six other people calling in, and they're going to run that old chief out of town. See what you started?"

Greg laughed, waved, and rolled down the hill. When he was out of sight, Jerry walked around the house. He waved at the neighbor who stood shirtless in his living room window, watching.

Jerry drove up the canyon, now out of his jurisdiction. But as a favor to the county sheriff, Jerry made notes of the motorhome license plates and noted the date and time they were parked by the river.

His radio announced a five-vehicle accident in the middle of town. He struggled to get around the chaos of tourist traffic trying to get around the wreck. The state patrol was on the scene, waiting for the city police. Two Range Rovers slammed into each other, head on, in the middle of the city. This set off a chain reaction of fender benders and snarled traffic.

An hour later, the street was clear and tourist commerce flowed freely. Jerry found Grady and Juarez in their hotel room.

"I'm ready. I've got three state troopers and one of our own who are going to be out of sight. I'll be in my brother's Jeep. We need to give him some more time. He's out for a bike ride." Fifteen minutes later, Jerry made a telephone call. "Okay, he's been home for a while."

"Informers?"

"Neighbor. Hates Lucas with a passion. He'll tell me anything. You want a radio?"

Grady nodded.

"He won't see it. I'll be listening and the others will respond on my count. When do you want us?"

"My count is 'Geronimo.'"

❧❧❧

The car seemed out of place. So many rustic homes, large sport utility vehicles. This red tin can without character rolled into Greg's driveway. Such a little car, and such a large man driving it. Greg stepped out on to the porch. "Can I help you?"

"The name is Grady. You're Greg Lucas, right."

"Yes."

Grady walked up the steps without an invitation. He stopped at the top and stood next to Greg. Greg was shorter by five inches, lighter, and showing a slight bit of gray at the temples. Healthy, strong, tanned. Grady turned and looked at the Tetons. "No snow. I was here in September once and they were covered almost down to the base. Is this normal?"

Greg sat in the rocker, leaving the bench for Grady. "Define normal."

"Harold sent me. Wanted me to share anything I had on the case."

"Harold didn't tell me that."

"I got a call last night in Denver."

"You sure got up here fast.

"The evidence Moro has is a trigger. Here's a photograph of it. Know anyone who might be capable of devising something like this?"

Greg looked casually at the photograph and then at Grady. "Moro sent you, not Harold. You want a drink?"

"No. I want to pass on information to you and leave. I have work back in Puerto Vallarta to tend to."

Greg stood and entered the cabin, leaving Grady on the porch. Grady watched a family walk along the broad, gravel trail that wove alongside the street. They seemed genuinely happy.

"You want some water?" Greg yelled from inside.

"No thank you."

"You should drink water. The combination of elevation and dry climate will dehydrate you quicker than you think." Greg sat smoothly in the rocker, setting his drink on the small table. "This trigger. Where was it found?"

"It set the bomb off that killed two boys and a cardinal."

"No it didn't."

Grady looked at Greg, who was looking at the photograph. "Okay, let's run with your theory."

"It's a dummy. The reason they call it a dummy is because only dummies would believe it was the actual triggering device. When the bomb went off, the signature trigger, the one the cops really want so they can trace back to who designed and detonated the bomb, is always blown to bits. That's why so few bombings are ever totally resolved. Take the Libyans. They learned with the flight over Locherby Scotland to always destroy the real trigger and devise a trigger that is so totally new and weird it probably doesn't work. Do you know anything about triggering devices?" Greg explained, admiring Doug's work.

"More than I want to."

"Not enough, I might suggest. Look here. This is where the electrical impulse travels to the explosives. Not even brown. This trigger was encased in something that was very near that point, something that would be destroyed in the blast, but strong enough to make sure this trigger survived. The fact they stumbled on the dummy device and called it the actual trigger so fast goes to show you why terrorists using explosives will not go away soon."

"You know so much, Greg. I'm glad Chief Grieg recommended you. You obviously don't need me anymore on this. You've got the cat by the tail." Grady crossed his legs and held his hands around his right knee. "But tell me something. This Harry Boyle. Who was he?"

"A friend of an enemy from my Central America days."

"Really. Did he go there on vacation?"

"No. I was special forces and he did missionary work."

Grady wondered why Greg would tell such a blatant lie. "I see. His suicide was a terrible loss, I'm sure."

"Sad. I could see him declining."

"Jerry Garcia wanted me to give this to you. Found it in a discarded copy of the Seattle Times."

Greg studied the photograph and read the article. "Jerry gave this to you?"

Grady nodded. He was not good at studying eyes. He wasn't even looking. He was more distracted by what he saw in Greg's mind—a man very nearby, a man with the same physical shape as the person wearing the leather jacket in the photographs, holding what looked like an ordinary garage door opener. The man could see them now. Doug Dorn. "Yes, Jerry Garcia, your poker friend."

Greg stared at Grady. "You looking for something?"

Grady turned back to Greg. "A bird. Something strange about it."

Their eyes met and held.

"Garcia said something about your friend Genelle. They talked about this and she said something strange about it. You might look in on her."

Greg's hand shook slightly as he sipped.

"Garcia also was saying something about the fact that Harry Boyle was in Seattle, and a new archbishop was installed there who didn't like Boyle. These events are so close together. The new archbishop arrives, goes to Mexico, gets killed, then very soon after, Boyle commits suicide."

"Garcia wanted you to ask me about that?"

"No. I'm just decompressing here. Stream of consciousness, maybe it will help you."

"I don't need your help."

"I agree. Maybe this is all just coincidence, the Archbishop of Seattle closing down an office Boyle was taking money from it and giving it away to people with AIDS. The archbishop dies. Boyle commits suicide. And you knew this man. But this is not my case any longer."

Grady stood and moved toward the steps. Greg sipped again from his drink.

"I met Captain Healy," Greg said. Grady stopped moving, staring at the Tetons. "I told him you had contacted me to do some work on the Riley case," Greg continued. "We got drunk together and he told me about your girlfriend. You ever shoot?" He was not looking at Grady to gauge a physical reaction. "He said she was a nice person, but you had to leave intelligence because of it."

Grady leaned against the railing. "I had my reasons for resigning."

"I'm sorry your girlfriend killed herself."

"Is that what Healy told you?"

"Drugs can induce many confusing emotions. I'd be very interested in knowing who supplied my girlfriend. I'd want to know if the supplier got her on it, or was she just a victim of the modeling industry?"

"My personal life—don't go there anymore. You leave this alone."

"I'm sorry. I should know better." Greg stood and walked back into the cabin.

Grady could hear ice clinking into the glass and the gurgling of another large pour. "You sure you don't want one?" Grady did not answer. He was reading a copy of the suicide note he had folded into his jacket pocket. "You don't believe Boyle had Archbishop Riley killed?" he asked.

Greg laughed when he saw the copy. "Did you bother reading all of that? The guy went over the edge. These are not the words of a sane man."

"Oh, I don't know. Much of it rings true. I mean the simple essence of the original Gospel message. I like the part about Judas. Money had old Judas by the balls. He'd do anything for money. Betray his most beloved friend, even." Grady set the suicide note on the table. He sat back on the bench. "You familiar with the Gospel story of the betrayal?"

Greg gulped large and set the glass on top of the suicide note. "Yes."

"Good thing Judas betrayed just Jesus. Kindly, soft-spoken Jesus, so easily given to forgiveness. I knew a guy once who pulled a Judas on the cartels. American GI, regular army. Got involved in smuggling heroin into the US. One of my first cases. He should have found a way to betray a guy like Jesus, but he went ahead and took our money, right along with the cartel's money, and flipped a dime on his Honduran contact. The Mexican police get their cartel guy and regular army walks to talk about it." Grady wiped his hands together, as if he was cleaning something off the surface. "They found parts of him in Mexico, United States—"

"I'm sorry for him and his family. This is Friday. Why the Sunday School lesson?" Greg picked up his drink and stared for a moment at the suicide note. "How many people have you killed, Grady?"

"Evil is an interesting subject, isn't it? What's the difference between a man who belongs to an aggressor army and a man who has children blown up in a cathedral?"

Greg flashed a look at Grady. His eyes shifted slightly. Grady decided many thoughts were coursing through his mind at the same time, and the alcohol was not allowing him to fix on any one of them. Sometimes that was a good thing on a Friday night after a long hard week—sit back in the recliner, put on some interesting music and slide. Grady figured this was not a good time for Greg to be drinking.

"Children are so precious," Grady continued. "Did Moro introduce you to the Ignacio boy? Loves cycling. Follows the races, has a Bianchi. Wants to race himself. Wanted to. His right foot was smashed by debris in the explosion that killed Riley. It also killed Ignacio's sixteen-year-old brother and their lifelong friend. Altar boys. Whoever did that bombing didn't care much for kids, did they, Greg? That Ignacio boy had his brother's blood on his hands when they found him. He's not going to be the same ever again, is he?"

"You think Boyle was affected by that and offed himself?"

Grady looked at Greg's hardened face.

"Interesting theory," Greg continued. "Boyle did not have the skills to do this. From my experience, he would have to find someone who would do it for him. Like you say, someone who was a puppet for money or some ideological cause."

"Doug Dorn?" No reaction from Greg. Grady looked away. "What ideological cause?"

"You know Doug Dorn?"

Grady shook his head. "Huge cocaine bust. Colonel Daniels tells me he's gay but no one knew it when he was in the forces. But it's not like that at all. The cocaine was for you."

"He tell you about his affiliation with gay activities?"

"No, Daniels didn't seem much interested in what Doug did in his personal life. Talked a lot about how you saved his life, didn't want anything in return. You get the Medal of Honor for that? By the way, where are Doug's pictures?" Grady saw it—the flash of pure hatred. The curled upper lip, slightly exposed teeth, squinted eyes. Grady felt for the radio strapped to his chest.

Greg stood and wordlessly entered the cabin. He poured a third drink and returned to the deck without offering Grady one. He sat in the rocker, holding the glass and looking out at the mountains. His eyes narrowed and his mouth moved ever so slightly, saying something to himself.

Grady stood. "Well, Greg, thanks for the time. I need to debrief when I get involved with something like this. Cleans up the system like a warm-water enema."

Greg nodded.

"You need anything else?" Grady asked. "If not, I'm out of here."

"Where did you say you were going, back to Mexico?"

"Yes. Since I'm off this, Moro thought I'd be helpful to her in solving some cartel thing with her son."

"I hear they can't drive too well. You okay, buddy?"

"Minor scrapes."

Grady started to walk slowly down the steps, almost sideways. He hesitated and pulled a folded sheet of paper from his coat pocket. "Doug sends his regards." He laid the last page of the suicide note on the table. "It's the missing page from the suicide note."

Greg glared at him.

Grady saw the Bianchi under the porch. "Hey, that's the same kind the Ignacio boy has. Exactly."

"Really?" Greg stood, holding his glass. "By the way. Healy said if you're in the neighborhood, he'd love to have lunch. He's always wanted to **ask** you where Dennis Hofburg ended up."

Grady smiled up at Greg, got into the car, and rolled out of the driveway. He tooted the horn lightly and waved.

Doug waited until the car drove away. He watched Greg on the porch, rocking, sipping, rocking, staring. Greg looked three times at the page Grady had left on the table. He got up for another drink. As he fixed his fourth drink, fire dripped from the ceiling. Something new Doug had thought up, made from the most elementary things found in a basement. Two thousand degrees of flames for fifteen seconds. No man would survive. And, besides, the house would burn down, leaving nothing but charred bones.

Doug smiled at the children walking on the bicycle trail. He stopped to talk with one young family throwing bread crumbs to the ducks. He quacked just like the ducks in the pond and they swam over to him, eating the bread crumbs out of the children's hands.

The children looked up, eyes ablaze, as the fire engines screamed by. "Fire engines," the father said. "Big red fire engines."

Ramone was drying himself by the pool, dripping on his books. "Long walk."

"Hey, you ready to go?"

"Yeah. I got two new CDs for the car. Where we headed?"

"Home."

Chapter 32

Captain Pillsbury sat heavily in the high-backed chair. He decided the first time he met Harold Brown he liked first-class police work. Tourist class was a retirement check. This was living. No more bad food, traveling in back with the screaming babies or drinking in shit holes. Okay, so he had to go along with this game of his—let's get all the prominent gay guys. Everything evil in the church was caused by the gays. Good thing Harold never asked him what Vatican II was all about. Pillsbury stopped going to mass when he was thirteen and got caught humping a girl in the Catholic school playground. The priest beat him so badly, Pillsbury swore he would get even. His first pedophile priest arrest was when he paid it back. Priests fought back, things got rough. Simple.

Ha. When Harold took him to a traditionalist church, mass was just like he had known it and the Latin flowed out of him like poop out of a baby.

Pillsbury made more in a month with Harold than he did in a year mid-way through his police career. For that kind of money, he'd find all sorts of queers and deliver them on a fucking silver platter.

"I'll have another, there, Aaron."

"Coming right up, Captain."

"What ever happened to that other guy…uhm…Peter."

"Not here anymore. Hand in the till and everything. Story has it one of Mr. Brown's men knew about it, like he was spying or something."

"Is that so? How about some more cashews?"

"Righto."

Harold was stooped and tired when he slumped into the chair. "Captain," he mumbled.

"You okay, Harold?"

"No first class seats on the plane so I sat in back. I couldn't even pay a first class passenger for their ticket. Oh, the food." Aaron set down the captain's scotch and a bowl of cashews. He returned in a moment with Harold's scotch.

"Very bad news, Captain," Harold said.

"Yeah?" Two cashews rolled down his chest on the floor.

Harold watched as Pillsbury tried unsuccessfully to retrieve them. *Probably to eat them*, he thought. "Greg Lucas died three days ago in a fire. His home burned to the ground."

Pillsbury nodded. "Chief Greig told me about that."

"He was a good man."

"I liked him. Seemed to take any news well, just got on with the job. Wish I'd had men like him on the force."

"We've got to replace him quickly. I spoke with Greg just a few days before he died. He told me about a fellow that used to work with him, a Doug Dorn. Homosexual. He was looking into some connection between Doug and these homosexual priests in Seattle. We could have gotten arrest warrants if we had established that. We need someone to find this Dorn fellow."

"This guy Grady coming back on?"

"I don't know. Right now, I think he is going back to

work for Captain Moro. I'll keep tabs on him. I need to talk to him about his commitment level. I'm not sure he's in total agreement with us."

"Maybe he's one of them."

"I don't think so. I knew his father. A very smart lawyer. Good Catholic family." Harold sipped lightly at his drink as Pillsbury shoved another handful of cashews into his mouth. "Colonel Daniels wrote to me and told me about another man. A captain who is about to retire. Same unit Grady was in. Captain Healy. He's Opus Dei, and a sharp fellow. I'm flying over there to talk with him. In the meantime, maybe you can start on these homosexual priests. I'll meet with Grady before he returns to Mexico."

❧❧❧

Gene Pillsbury was a good man in search of an easy retirement. His success as a policeman came easy because he was smart and kind, attributes that served him well when he needed answers from the Blacks, the Hispanics, the gays, any one in Seattle. They talked to him because he genuinely liked good people and most of the people he met on the street were good. He rewarded them with the respect no other straight, white male would afford them. He kept his promises. In return, he solved more crimes.

To narrow in on one segment of the population never was his style. If Harold Brown was half as smart as he was rich, he would figure out that Captain Pillsbury's name never came up when it came to delivering he punch to the men they chased after.

"Father Carol."

"Yes." The priest was dressed in a jogging suit.

"My name is Gene Pillsbury."

"You used to be with the Seattle Police."

"Yes. Can we get out of this rain? Let's get some coffee."

They chatted about the bad September weather as they waited their turn. Father Carol ordered chai.

"What the hell is chai."

"It's like a tea. Would you like some?"

Pillsbury grunted and shook his head. "You know Father Jurevics?"

"I'm sorry. Are you still with the police?"

"No. I work for a private individual who has hired me as a detective to investigate some of the events surrounding the death of Archbishop Riley. Do you know a fella by the name of Doug Dorn." Father Carol stared at him. Pillsbury stared back. "I see. It's funny, we think this Dorn character set off the bombs in Mexico, even the one in Mexico City. Or maybe he's got a contact there who followed his design. A message is sent from a computer owned by your roommate, and then the bomb explodes. We're obviously looking for a connection."

"This is an odd way of going about it. Usually you don't tell people what you have unless—"

"Yes."

"You've been pretty popular in the gay community here in Seattle."

Pillsbury stirred more sugar into his coffee." "I tried to get along with everyone. I'm not in the business of judging people's morals, Father Carroll."

"You just warned me."

"About what?"

"I'm not sure, but I think I need to thank you."

"Oh, don't thank me. Just tell me something. I've been candid with you, see if you can answer this. The threat sent to the pope. Jurevics do it?"

Father Carol shook his head. "Seattle has more computer whiz kids than it knows what to do with. I know eight people who could reinvent computers. One woman in my parish traced the computer messages to a guy in Wyoming. We gave the FBI the information last week. Jurevics looks like he's in the clear. They haven't called him back yet."

"Good job. That's pretty clear then, isn't it? You guys had nothing to do with it."

"No, we didn't."

"I'd hate to find out you're lying to me and you really know Doug Dorn."

"You won't."

When Captain Pillsbury went home to his wife Ling, he always remembered when her family ostracized her for marrying him. More painful, however, was the treatment he received from his fellow officers when he married a Chinese woman. In spite of this, their children grew up handsome, tall, and proud of themselves. Gene Pillsbury saw to that.

Especially his son, Brent. Pillsbury knew he had no interest in women when he first observed the boys sexual awakenings. He'd prepared himself then for the inevitable day when Brent would feel it necessary to tell his mother first, gauging the reaction his father might have to the news. Ling laughed and waved the nervous eighteen-year-old into the living room where the then "Captain Gene Pillsbury" was resting from a rough and tiring day chasing windmills with Harold Brown.

"I know a lot of gay men, Brent. You're the finest among them."

Brent now asked about Harold Brown and the great gay hunt Pillsbury was conducting.

"Well, have you ever wondered why the most decorated captain in the Seattle Police Department can't ever seem to find them?"

"So, it's a scam?"

"No. Harold Brown needs a babysitter so he doesn't get himself into trouble."

Pillsbury was in love with Ling and nothing could stop love. He kissed her solidly when he got home.

"Did you have a good day with Harold?"

"I did." He poured himself a scotch and rummaged for ice in the freezer.

Ling was cooking his favorite; lasagna. "How do you stand that man?"

"It's like a play, sort of. I keep feeding him lines, he acts a certain way, I line up information, and he says the right thing. And we keep on chasing windmills."

"You're a smart cop, Gene Pillsbury."

Chapter 33

After dropping Inspector Juarez off at SeaTac airport, Grady drove back down town Seattle for a meeting with Harold. Grady did not want to meet at the Rainier Club. He chose Ivars Fish House instead, next to the Coleman dock, and he insisted Sandy finally meet Harold in person. They sat at an outdoor table in the bright sun. Grady bought a large order of fish and chips. Harold first claimed not to be hungry, but eventually nibbled at and then ate two large pieces of fried cod. The Seattle waterfront in late March was balmy, even a bit uncomfortably warm. The fresh breeze blowing in across the water tempered this. Harold looked at Sandy then at Grady.

Grady smiled. "She stays and whatever you have to say to me you can say to her."

Sandy smirked. "So good to finally meet you, Mr. Brown."

Harold wiped his hands several times on a napkin, looking to see that he cleaned all the grease. "So, we never resolved this."

"I think it was resolved, Harold. When Greg Lucas died in that fire, I think we were being told who was really responsible."

"Well, yes, of course we know that. Don't fret, I'll pay you anyway. I just don't think we got to the bottom of all this. Those homosexuals who fomented this are still out there. Where will they strike next? And, that lunatic Harry Boyle. What he wrote is very near unforgivable. I think he was of diminished capacity."

"Boyle may have had the idea, but he wasn't able to kill anyone. Nor do I believe he really wanted to."

"If your theory is correct, we need to get on this Doug Dorn—"

"Dorn is innocent."

"Who are you suggesting was primarily responsi—"

A long, shattering blast of a ferry horn interrupted the conversation. The screeching seagulls, frightened by the horn, prolonged the interruption.

Grady took the opportunity to eat some fries. "Greg Lucas."

Harold's face drooped and his eyes narrowed. "I don't believe this. What evidence do you have?"

"He met with Harry Boyle a week before the bomb was detonated in Puerto Vallarta."

"They knew each other, from Lucas's army days?"

"No. Boyle never went to Central America."

"Greg Lucas was a good man. The work he did for the Jackson Hole Police, do you know about that?"

"Yes. Good work. He put a big-time scam artist where he belongs. He also planned the death of Archbishop Riley."

"Why? What motive would he have for doing this, after demonstrating his heroism in Central America and working so closely with the police in his retirement? What motive would you suggest?" Harold's voice strained and he was shaking. Grady watched him carefully. "What does Olivia Moro think of this theory of yours?" Harold demanded.

"She completely agrees. In fact, she was the one who put me on to her suspicions when I got out of the hospital. And thank you for taking care of those bills."

Harold nodded. "Captain Moro believes this? I'll visit her next time I'm in Mexico. They're looking in the wrong place. These homosexual extremists are responsible—"

"Now, Harold, I have just about heard enough." Sandy stood up from the small table to dispose of the empty fish tray.

Harold studied Sandy and then Grady. He decided he had said too much and not to hire him again. He would pay him and not invite him to consider the merits of his greater plan—to expose the festering underworld violence of the extreme homosexual left. "I owe you some money."

"I can't charge you for the days I was in the hospital."

"Nonsense." Harold studied the invoice and expense report and added the sum appropriate for the time Grady had spent in the hospital. He signed the check without flourish. "Who gets this?"

Sandy held out her hand and smiled. "Thank you, Mr. Brown."

"I think you and I will part company here, Grady. I am sorry for that. I liked your father very much, and you have served me faithfully. But I am getting older and my work has taken on a focus that I believe you are not convinced needs doing. I will find someone who will look where—"

"Captain Healy? You could do better than that, Harold?"

Harold rose from the table, his eyes fixed on Grady, his lips quivering. "I will not ask where you got that information." He walked slowly away toward the Jaguar parked on the street with the portly Sam Pillsbury leaning against it, patiently waiting for his employer. Harold hesitated mid-way and motioned to Grady, who walked over and stood at his side. "I may have to recant what I just said about you," Harold admitted. "If I called, would you answer and consider another assignment?"

"I get to accept or decline any job, okay?"

"That's fair." Harold continued walking slowly and stiffly toward the Jaguar. Pillsbury held the passenger door open. "Tell your wife I'm sorry if I appeared rude."

"You can tell her yourself."

Harold shook his head and got into the Jaguar.

Chapter 34

On Saturday evenings, Olivia Moro used to go with Hektor to the movies, something she did often alone when she was a student in the United States. She now spent weekend nights working.

She often walked the gravel path to her own mother's grave where Hektor was praying when they took him. She always hesitated a few feet before the grave, flowers for the mother in her right hand, the gold crucifix clenched tightly in her left, a memorial of her son. On cold nights, she did not stay long at the grave, but instead sat silently in the cemetery chapel. On warmer nights, she sat on the cement curbing that surrounded the family site. It was then she allowed herself to cry. She would usually return home at nine. She knew her escorts were always there, out of sight, protecting her, but they never interfered.

Her cell phone rang and her first instinct was to not answer. She looked at the caller ID. The minister. "This is Captain Moro."

"Captain More, Minister Teresa Chavez here. I am to understand you have gotten some resolution to the matter of the archbishop in the cathedral." The minister was driving and she had to speak loudly for the hands free device to catch her voice. "Good work."

"Thank you, Minister. I have a very good team, and we had some help."

"Oh, stop being so modest. You're a talent on the rise. I need to ask you some questions about the information you passed on to the federales about the possibility of money laundering. I will call you tomorrow, but I want you to start thinking about moving up so you can lead that investigation. That could be the kind of thing that makes your permanent career."

"Minister, I have a good home here and a very good team—"

"Buy a new home and bring your team. You think about it, Olivia, and I will call you tomorrow. Good night and good work."

"Thank you, Minister."

About the Author

Shawn Rohrbach earned his BA in Medieval Philosophy at the Seminary of Christ the King in British Columbia, Canada, and his MFA in Writing at Naropa University in Boulder, Colorado. Rohrbach is the author of nine books, having won the 2008 Indie Book Award for Sports and Fitness. He lives and writes in San Diego, California, and travels frequently through the Southwest and Mexico to inform his stories and sample the tequila.

www.ingramcontent.com/pod-product-compliance
Lightning Source LLC
Chambersburg PA
CBHW060952120726
47910CB00002B/604

* 9 7 8 1 6 2 6 9 4 5 8 2 1 *